A VENOM BENEATH THE SKIN

Also by Marcos M. Villatoro

FICTION

Minos: A Romilia Chacón novel
Home Killings: A Romilia Chacón novel
The Holy Spirit of My Uncle's Cojones
A Fire in the Earth

NONFICTION

Walking to La Milpa:
Living in Guatemala with Armies, Demons, Abrazos, and Death

POETRY

They Say That I am Two: Poems
On Tuesday: When the Homeless Disappeared

A VENOM BENEATH THE SKIN

A ROMILIA CHACÓN NOVEL

Marcos M. Villatoro

Kate's Mystery Books
Justin, Charles & Co., Publishers
Boston, Massachusetts

FIRST EDITION 2005

This is a work of fiction. All characters and events portrayed in this
work are either fictitious or are used fictitiously.

Library of Congress Cataloging-in-Publication Data is available.

ISBN 1-932112-37-5

Published in the United States by Kate's Mystery Books,
an imprint of Justin, Charles & Co., Publishers
www.justincharlesbooks.com

Distributed by National Book Network, Lanham, Maryland
www.nbnbooks.com

2 4 6 8 10 9 7 5 3 1

Para las Girlfriends de la Montaña,
y también para Mi Vida

ACKNOWLEDGMENTS

The good folks at Georges Borchardt, Inc., have taken such good care of my books: *muchas gracias*, Valerie, Anne, and Georges.

DeAnna Heindel is a friend to me and to my books. Her keen eye, her honesty and her kindness — I will always be thankful for her.

Thanks to Dr. Cynthia Moore and the Physical Therapy Department of Mount St. Mary's College for help regarding prosthetics.

Steve Hull and the crew of Justin, Charles make beautiful books. Gracias, gracias.

Caitlin Alexander is brilliant. She has the true art of editing. I genuflect before her green pen.

Michelle, *vos sos mi vida. Tanto que te quiero que quiero quererte otro tanto.*

There is a venom beneath the skin
That cries at night.
— R.M.

A VENOM BENEATH THE SKIN

Special Agent Romilia Chacón drives her old Taurus out of the neighborhood of canals of Venice, California, and toward the freeway. Venice Boulevard has little traffic just past midnight. It's a straight shot of green lights all the way to the 405. She does not speed. There is no need for that.

I can see her easily, even without the streetlights, from the roof of this old apartment building. The Steiner Nighthunters with their twelve by fifty-six range can peer into near total darkness. The binoculars, manufactured by a private company for the U.S. Army and used by the high military command in the Iraq war, and bought at Internet prices (eight hundred forty dollars, a *steal*), make Romilia's face large and sharp. She does not cry. This does not surprise me; she's not in love.

She has a lover. The man who lives on the banks of these canals, in one of the smaller homes but one that he can barely afford. Special Agent Samuel "Chip" Pierce. Living off a Fed's salary, bringing in a little extra income due to his wounds, Chip can manage the payments, along with the help of an inheritance; and he means to enjoy it. The loss of body parts has that effect on some men: Either you drink yourself away or you slam down the pain pills or the heroin or all three; or maybe you get existential, you decide hey, they took my leg, my eye, they took a chunk of my hand, fuck it; I'm living. I'm going to live, and if I can, I'll live in one of the nicer areas in Los Angeles. Sure, it's not the real Venice, no gondolas plying the waterways; it's just L.A. with canals running by the houses, but it's expensive and that's what Chip wanted and I can't disagree.

I understand Pierce's perspective. I know how much it costs to ease pain. But I have become an existentialist, too; I've learned that pain means life and that death is the absence of pain and sometimes I'm not sure which one to choose so I've chosen this.

I lean against the concrete banister of the roof, adjust the Nighthunters so as to look up the street, through the space between two jacaranda trees and into the window of the small canal home. Chip Pierce places a drink on a glass table. Now he looks out the window, no doubt at the road that Romilia Chacón has just taken home. I can't adjust the binoculars anymore, can't see the look that may be regret pass over Chip Pierce's face. But the stance is there, a cock of the head downward, a decision not to drink from the glass for that moment. A pause. Who is more solid: Chip Pierce, or me?

Or Romilia Chacón? She's done well for herself here in Los Angeles these past years. No doubt she is the most solid of all, even with that knife-scar over the left side of her neck, even with that sister long in the grave. I know her, I've had to get to know her.

But she's not my target. Nor is Chip Pierce. Though later, police and witnesses will be hard put to believe that. I'm painting a picture that they won't forget.

I watch, carefully, as Chip cracks ice for another drink. My ice, the tray I made for him.

He sits in a large chair and drinks scotch, then starts to shake his head. Another sip, as if to toss off the sudden whirl. He stands to walk it off, means to set the scotch on the table but doesn't quite place it correctly; the glass tumbler totters on the table's lip. It falls, but does not break. And poor, half-drugged Chip is on his way to sleep.

I leave the roof and make my way across Venice Boulevard. After popping the lock on the front door and entering the six-digit code that will disarm his alarm system, I will find Special Agent Pierce on his back, just below the window, the empty tumbler next to his head.

Get to work. Wrap Pierce's limp fingers around objects. Open drawers and leave the objects behind. Prick and shoot. Pierce has only a slipper on his right foot. This makes it easy.

Now, wait for his body to go through the motions, the rush. The first venom streams through him, like it streams through the blood of so many others across this country.

A great country.

Enough. Pierce's body has relaxed. Now, dip and stab. Snap the dart, leave a splinter of wood behind. Help Chip Pierce die.

Then I draw the blade across Pierce's stomach. At first it's simple, like cutting on a mannequin. But then it gets harder, even though he's dead.

Still, there is rage, though it is not sure which way to go. Rage against the poison that you've just shot into him. Rage against those who buy and sell it. Chip has been like me, hurt in the line of duty. Too many parallels. That's why there is regret. Still, I do the only thing I can think of doing: I take off Chip Pierce's left leg. I fight with the silicon sheath, peeling it down over the stub. Finally it comes off. Over and again, I drop it down hard on his face. It works. It looks close enough to my own rage that it seems all very real. This will bring everybody out of the bushes, make them all run across open fields, crisscrossing one another's paths, making it that much easier for me to hunt.

This is good. Really good. Now that I'm not a coach, this is just fantastic.

Sergio kicked the ball right between two opponents' legs, and all of us parents on the sidelines whooped it up. He was playing defense, as always; Sergio hadn't had his chance at scoring a goal yet, but at this point, it didn't matter to him. His teammates nicknamed him *Firewall Chacón*. He was not about to let that ball get by him or into the goal.

"Keep it up, Firewall, stop every ball that comes your way!" said Matt, a good-looking fellow with a thick mustache. Matt kept the game positive by emphasizing the fun of it all; still, he wanted the team to win as much as the rest of us did. He was better at maintaining a balance between the two — much better than I was.

Last year had been a disaster. I learned quickly, after only two months, that being a coach of the Sherman Oaks Soccer Association was a bad idea. Not just because I was sometimes away on a case, which meant leaving The Mighty Slayers without a leader; but because when I was there, my reputation overshadowed Sergio's. More than once I heard it whispered among some of the moms: *that Latina hothead.* Here, in good old liberal Los Angeles, and those wondrous stereotypes just keep pumping along.

But I suppose I didn't do much to help snuff the stereotype out. One Saturday morning the coach of the other team (The Red Terminators) had decided that the ref's call was bad: His goalie had stopped the ball even though the goalie had fallen back with the ball in hand, right into the goal net. The ref had given us the point, rightly so. The opposing coach launched into the ref. I made my way onto the field to calm the situation only to have him start breathing down my throat. And even with my mother on the sidelines saying, "*Hija*, just let it go, come on, we're winning," I stayed out there and said my piece. And am I to blame for him calling me bitch?

Though I am to blame for flipping him over my calf and slamming him on the full of his back, which had a very interesting way of silencing both sides of the field.

I lost my coach position that same weekend. He didn't. I wanted to fight that, but my mother talked me out of it. And it had gotten busy at the Bureau, what with all the buildup around antiterrorism, so I decided, one less battle.

Which, my mother could tell anyone, was quite a change in my life. "You're getting wiser in your old age, *hija*," she said to me. I had turned thirty that year. I didn't need her to remind me.

Still, I had recognized it as well. I can still lose it, but after a short time, I regain . . . whatever it is we're supposed to regain. Patience? Acquiescence? I'm calmer now, that's what Mamá tells me. Everyone agrees that it's good. I suppose they're right.

But this year was much better. Sergio turned eight in August, and he seemed less stressed out once his mother was no longer his coach. And, I had to admit, I enjoyed the game more. Matt was a great coach. The kids loved him; Sergio was always one of the first to run up and give Coach Matt a high five. Matt was married, though. Too bad. His wife was always there: a good-looking woman, blond, nice figure, maybe four, five years older than me. A little shorter, though her legs were thinner than mine and I didn't doubt those breasts were silicone. Or, maybe they weren't. She was nice, in a soccer-mom way. "Come on, Slayers, move your behinds up that field!" She would belt her demands across the grass, but in a way that felt more, I don't know, positive.

I hadn't warmed up much to the other mothers on the team. There were differences between us, like shards of glass strewn over the sidelines. They gathered under sun umbrellas, talked to one another in familiar, though elevated ways. If they had been Latinas, they'd have been using *tú* between one another. But they weren't; somehow, in a game dominated by Latin Americans, and in a city where Latinos have become the majority, my kid had landed on an almost all-white team.

But that wasn't the main difference between us. It was the differences in our lives. "Gosh, I hope Jessica's careful today," said one woman. "If she gets hurt or anything, well, that'll just ruin her filming tomorrow."

"What's she on?"

"It's another Kellogg commercial."

"Really? Animated?"

"Oh, yes. She's gotten *very* good at pretending to talk with Tony the Tiger. She practices all the *time* in front of her mirror. But I've got to get her home right after the game. We've got a party tonight. You know Steve, the director from Sony? He and his wife are coming over. Marta's cooking salmon with fois gras. I hope that'll do."

"You're just multitasking today, aren't you?"

Not my style of conversation. And they knew it, after the one time they were kind enough to invite me under the umbrellas. I had been at a scene in Culver City the day before. One of those late nights when LAPD and we from the Bureau were trying to figure out if a new case was local or federal. I don't know, something I said to the soccer ladies about the lacerations around the girl's neck, it didn't look like it had been done with a wire, but rather a hemp cord, which wasn't our boy's M.O., and besides, she was fifteen, not twelve, which was another red flag, so we handed it to the blues. The other moms never asked me under the umbrella again.

My mother would say I had meant to do that. My own way of marking territory. She's right, some things never change. I hate wasting time. Any time.

The soccer was not wasting time at all. It was part of our days together: Sergio, his grandmother, and me. And I liked the game. The kids had developed over the year; last season they looked like a flock of seagulls fighting for the same piece of bread. This year they actually understood *positions*. The game got my mind off work, off the drug traffic killings that I had an impossible time keeping up with. The soccer let me forget, for an hour or so, the other Los Angeles that I had learned about in the past three years: a silent city that seeped into this real, bustling city, kept hidden but still right here. I knew. I didn't doubt that, while standing here, my mother to my right on her fold-up easy chair with her sunglasses and her diet soda, there was, within the radius of the three soccer fields we stood in, no doubt a good, I don't know, twelve thousand dollars' worth of coke, grass, meth, ice, heroin, all tucked in purses, pocketbooks, in folded plastic liners under baseball caps.

Mamá used to tell me that I worried too much about this. Even back in Nashville I worried about it. But she doesn't say that anymore, once she learned, through me, how many doctors and teachers both bought and sold in Music City. And the day that she saw her grandson overdose, all because he mistook a babysitter's meth for rock candy, changed her mind entirely.

Sergio was doing well. He was in second grade in a good school on Kester Avenue here in the Valley, where they taught drug-awareness regularly. They even had me come in a couple of times to speak to the older kids about the dangers of narcotics. I used the traditional scare tactics: pictures of overdosed women and men on the street. I even snuck in a couple shots of street assassinations, which the teacher didn't care for, though that had made the point clear, that too many people die because of their bad drug habits. Then I got stopped by this one fifth grader, an Asian American girl, who said, "But, Miss Chacón, if drugs are so bad, then why do people do it so much?"

I had never been asked that before. I promised myself to be honest with them: "That's a great question, honey. It's because the drugs feel so very, very good."

That bothered the teacher, too. So I followed up quickly with more lessons, about the addiction, and the sicknesses. But I told them just what their future drug dealer was going to tell them: It feels so very good.

"Hija. Mirá vos."

My mother stood from her chair, which woke me a bit; I was tired, had been up way too late last night. She saw it before I did: Sergio had not only blocked the ball, he was moving forward with it. And though he usually was very good at staying in Defense position, he couldn't avoid the temptation of the clear pathway to the goal. He ran it, moved the ball through the space left by both teams, and was alone with the opposing goalie on the other end of the field. Our voices followed him in a crescendo, the umbrella women yelping his number, one of them asking, "What's his name? What's his name?" So I screamed it, "*Corre mi hijo*, Sergio!" And he did. He ran, faster than I've seen him run before. Then the pop: his foot sideways, his leg forming that perfect arch. The poor goalie reaching but not touching. The net, pulled back with the force of the ball.

Glorious. Just beautiful. Something we all needed. Something, these days, ever since the bombing on Olive Street, all of Los Angeles could use: a sense of victory.

Later I would be happy that the phone call did not come until after the kids had torn open their snacks (Oreo cookies, Gatorade) and hovered around Matt as he told them what a terrific group of players they were. I could enjoy that as well. Mamá and I stood with a few of the other parents, giving our attention to Matt so our kids, all sweaty and walking off their heat, would listen to him.

Other cell phones were beeping and buzzing around us, so I didn't feel so bad when mine went off. Then I saw the phone number: the Field Office.

"Romilia, hello, this is Leticia Fisher."

Not a good voice to hear. The Special Agent in Charge, calling me on a Saturday morning. Even the SAC should have had the day off; but since Olive Street, days off were hard to come by.

"I'm afraid I've got some bad news. Chip Pierce is dead."

As Matt praised The Mighty Slayers for their great teamwork, I walked over to one side of the field to listen to Fisher. "I'm calling everyone in Chip's squad, but I thought you would want to know as well," she said. She did not need to explain. No doubt Chip had told Fisher about us. "Karen in Media Rep already has her hands full with this, and the LAPD's hovering around the scene, calling it theirs until we can prove otherwise. Romilia, you there?"

"Yeah. Yes, sorry, Agent Fisher, I'm . . . Jesus, what happened?"

"I don't have all the details. But it sounds like it *might* be an L.A. case. They beat him to death. Apparent robbery. But there's the fact that he was working on the Olive Street bombing, and this may have been connected. We're still talking to the Venice cops."

She continued with a few other details, but I could hear her voice faltering and picking itself up, in spasms. She was a friend of Chip's. As she roused up a professional voice, I was trying to make a decision about right or wrong. My mother would tell you that this was also a sign I was getting older: I chose what seemed like the right thing. "Agent Fisher. I was with him last night."

A long pause. She asked the obvious questions: What time? (Ten o'clock. I stayed until after midnight.) Were we still seeing each other? (No.) Then why were we together? (Just a drink; and, okay, so we were still trying to figure things out, had been playing the platonic/erotic game the past few weeks.) The blunt phone interrogation ended with her saying, "You need to get on down here."

"Who was that?" Mamá asked.

"Work. I've got to go."

"Ay." That was her fed-up *ay*. But she saw worry on my face. "What happened?"

She had known Chip, though she had not approved of the relationship, and had been glad when we ended it. Still, she could be shocked and saddened, when I told her. "Oh no," she said. "Who? Was he working? How—?"

"I'm not sure yet. I've got to get to the office."

She squeezed my fingers. "I'm sorry, Romilia." She kissed me on my left cheek. "I'll take Sergio. We'll go over to Chepe's together."

"All right. Thanks. *Te quiero*," I said.

"*Vos también.*"

I walked away from the noise of the field, from the sounds of children and coaches and refs and parents. All that faded. Not just from my walking away from it; it was more the moving from one Los Angeles to that other one, from the bustle into the silence.

My mother's *I'm sorry* was not just for Chip's death, nor for my own sadness over his murder. It also meant to cover, like a mother's blanket, the whole truth of our relationship. For my mother knew that, though we had been lovers, I had not been in love.

She was okay with this. She had liked Chip, had seen him as a fine man, not necessarily young (eight years my senior), but still in good shape. She wasn't sure about my dating a man with a prosthetic, but said little about it. "Does he make love with it on?" she once asked, then laughed at her own ignorance. "But the eye patch, well, it looks kind of sexy," she said. "*Hacer el amor con un pirata. Hmmmm . . .*"

She knew we were having sex. And though tending toward the traditional, she said nothing against this. It had been a long haul, since the days we lived in Nashville. I had not been with a man since my own husband had died. The only man in our life now was little Sergio, and though he certainly filled our days and filled a certain need in both of us, he couldn't fill in me what I finally started to recognize was desperately lacking. I couldn't recognize it, not until several months after taking down the monster who had killed my sister.

Mamá and I made decisions quickly after that: It was time for a drastic change. Even though we had been in Nashville less than a year (after an entire life in Atlanta), the option to move to Los Angeles was too tempting for either of us to ignore. The FBI had offered me a job in L.A., one of the largest field offices in the Bureau. My uncle Chepe, Mamá's youngest and only surviving brother, lived out here, and was a successful caterer to the stars, spending his days on movie and television sets. It was no big deal for him to cut up carrots for Dennis Hopper or make a blended seaweed shake for Angelina Jolie.

The thought of his big sister moving out to southern California pleased Uncle Chepe in a way that no one could understand unless they had walked the road he had walked: all the way from El Salvador, as a teenager. After he had escaped from the army and avoided forced draft by the guerrillas, my mother made sure Chepe had a clear pathway to America. She paid for all three coyotes — men who deal in people-running across the border — between

San Salvador and Tijuana. Chepe was ready to leave. In the old country the military had him on a list, all because he had acted in a *sociodrama* at the age of fifteen, with a group of street actors who liked to thumb their noses at all authorities, including, from time to time, the military. Three of their thespians wound up dead, their testicles removed and shoved down their throats, with *comunistas jodidos* (fucking communists) carved into their chests with razor blades. That was in the mid-seventies. Mamá spent a lot of money to get Chepe to the States. From that point on, Chepe has been trying to repay her, always saying, "My debt to you is one of my great blessings." He helped us put a down payment on our house in Van Nuys; he gave Mamá a job in his business. Sometimes she cooks, but most of the time she takes care of the bookkeeping.

It was all too good to ignore. While Sergio and Mamá packed up our belongings in Nashville, my new employer had me sent to Quantico for fifteen weeks of training. I spent my time in the Behavioral Science Unit and did drills in Hogan's Alley, the simulated town where aspiring Fed agents train to bring down fleeing bank robbers and search seedy pawn shops. Special Operations and Research, Forensic Science Research, Bomb Data and Basic Diffusion, I did it all.

It was strange, being among the cadets. Word had gotten around about a couple of my cases. That I had brought down a serial killer through actual detective work astounded them. I wanted to correct them, say that it was not detective work, but obsession, bordering on pathology, that helped me bring Minos down.

It was strange, being a cop who had taken care of family business. I had done what I had set out to do, long ago: Find the man who killed my sister, and kill him myself. He was the reason I had become a cop and, finally, a homicide detective. He was the reason I had actually become successful in life.

And now, to be a cop without that vengeance, rather, to be not just a homicide detective but a *federal agent*, was strange, unfamiliar. Or so I thought, until the day I visited Catalina's grave in Atlanta.

My mother and son had already moved out to the house in

Van Nuys. I had finished the training at Quantico and wanted to go back to Nashville to say a few good-byes to my boss, Patrick McCabe, and my friend Doc Callahan. And to Catalina.

It was sad to leave McCabe and Doc, as we had worked hard together for that year in Nashville. I always wondered if Doc, a good-looking man in his fifties, had a crush on me. He cleared that up on the last day: "Romi darling, you'll always be my girl." He had smiled, kissed me on the cheek, and turned away, quickly, as if not wanting me to see his eyes water over.

Lieutenant McCabe had been more stoic. "What'd I tell you? No more local gravy for you. You're with the Feds now." He had shaken my hand, had smiled. "You're a great cop, Romilia. They're lucky to have you."

This was all new to me: a life of good things, a life with fewer shadows. I wasn't sure whether to trust it or not.

I visited Catalina on a cool afternoon in September. The sky in Atlanta was clear, the wind crisp. I placed flowers on her grave, then sat to one side with a cup of Starbucks in hand. I talked a while, which was not my way. I haven't prayed in years, since the day she died. My shadow graces no church pews. I have little desire to sow that sort of hope. Too many promises, very little proof. And my job, my life, is about proof.

But I sat there on the cold, dry grass and talked with my sister. Talked about those days when we used to sneak some of Papá's whiskey, take it up into our room, and sip it and giggle until the headaches came on. Then later, when we graduated to weed, how we'd get together in her apartment and smoke and talk about our boyfriends, and how she shocked Mamá once by saying she considered going lesbian, how it seemed a lot less complicated. "But no more grass for me, Caty," I said to the grave. "FBI does these spot checks with pee cups." I talked. I told Catalina that the finest plastic surgeons lived in Los Angeles, and Uncle Chepe thought one of them could get rid of this scar on my neck. He didn't say who would pay for it, though I had a feeling Chepe was offering. I even talked about Tekún Umán, and there, at the gravesite, I could express how I felt about a man in a way I had never shared with anyone else, and perhaps never will. "I've got to go, Caty. I miss you. I will always miss you."

I wept, which felt good. Really good. Until I bent over, and was about to kiss her gravestone, in some forgotten Catholic tendency from my childhood or my Salvadoran-ness. Something, I don't know, worthless. I recognized this the moment I glanced down, right before kissing the stone, and saw the word scratched upon the marble, just above the grassline:

FRANCESCA

I had been there the year previous, with Mamá. That was not on the stone then. Which meant that before Minos had gone on his killing spree, he had visited Catalina as well. And left this little memento.

It was too much. Just too much. It sucked away my tears. It raised in me a familiar rage that I had had for years — that though I'd killed him, I'd not snuffed him out, not completely.

I had my gun that day in the cemetery. I pulled it out and aimed it at that graffiti, the adulterous name from Dante's *Inferno*. Minos, now dead, and yet it felt like he was laughing at me, at my family, at my sister. I almost shot that word off the marble. But did not. No, did not; I made a smart decision, though, Jesus, I don't know how. I stumbled about the cemetery, looking for loose stones, finding none. So I opened my car trunk and pulled out the tire wrench and spent five sweaty minutes beating on my sister's gravestone until I shattered that word. Then I fell on the ground, atop her, and lay there, breathing, sweating, my bruised hands still aching with the vibration of the wrench.

I left the cemetery, left my sister. Got the hell out of Atlanta, out of Georgia, out of all this, my past. Headed to L.A. Pretended to start over.

LAPD swarmed Chip's house. They already had the yellow tape up. People walked by, individual women running, with their babies in large, three-wheel strollers; two men, walking together, hand in hand, until they saw all the cops. The blues kept them all at bay.

I parked quickly in a lot over on Virginia Court, walked across the street and into the neat labyrinth of paths that stand between the homes and the canals. It wasn't until I got to the corner of the Carroll and East Canals and put on my surgical rubber gloves that I stopped flat.

He was dead. I had just seen him, what? Nine hours ago.

At thirty years old, I'm not sure what to think about my own brain. Doctors have told me I tend toward the depressive; my mother just calls me moody. Neither seems right. I am . . . a rattle of thoughts, especially in these moments before approaching a crime scene. And then there is the personal, which my mind, over these past few years, had trained itself to keep at bay.

Nine hours ago. At one a.m., I left.

He's been dead less than nine hours, no doubt less than eight. It's nine-thirty now; they've checked his body temperature, plugged a thermometer into his liver.

He was bothered by something last night, more than just me. He was in love, but it was more than that. He was shaky. About something. Something was wearing him down.

He had a perfectly round mole on his left buttock. Once we played with my handcuffs. I liked it, he didn't.

He likes eggs Benedict. Liked.

Dead.

"Don't go in yet."

Special Agent in Charge Leticia Fisher walked up from one of the side paths, along with another agent whose name I could not remember: a young woman, white, a real blondie and new to the field office. "Agent Pearl, talk with the head homicide detective, Sergeant Clocker, see where's he's at so far. I'll be there in a minute."

Blondie left. Fisher turned to me. "So why were you here last night?"

"He asked me to come. He said that he was thinking about retiring."

"Retiring?" Fisher looked suspicious. "He never said anything about that to me."

"He seemed pretty stressed out."

She said nothing to that, but turned away a moment, looked at Chip's house. "Anything else?"

"Olive Street. He also mentioned the Crack Killer. But just in passing."

"Yeah? And?"

". . . He wanted me to marry him."

Fisher looked straight at me. Her eyes turned hard: Latina angry, African American solid. "No doubt, then. This is our case."

Chip Pierce was the head of my squad when I first came to Los Angeles. We knew a little bit about each other, having worked on the Minos case together. In L.A., we dealt mostly with narcotics, investigating drug killings in the southern California area. He had considered moving over to counterterrorism, but decided to stay on in narcotics, in part to help shepherd me into the Bureau.

Or so I thought. At first I didn't realize Pierce had something for me. I admired him as an agent; and he was the reason the FBI considered me in the first place. I want to believe that Pierce had submitted my name for consideration because of my skills as a homicide detective, rather than for any other reason.

For the first year, Chip and I only saw each other during squad meetings. He was Squad Leader; each of us under him had our own partners. I kept dropping partners like discarded poker cards. This didn't go well with the Squad. Some said I had a problem with trust. Maybe it's true; the relationship with my first partner almost got me killed and left me with a permanent scar on my neck, so gosh, perhaps I *do* have a problem with trust.

Then came the day when Chip said, "You want to ride with me to San Diego? Double-homicide. Sounds like something you'd be interested in."

"Why's that?"

"Strange markings on the bodies. Like a signature."

"Oh. And I'd be interested in strange?" I smiled at him.

He filled me in: Both bodies had been found near the border on the beach, right where Mexican and Californian sand meet.

Two men, one of them Mexican, the other white, both shot in the head in true *tiro de gracia* fashion. It had looked like the M.O. of the drug running Arellano brothers, though the brothers had been brought down that same year.

"Locals said there were scratch marks on the bodies," said Chip. "They looked too . . . formal for accidental scratches."

That long drive was the first time we had spoken privately since the Minos case. It was a languid, informal conversation, which started out with "So, you look like life's treating you well," and "How old's Sergio now? The only man in your life, right?" Then other questions, about my mother, and her hometown in El Salvador, a village called El Comienzo. Then the politics of El Salvador, and the fact that there were pupuserias all over L.A., where I could get my favorite Salvadoran dish. And then: Did I get out much? Did I like to go to movies? Once I told him I was a pretty boring home-girl, preferring to curl up with a book rather than drive around town looking for entertainment, he said, "Well, there's something very appealing about that."

It was very engaging; and I engaged, for the first time in a long while, with a man. It was a two-hour drive, so we could talk about personal details a bit more, though it always seemed to dovetail into our professions. The scar on my neck; his lost leg and missing eye. We got to that. "Smoky Mountains," said Chip. "Remember that case?"

"The guy who killed all those gay rights activists, and then hid out in the hills? Yeah, I remember that. Did they ever catch him?"

"No. They think he's dead, though they never found a body. But he was the one," Chip said, raising his open hand to his eye patch. He said it crisply, matter-of-factly, as if having mastered that tone with practice. "It was a setup. And I was cocky. You know, young new special agent in charge of his first squad, assigned to head up the task force in some small town in the Smokies. I went in with a crew. He had planned for us. Plastique explosives inside a small cove. We should have seen it, but we didn't. I was lucky to get out alive."

"You sound okay with it. Or, at least, reconciled."

He slapped his leg. "They took care of me. And they didn't

force me out, though they offered me a decent pension. I almost took it. But changed my mind, pretty quickly. The Bureau is my home. It's screwed up, but hey, what family isn't?"

We got around to my scar. How, in Nashville, handcuffed, I had used the cuffs to choke a perp from behind. He had reached back and slashed me with his blade. I was lucky, too, I supposed: he hadn't killed me. "But he left me with this damn, ugly thing." I covered it, as I always do, with my long hair.

"It bothers you, doesn't it?" Chip was driving. He turned slightly to me, then turned back to the road.

"Yeah. Yeah, it does. I hate how it makes me look." That slipped out before I could stop it, but it was that type of conversation, that certain, sudden intimacy between the wounded.

"It doesn't do you bad."

"Shit, I feel ugly."

He paused, then, on a long stretch of highway, turned and looked at me and said, "No scar could make *you* look bad."

That was it. And we both knew it, right then, though we said nothing about it until later. We got to San Diego, did our work. A cold day: They had the bodies out still on the beach, covered, left for us to check before the local Medical Examiner took them away. Both of them, yep, shots to the head, dead as dead could be; and one of them, very recognizable as Frankie Muñoz, a peon of the Arellano brothers. No doubt seen as a turncoat and executed by the brothers' retinue. Left here on U.S. soil, rather than inside Tijuana, as a sign of sorts. Bought by the gringos, these two stiffs were found out as *orejas*, "ears" or narcs, and were taken care of. Chip and I assessed the scene while walking around the bodies. I said I would write it up. The Medical Examiner turned the bodies over carefully, looked at their backsides, at the scrapes over their lumbar areas. "That what you were talking about?" Chip said to the local detective, who confirmed it. The scrapes looked uniform, as if placed there meaningfully: a perfect square, right across each man's lumbar. Almost like the stroke of a brush, only with the raking of a sharp edge across the skin.

"Might want to report that to D.E.A.," I said. "They may want to tag it to measure it up with the Crack Killer."

"A little out of that region, don't you think?" Chip said. "The Crack Killer's out east. If he even exists."

Still, he made a note to send the stats to the Drug Enforcement Agency in D.C.

We spent the afternoon there, combing the sand and talking with the people who had found the corpses (a young family from Des Moines, on vacation; there were other folks on the beach, mostly Latinos taking a Sunday off). Then we wrapped it up, maybe a bit more quickly than we were accustomed to doing. We got in the car and drove off, but wouldn't make it back to L.A. until later that evening. Not with a Holiday Inn Express on the road, where he checked us in and I made my way down the hall as if I didn't know him, then met up with him after he got the plastic door cards.

And it was good. Really good. Later I worried that he found me a bit more, I don't know, rapacious than what he'd expected. But I was hungry in a way I had not allowed myself to be hungry in a long while. At first we stumbled; I wasn't sure what to expect of him, once he shucked himself out of his pants and I saw, right there, the full of his prosthetic. An aluminum knee joint and a carbon fiber tube below it which took the place of his lower leg, and a fake foot below, really nothing but a curved piece of hard plastic. He rolled off a plastic liner (he corrected me, "It's made of silicone, fits like a tight glove.") from the nub of his leg, which freed the prosthetic. His leg looked slightly atrophied, as I had seen in other people who had lost limbs; yet it held form, probably from the stress he put on it while walking. He leaned upon the knee and the nub as he placed the fake leg carefully on the side of the bed. "Sorry. I'd rather have it off. I hope it doesn't bother you. I'll try to make up for it." He said that as he smiled and stripped off his tie, unbuttoned his shirt and peeled away his T-Shirt, and damn, yes, he made up for it.

He looked good, thin, taut, underneath. He was thirty-seven, maybe a little older, white skin, pink, with arms that showed off layers of muscle. When he squatted over me, his knee to one side of my thighs, the nub to the other, it looked as if he were merely kneeling, and that his missing leg was not missing; it was just hiding behind that gorgeous, smaller thigh.

Catalina and I used to trade notes. She talked more about men's bodies than I did; I tended more toward the "nice guy, caring, engaging, intellectual" talk. That was then. It still was important; but looking at Chip Pierce above me, wearing nothing but tight black underwear and that matching black eye patch, well, such wholesome talk didn't become necessarily secondary; but I suddenly got real hungry for the feel.

Hungry, and a desire to be unwound. Not just to relax, though that too happened. He worked his mouth over me, and shit if it didn't feel like he was unspooling tight springs out of my bones. When his tongue probed the dimples of my lower back, I squealed; the people in the room next to us, who I could hear talking, shut up. I laughed, buried my head in the pillow; and Chip kept going. I wondered if this would have happened with any guy, if I was just so tense that having any man slap me on the ass would have undone me, but no, Chip was good. His form of foreplay wasn't, "Brace yourself girl," but rather the long way home. I creamed once, even before he got to my button; it had been a long while since a man worked on my nipples like that, not since, well, not since Sergio breast-fed. "Jesus," I said. Chip smiled at me, his head right above mine. "God, you're gorgeous," he said, then nibbled around my forehead, down my left cheek, over my neck; right over the scar. Something only one other man has done in my life: again, my son. One day Sergio kissed that scar in a sudden burst of love for a mother, and started some strange sense of healing. Now, here was this blond white guy, my squad boss, Chip Pierce, kissing it, which was just fine by me.

"Now hang on," he said. He made his way down. It was candy time, I could feel it; yes, it was, and he used all his strength for it: He threw my legs over his shoulders, my knees to either side of his head. He lifted my pelvis, tucked my feet in the curves of his chest. He brought me up, held me in a grip, locked his mouth over me and didn't stop until I melted, right over his face. I must have been loud; the people next door got quiet again.

When he rode into me, I locked my right leg around his left. My left did not know where to go, so it lay there. I could feel the stub of his knee against mine, nothing below, but it didn't matter.

The way he moved in me there was no doubt that he was all man, all whole.

Months passed and we were both happy, though for different reasons. Chip may have thought, or hoped, that I was opening up to a solid, long-term relationship. Which meant he was soon disappointed.

"Don't you think we could take this further?" he once said, one night after a fine roll, when he made me breakfast around midnight.

"How could we go any further than what we've done?" I said, chomping on bacon. "I hear some of our movements are illegal in certain counties in Georgia. You know, sodomy laws and all that."

"That's not what I'm talking about. You want to get married?"

"Whoa." Then I sipped the wine and said, again, "Whoa."

"Come on, Romi. Feels right, doesn't it?"

But he must have sensed a change in me after that. A "holding back," as he once put it. I don't know if it was holding back; it was, for me, a simple distinction between sex and love. I was not in love. But I had found that I was horny as hell. And yes, the sex with him had allowed for some loosening, a nice waking up to days with a bit of a sigh and not minding it so much that Sergio had wet his bed. I knew in those first few months that I was on the dangerous edge of being labeled, that my desire to have a fuck-buddy would have, even in this oh so liberal town of L.A., defined me as a puta, whore, prostitute, loose woman, bitch.

And maybe I *was* holding back. Something about getting completely involved with a man bothered me. Frightened me a bit, made me gun-shy. Traits that we expect more from a man; but, considering the latest roads I had traveled, traits that seemed to fit my profile aptly. So I suppose it confused Chip whenever we competed with new moves in bed and I still would not give in to a long-term relationship. He was older; no doubt he had needs I didn't. So though I was saddened, I was not surprised the day he said, "We've got to stop. Lettie knows, and she doesn't like it, and she's not going to cover for us."

I knew what that meant: He and our boss, Lettie, were friends from years back. She had a warm spot for him, had helped make sure he could continue being an agent, even with his disabilities. Made sure he had gotten jobs that were not necessarily simply desk work, but also not so dangerous fieldwork, either. And no doubt, Lettie may have been happy that I had come along. I had given Chip one final sense of acceptance, in a world that does not accept broken people. But agents as lovers was not something Leticia could ignore forever.

"And besides, I need . . . more," he said. We both knew what that meant; and we both understood it would not happen. I said little. He explained the upcoming changes: Lettie was moving him to head up Counterterrorism. Then Chip paid for the coffee, stood, touched my shoulder. "See you around," he said. "Yeah," I said. I watched him leave. Then I got up and drove home.

In Counterterrorism he was busier than ever, what with all the threats placed upon Los Angeles: from the real bomb scares against LAX, to the crazies who called in with bad Arab accents saying they were planning to blow up the Getty Center only to be outed as some American nutso who had it in for a Muslim taxi driver who supposedly had stiffed him by driving him home the long way. I stayed with something more familiar and consistent: narcotics. In the months following, Chip and I would run into each other in the cafeteria or in the elevator. As of late, however, he went out of his way to run into me, which should have been a warning sign. Still, I was surprised when he called me last night and said, "I want to talk."

I made the trip over there. That house in Venice, where we had crawled over each other in every single position we could think of.

He kept a clean house. Maria, his cleaning lady, came in once a week. But she left his work, which he always carried home, alone. There, on the dining room table, where he never ate (we always ate in the kitchen, on the counter), there were books, files, maps of Los Angeles. Just like always. That night the table was piled with photos. One pile was of the Olive Street bombing. Two were from other areas: just some buildings, graffiti scrawled across their bricks.

He poured me whiskey, neat, from a bottle of Wild Turkey that he had bought me when we were lovers. Then he started talking. Not only had he decided to give it one more try; he meant to give up everything, for the woman he loved. "I'm going to retire," he said. This, I could not believe. "I'm tired. I'm just tired . . ."

"Chip, what's the matter?"

"What's *not* the matter? Olive Street. It's like investigating air! Just like the Crack Killer, Jesus, what the hell can you do with that? We should give him a medal rather than bring him in. He's doing a better job than we are, hell, just let him keep going . . ."

Why he would worry about the Crack Killer, I was not sure. That was more rumor than anything, a folklore among drug dealers. But Chip might have been drinking; it had gotten back to me, how much scotch he was putting down lately. I had seen this sort of stress on fellow agents, but never on him.

"Tell me something," he said. "What does 'ojala' mean?"

"What?"

"It's a word I ran across. Never seen it before."

"How do you spell it?"

He took a pen, paper, and wrote it out.

"Oh. *Ojalá*. You were pronouncing the 'j,' which should sound like an 'h.' Yeah, that's Spanish. It means, 'Oh how I wish.' It's a word that shows strong desire."

"Really?" He stared at the word. "Is that right?" He laughed, as if catching a joke no one else would understand.

"Where'd you learn it?"

He ignored my question; he was thinking hard. Then he said, "*Ojalá* . . . you'd marry me."

"Oh, Jesus, Chip."

"Romi. I'm going to hand in my badge. It's time. I've still got a life, and I want to live it."

"Don't quit for me, Chip."

"I'm not! I'm not at all. I'm quitting because I'm tired. And, once I quit, there's no conflict of interest. We're not partners. I'm not in the Bureau. You go work. Come home. I'll cook, clean up, I'll get Sergio to school. Your mom can live with us."

The conversation didn't go forward much. I felt I had broken something in him.

It was hard, leaving; and yet all I wanted to do was leave. He seemed, if not unstable, at least erratic; and at the moment, I thought I was the only thing making him so. My rejection, how it hurt him.

But now, walking behind Lettie Fisher into Chip's house that was now a crime scene, I wondered if there were other ghosts besides those of rejected love in the room with us last night.

I walked through the small foyer, into the front room, then past
the dining room table, with all his case files and books and maps
and photos, apparently untouched. A quick glance: It looked the
same as last night. Crime files, something he no doubt shouldn't
have had in his house; but such things slip by with obsessive
agents, and he was one.

The Crime Scene usuals: Prints, photographers, and the two
Venice detectives who got the call, hovered around one area, the
back dining room, with the large window that looked out beyond
Carroll Canal and toward Venice Boulevard. He was there, among
them, at their feet. They stepped around him, careful not to have
to step over him.

One fundamental thought hit me: I was necessarily a suspect.
No doubt I was the last person to see him alive. While running
the fingerprints through AFIS and, inevitably, through the ten
million-plus records of the National Crime Information Center,
they would also quietly pull up my files from D.C. and have a good
look at my prints. This didn't bother me too much. I hadn't spent
time in here in months. Maria was a good housekeeper; she had
cleaned any remnants of me out of Chip's home, enough to keep
the detectives from getting confused or forming flimsy theories. My
story would match the proof: I was here last night. I had touched a
glass of whiskey, the couch, the toilet when I flushed. I touched the
inner doorknob upon letting myself out. There was little of me
here.

Before I got to the doorway of the dining room, Letty touched my shoulder, warned me, "It's not good."

It never is, I thought. But I knew what she meant.

His face, barely recognizable, like a shattered mirror of Chip Pierce. It was rage, that was the first thing I saw; a rage had beaten itself out onto his skull. Broken nose, broken cheekbones, no doubt some teeth missing. All this I could see in just a glance. And there, so obvious, his prosthetic: bloodied and blunted and bent, lying next to his left shoulder.

"Why," I said, then stopped myself. For I was just about to ask Letty, *Why is this our case?* But then I saw the seep of blood through Chip's pullover shirt. Right over his abdomen. Not thick blotches, but curved lines. Then I knew why Letty said what she did, why this was our case. The shirt itself almost made the word, but not quite. "Have you already looked?" I said to Letty.

"Yeah."

She did not stop me from leaning over. With my gloved hands I peeled the shirt up and saw the scar of word. CABRON.

I just stayed there, leaning over him, but I turned away from the word and placed the shirt carefully back down. I didn't get up, as if this was the closest I was going to get to prayer position. But I wasn't praying; I was just thinking, *This is more complicated than anyone realizes.*

Meanwhile, my boss made one last argument with the head LAPD detective, saying that we had jurisdiction over this killing, for not only was Special Agent Pierce one of our own, but this was done by a man we and the DEA had been looking for for a good three years, so LAPD's Finest could go on home now, let the Feds take this one. Nothing about the Olive Street bombing. I could hear it in her voice, an anger known by all law enforcement officers and Bureau agents and every single man and woman who has lost partners in these jobs. I understood. Still, I shivered when Fisher turned to the young blond agent Pearl and said, "Send it back to the office, that Rafael Murillo is in the Los Angeles region." Pearl gave her a blank stare, so Letty repeated it and spelled it out: "Murillo. He goes by the name Tekún Umán."

He had made it onto the Ten Most Wanted List. Yet no one had heard of the whereabouts of Rafael Murillo for three years. Not since the day he had escaped from Nashville, after trying to set up various nonprofit organizations as fronts for his drug trade. He had planned to make Nashville the headquarters for all his traffic throughout the southeast United States. He had gotten pretty far, setting up meth labs all over Tennessee's capital, importing cocaine and heroin from Miami and Corpus Christi via truck lines that he had acquired, and washing the money through fake homeless shelters that really took care of homeless people. Not only took care of them; he made sure the homeless who stayed in his shelters drank Starbucks and had cable. Every Sunday night the shelters filled with people from off the streets who didn't want to miss the next episode of "The Sopranos."

Then I came along and messed up his plans. While handling the Jade Pyramid serial killings that had haunted Nashville for an entire season, I outed Rafael Murillo from his philanthropic façade and showed the Nashville world what a slippery drug runner he was. Something Murillo threatened to kill me for, until I saved him from a man who hated him enough to leave a wake of killings on the Nashville streets.

Murillo. No, not Rafael Murillo. Everyone knew him for who he was: Tekún Umán. Named after the great Mayan Indian warrior who had died fighting off the Spanish conquistadores. At first I thought this was Murillo's own self-praise, a demonstration of his narcissism, but I was wrong. He had not named himself that; others in the Latin American drug world from where he had come had given him the name. For some, he was a hero (I can't help but think of all those homeless he fed); but the rest of us knew what he was capable of doing.

He was capable of carving a man's stomach with words, with that damned emerald Harpy Knife of his, a knife that I had gotten a good close look at a couple of times.

And yet he loved me. Or so he had pronounced, loud enough for most of the world to hear. That's why this was our case; that's why my boss Letty made it our case.

And that's why I wanted to make it mine.

Tekún was Guatemalan; but he was also still very southern. A Central American father, a mother from Chattanooga. I had never heard of such a mix, what he liked to call a "Latino Hick."

He still had relatives in Tennessee. One of them had once filled me in: Tekún had lived most of his childhood in Guatemala, in the northern, jungle region of the country. His father, supposedly an upright businessman, had been gunned down by a competing cocaine-running family. This was too much for Tekún. He joined the Guatemalan army, one of the more shadowy militaries in Latin America. But even that wasn't enough: He joined their Special Forces, became a Kaibil soldier. Trained in all the arts and crafts of killing. That's where he developed this little signature, leaving words carved into people's bellies.

Fisher slapped her cell phone closed and turned to me. "That was Terry Lyons, at DEA," Letty said. "You can't imagine how, well, I won't say happy . . . excited he was to hear the news that we're back on Tekún's ass."

"I want this one."

Letty looked at me. "I didn't call you to take the case. You said you were with Chip last night. We need to question you."

"I know. That's fine. But I want this."

"You're too close."

"No. No, I'm not." And it came out like regret. She caught it. "Chip and I, we didn't work out."

"I know. That's not what I mean."

"What do you mean you 'know?'"

"I'm not stupid, Romilia." She lit a cigarette. We were outside Chip's house, on the sidewalk next to the canal. "Look,I know how much you meant to Chip. In fact, I was happy to hear about it. He didn't tell me everything, but I could tell you made him happy."

"I think I let him down, too."

"No, you didn't. You were honest. Chip wouldn't have wanted you to be anything else but honest." She dragged, then blew, looking toward Venice Boulevard. "I thought you were pretty discreet about it, too, especially when he asked to be moved over to C.T. But looks like it's true what they say about Tekún: He's still obsessed with you. And that's why you can't take this case."

"With all respect, Agent Fisher, I know Tekún Umán better than anybody."

"And it seems he knows you. Your daily movements, who you hang out with, who you're seeing on an intimate basis. And now, presumably out of jealousy, he's killed Pierce."

I did not contradict her. "Please consider it."

She smoked, crushed out the butt. "Report to Wilshire Street for questioning." The tightened quiver of her voice gave it away: She had lost a friend.

Two male agents I did not know but had seen walking the hallways of the Wilshire Field Office questioned me. They were nice enough about it. I was one of their own. But that did not make them my friends. Agent Randall asked the questions. Agent Shrieber wrote notes. They were both younger than me. Which I believed made them hungry for ladder-climbing.

I was honest with them: how Chip had asked me over, saying he needed to talk with me. How erratic he had acted, as if he was overloaded from the job. No, we had never talked about his work in counterterrorism; we had talked little in the past several months, as we had broken up our relationship, and why? Due to the job. The job consumed us both, and we both realized the dangers of being too involved with another agent. So we broke it off. But yes, Special Agent Pierce had asked me over to propose to me, that he was willing to give up his job and take disability, finally, after so many years of serving the government. He was ready to hang it up, get married, settle down with a wife who would still work as a federal agent. All of which, I told Randall, was why I thought he was erratic.

"What do you mean?"

"Something was bothering him. It had to do with the counterterrorism unit, his work. It wasn't like Chip to run from a fight."

"Was it the work? Or are you saying something was happening in his squad?"

"I don't know. All I know is what I've told you. He was behaving in a manner not consistent with his usual demeanor."

Those were enough big words and complex enough syntax to keep Randall thinking and Shrieber scribbling.

"But I don't know why Tekún Umán did Agent Pierce like that," said Randall.

"Seems simple enough for me," said Shreiber, looking up from his notepad.

"Yes?" I looked at him.

"Well, the perp had the hots for you, right?"

"The perp was known for his uncanny ability to smoke screen," I said. "Don't believe everything you hear. He's a fucking drug runner."

This did not mollify their curiosity. "But it's true that you and Agent Pierce were involved sexually, that perhaps this Tekún Umán might have come after him for stealing you away from him?"

"Yeah," said Shreiber. "Can't tell with these narco guys. When they want something, they go after it."

"Sure do. And, hey, that word on Chip Pierce's stomach, what's it mean?

"I dunno."

They both looked at me. A nickname came to mind: Klick and Klack. A little more updated than Tweedledee and Tweedledum.

"You know?" Klick asked me.

"It means 'cuckold,'" I said.

"That's, uh, what?" said Klack.

"A man who's wife is in bed with another guy."

"Oh, being two-timed, right?" said Klick. "Yeah. Two timer."

"Well, there you go," said Klack. "This Tekún fellow, he gets mad at Pierce for two-timing with you. Man, this guy's a sicko."

"A smart sicko," said Randall, who turned to me again. "You've got to ask how it was that Tekún knew about you two, and all that you did." He cleared his throat, adjusted his glasses, drew his gaze from my breasts up toward my face, and said, "I mean, just how intimate were you two?"

As if I would give him anatomical maps. "Intimate enough." I wondered, was this sudden good-ol'-boy talk, this smoke screen, to get me to confess? Or to stumble into erotic details?

A cell phone buzzed. Shreiber's, who I now, silently, referred to as Klick. He talked while Randall asked another curiosity-quencher: "Isn't it true that Tekún Umán gave you that?" He pointed, with his pen, toward the long scar on my neck.

"No. That's not true."

He stared, waiting for me to tell him the truth. I said nothing. I just looked at him, with my arms crossed. I flipped my hair back and turned my head so the full of my scar filled his eyesight. He turned away.

Shrieber closed his phone. "We're done. Agent Chacón, Special Agent Fisher wants to see you."

Both men stood. Randall looked a wee bit shaken. Perhaps that scar was more than he'd wanted to think about today. Too bad.

I looked over at the one-way mirror, knowing my boss was on the other side.

"Take Agent Pearl with you back to Pierce's place."

"Pearl? Why?"

"You need a partner on this one."

I do not. "Isn't she kind of green?"

Fisher looked at me. Sometimes all she has to do is look at you.

"So, did you know Special Agent Pierce very well?" Agent Nancy Pearl asked. Her voice was peppy and kind, which got on my nerves quickly.

"Yeah. We worked together, years ago. On the Minos case."

She wanted to ask more about that. But I looked at her; it must have been enough of a look to clue her in.

She spent the rest of the drive talking about her journey into the corridors of the FBI: She had seen *The Silence of the Lambs* so many times, all those scenes at Quantico, of a young girl from the sticks becoming a great federal agent. She loved movies, especially since she really hated reading, much preferring to see a book on the screen rather than having all the works of Mark Twain shoved down her throat. . . . She talked, way too much. Pearl may have been only three or four years younger than me, but there was a canyon of experience between us.

"Agent Pearl, sorry, don't take this wrong: Would you mind being quiet a few minutes? I'm trying to think about where we're going."

"Oh, yeah. Yeah, right. Sorry."

I turned on the radio, flipped it to the jazz station. Coltrane. She just couldn't keep her mouth shut. "Oh, you like jazz?"

"Yeah. Partly."

She laughed, just slightly.

"What?" I looked at her.

"Oh, I don't know . . . aren't you Mexican?"

I sighed. "Salvadoran."

"Right. I just thought you'd like, you know, that mariachi music more."

As if it mattered what kind of music I liked. "Agent Pearl, are you from . . . the Midwest?"

She smiled, surprised. "Yes, I am."

"Let me guess," and I played in my head her voice, her accent, her pick of movies, and the string of stupid things she said. "I'm guessing rural, but not southern exactly, but something like it . . . far from a city, right?"

"Yeah . . ." She was intrigued.

"Iowa or Missouri?"

"That's right." Her mouth opened, her jaw slackened.

"Oh, let me take a stab at it . . . somewhere near Hannibal, Missouri!"

"You're *right!* I was born in Palmyra. Oh, my gosh!"

She almost screamed. I faked a laugh, then looked ahead and muttered in Spanish, something close to *Holy fuck, who has Fisher stuck me with?*

How could I toy around with Agent Pearl like that? Especially with what waited for me at the end of this drive. A return to Venice, to his home. In the past three years, one of my mother's complaints has been that I've become a bit distant. This, from a woman who always said I got too close, became too dark, too obsessed with incidents. Such as my sister's murder. And she had been right. So after burying that past, I got more objective. FBI. Special Agent. This was the big time. This was a job offered me because I had done well on local cases, and my screwups had not brought me down. I had decided, three years ago, to make fewer screwups, try to keep my head on straight, do the right thing. Like telling Letty Fisher that I had seen Chip last night. Like being as honest as necessary with the two little Feds who were so interested in my sex life and my scar. I had become objective, distant; and these days, my mother complained about *that*.

Toying with Pearl was part of that objectivity. It was a harmless game (harmless to me, at least;), a way of dealing with some inconsistencies: the FBI, the best of the best, and yet they still let in someone like this Pearl. A younger agent who had heard about me, just like the two guys who questioned me had heard about me.

I remember where I was, at what time, by the gauge of a book. *Paula* during the move to L.A. *Atonement* once we settled in and during my first case, when Chip and I got together. Nowadays I've gone to Faulkner; Pearl didn't know that, in the backseat, an old paperback of *Absalom, Absalom!* was shoved in my backpack. All books that have not been accidental reads; each one had a way of approaching whatever it was I needed to approach, or to distance myself from.

In the six months spent hunting Minos, I read no novels. Only downloaded Bureau documents and a well-thumbed copy of *The Inferno*. That was enough Dante for the rest of my life. I needed novels again.

Something I did not think I could talk much about with Pearl. She had already shown her disdain for reading; perhaps that's why I had turned her off so quickly.

LAPD's Crime Scene Investigation Unit had done most of the work. Prints had used black dragon's blood to lift latents from glasses, doorknobs, windows, plates. All the case files on his dining room table were gone, packed up after Prints finished with them, boxed and sent them back to the Bureau offices. Chip was gone; his body was gone. But his leg was still there, spattered with black powder and the red of his blood. That had been the work of the LAPD, before Agent Fisher had called it a federal investigation. Right there and then, LAPD stopped their work. Our crime scene crew was here now, gathering more information. Most of the fingerprint powder was around the prosthetic's shoe, encircling the ankle, which was right: That's where the killer grabbed it in order to use the leg as a club. That was the only thing that was right.

Pearl walked around me, her head bent slightly, her hands behind her back. That was a good sign; I had to give her credit, just by her position at a scene. "Watch out, right there," I said.

"What?" She stopped, looked at me, then at the empty space before her on the rug.

"They've already lifted the glass. But it was spilled, right about there. They should have circled the spot." I looked around for the head of the Crime Scene Unit. A woman, a number of years older than me, walked through the front door. Asian American woman, pretty, though looking tired, and maybe a bit tense.

I introduced myself. Her name was Huong. "Was there a glass right here?" I pointed to the place.

She flipped through her notepad. "Yes. A tumbler. Fallen on its side, the top of the tumbler pointing northeast, toward that corner." She turned and looked. I scanned her notepad. She had an intricate map of the entire room, the positions of every piece of furniture in the place. "We've already lifted it," she said. "They'll check it for residue."

Meaning toxicology. "But poison didn't kill him, right?"

"As far as we know, probable cause of death was the beating to the head, with his own prosthetic."

"Did the M.E. say anything offhand about the body? Signs of struggle, a fight, maybe some hair torn?"

Huong smirked. "Dibbs doesn't say much."

I would be meeting Dibbs soon, so it was best to inquire as much about him as possible. "He hard to work with?"

"Oh, he's just trying to fill Noguchi's shoes. You know, the Coroner to the Stars? Hard act to follow."

I stared at the area where Chip had died. I remembered what I had seen before: It would have been easy to have forgotten details, with that Spanish word looking up at me from his stomach. But I had not. Maybe because I had seen words carved on the stomachs of other people. Or maybe because I knew not to focus on the carving. From what I could remember from looking at Chip's body, only his head had taken blows. The rest of him, I guessed, was not bruised, from either a beating or a fight.

"When toxicology checks for residue, what do they check for?"

"First sweep, any toxic substance. Second, any pharmacological residue. After that, any anomaly that might show up."

"Focus on the anomaly," I said. "Have them look for muscle inhibitors."

"Like a tranquilizer?"

"No. Not tranquilizer. Something that can paralyze you. For just a few minutes. But you might not get it from the glass. I'd suggest taking out part of that carpeting." I pointed to the place where the glass had fallen.

"Is that what the suspect did last time?"

"He's known for that."

Huong nodded, motioned for one of her men to start cutting into the carpet to take it back to the lab.

Pearl and I spent another hour in and outside the house. Much of our investigation would be at the Crime Lab. For now I wanted to see what Pierce was like in his last days. And I was relieved to see that his last days were not about me. There was only one photo of us together, and it was amongst a gathering of photos on the dresser in his room. Taken during a walk in the Santa Monica Mountains; I remembered the elderly white couple who had been kind enough to stop and use our camera. "Such a lovely pair. Looks like you two could be happy the rest of your lives," the woman had said. Happy, like them? They were in their seventies, and there they were, climbing the Backbone Trail together.

The photo had once stood prominent, and alone, on his lower dresser, where he could look at it as he tied his tie or combed his hair. But he had moved the photo to the taller dresser, relegated it to his collection of memories. Pictures of his parents, both dead now. Pictures of friends in the Bureau, him and Letty, some other pals whose names I did not know and had never asked about. The signs were there, back then: I had not asked about his friends, had asked little about his past. That was not important to me in this relationship. What had been important to me was Chip, and the sex, and how good it had felt and how nights with him had led to a calm during the days.

He had not rejected me. He had placed me with the people he cherished. At first I was not sure what to think of this: He had not stuffed me into a drawer like an angry lover would have done. Nor had he left me on the lower cabinet, like a lover bemoaning his fate. He had placed me with the rest of his memories, the good memories, friends who were living and dead. That, to me, showed a certain acceptance; though regretful, he had kept me as a reminder of good things.

Which did not make sense, compared to our last conversation, of what? Just thirteen hours ago.

Thirteen hours. Twelve hours dead.

"Okay . . . Pearl, where are you?"

"Yes, Agent Chacón?" She had been studying the area around the marker of Chip's body.

"Let's go."

"Oh . . . are we done here?"

"I'd say that's what 'let's go' means, yeah."

I drove. I put on my sunglasses. I gave her instructions: We were going back to the Bureau offices, on the way to the Coroner's. Just a quick stop. I wanted to pick up some files, then we'd head on over to meet with Dr. Dibbs. She asked no questions, and knew simply to acknowledge my demands. That made it easier for me to park the car quickly, tell her I'd see her in half an hour, back here at the car. I made my way to the bathroom, where I could take off my sunglasses and blow my nose. Acknowledge the full image, the memory of Chip that had cut at me like a scalpel since the moment I had seen my photo on his dresser: Chip over me, in me; almost ready to spill into me, a man turning into a boy who is happy. He had been happy.

There, in the women's restroom, for the first time in a long while, I had a simple, pure emotion: the singular sense of mourning. No one came in, thank God; no one could hear me sob in the stall.

I called ahead to see when the M.E. would be ready with the autopsy report. He needed another four hours. This was not from him; he had his assistant give me that information, and though the young man named Phil was nice enough about it, I couldn't help but hear the residue of Dibbs's curt voice coming through.

"So, around five o'clock?" I said.

"Well, better around six," said Phil.

"Okay. Will he be there?"

"Oh, yes. Dr. Dibbs said he would stay for you. But please be here at six."

Dibbs had trained the boy well. "Okay. Six it is."

I gave Dibbs Junior my cell number, then called down to our Evidence Lab. "I'm Special Agent Chacón, I'd like to come down and see the bags on the Pierce killing."

"I'm sorry, which case was that?" the woman said. She must have been new.

"Pierce, Special Agent Pierce. I need to see the evidence bags."

"I'm sorry, nothing has come in under that case name."

"Oh, shit," I muttered, "sorry. I just remembered, thank you . . ." and I hung up on her, then looked up the number for Venice Homicide. They connected me to their Evidence department.

"I think you've got the workup on the Pierce case?" I said.

"Yeah, sorry, we just got the word that it's yours. I was going to send it over, but got caught up registering another set of bags. You need it now?"

"Soon as you can. How much is it?"

"We only did a partial pickup, when your boss called it a Fed case. But yeah, we've got oh, five, six plastics for you."

"All dusted?"

"Yep."

I was drawing a blank on what they would have dusted before Fisher had called it ours. "What's in the bags?"

"Well, his wallet, a short drinking glass, and, uh, the needles."

"Needles. What needles?"

"Well, we found needles in his house."

"For what?"

He must have taken my confusion for thick-headedness. "For injections, ma'am."

"What injections? Agent Pierce wasn't on any special medications."

"His prints were on them. Ma'am? You there?"

"Yeah. Listen, I'll come by, pick it all up. I can sign out for it."

"We'll be here." A congenial tone. Maybe he was trying to cover over the embarrassment. Which meant the needles were not regular hypodermics.

Half an hour later, Pearl and I were at the Evidence office on the outskirts of Venice. We both showed our shields, and she watched as I signed out the wallet, the glass, and the three thin hypodermics filled with a brownish liquid that looked too close to the real thing. "Shit," I said.

We drove back to the offices on Wilshire. I said nothing along the way. She chose to keep quiet herself; a good decision.

After checking in the evidence bags, I looked for Fisher, who was not in the building. It was probably best; I could come back later, after the autopsy, and give a full account.

"Okay, Agent Pearl, listen. We've got four hours before Dibbs is done. We'll probably be working overtime tonight, so I'd suggest taking the afternoon off. Meet me at the Medical Examiner's at five forty-five." I spoke to her like I would have spoken with Sergio during one of those long days of homework, baths, and piles of toys to pick up. "I'll see you then." I turned to walk down the hallway.

"Special Agent Chacón?"

I turned back to her. "Yeah?"

"My first name is Nancy."

"Yeah?"

"You can call me Nancy." She smiled.

"All right," I said while walking out of the building.

I took my own advice and went home. Not to my house in Van Nuys, but to my Uncle Chepe's business, down on Sunset, in Hollywood. Where I could eat a free, Salvadoran lunch. I could check my e-mail there. Uncle Chepe has high-speed Internet, while at home we still have dial-up. I'd have a chance to catch up with Mamá, who would want to know as little as possible about Chip's death, but would not mind at all talking a while about his life. I wasn't ready for that, but I was ready to eat and chat with her and Chepe and have my boy sit on my lap, where we could praise him on his most awesome goal this morning.

Uncle Chepe's front kitchen smelled of every food you could think of except Salvadoran. He had a client from Universal filming a new Russell Crowe flick in Long Beach, and he had to feed them through the night. I walked back into the second kitchen, the family kitchen, where he prepared real food. "You're just in time," Uncle Chepe said to me, kissing me on the cheek. "We've got *pupusas* on the grill."

"You got cheese?"

"Yes, dear." He smiled. Following our little joke.

"And *chicharrón?*"

"Of course, *mi hija*."

"But not together, right?"

"Why would I do that? Everyone knows how Romilia Chacón feels about *pupusas revueltas*."

"You've made my day."

My mother walked by. "I'll never understand that," she said. "They mix in your stomach, why not mix them in the *pupusas?*"

My son was in a back room, playing a Nintendo game with his cousin Felix. I called for him: "*¡Hola, mi cipote!*"

He turned, looked at me. "*Hola, Mamá*." He kept punching the buttons on that damn game.

"Hey. I walk in the door, you jump up and show me *cariño*, you got it?"

He smiled, embarrassed, dropped the control board, and tackled me. "You were Superman out there today, you know that?" And all the adults — Chepe, my mother at the stove, and a hired cook — all joined in the praise with me. It satisfied us both: I let him go, and Sergio ran back to the Nintendo game.

I ate, talked with my mother and uncle. They did not ask about the case, though I was sure Mamá had talked with her little brother about Chip. But they knew better than to ask. There was no point in it, as I would say little, and they knew that was as it had to be. And I don't doubt that they didn't want to hear it, really; they didn't want details. They were curious, but they didn't want images from my work floating in their heads.

And not because they were innocents. Both my mother and my uncle had seen too much in their past, in our old country. They had seen back in El Salvador what I stand over every day; only they did not have the chance that I have: they could never try to make order of the chaos. They had no tools of investigation; they had no access to a group or a company or a government that would help them figure out the who, and the why, of so many killings. Mamá had given up on wishing me out of the law enforcement world. She had not acquiesced, but rather had chosen to see it as a type of poetic irony that her daughter would deal with the very thing that had driven her away from her homeland. Violence. Killings. She didn't like my job, but she was a big fan of justice. "Did you learn anything?" was all she asked me.

"It's still early," I said. My pat answer.

"He was a good man. We wouldn't be out here if it hadn't been for him."

To that, my uncle raised a glass of wine. "To Mr. Pierce," he said, "for bringing my big sister to me."

We joined in the *brindis*, Mamá with her can of beer, me with my soda. After we finished eating, Uncle Chepe took me to his computer. He put in his password (we all knew it, *pupusa*, but he still typed it in). "Take your time," he said. He patted me on the shoulder, then closed the door behind him when he left. I made my way into the secured section of the FBI VICAP files. This was my way of being a good Mommy and a good agent: bringing work home. And my family put up with it, even learned to love me for it.

The last time the authorities had known of Tekún Umán's whereabouts, he had shot me with a poisoned dart in New Orleans. Before that, they had spotted him in Chattanooga, one of his hometowns. Just weeks before that, he had left a DEA agent bleeding from his scrotum in the jungles of Guatemala.

The last time *I* had seen him was the day I brought Minos down. Had it not been for Tekún, I wouldn't have made it out of that house alive.

Thus we were even: I had saved his life once, and he had saved me. So I had let him go. As if I could have stopped him.

DEA had other information on him: rumors that he had been trying to break into the business with the Arellano brothers, the heads of the Tijuana cartel. Just before slicing up the DEA agent and running out of Guatemala, Tekún had had a free shipment of coke sent to the brothers as a gift, and a signal that he was interested in joining up with them. No doubt he had planned to use Tijuana as a new port of importation into the U.S.

But much had changed since giving them that gift. The two Arellano brothers, Ramon and Benjamin, had been brought down: Benjamin in a sting operation in Puebla, Ramon in a shower of bullets in the streets of Tijuana.

So where did that leave Tekún? No doubt scrambling, like a lot of other smaller cartels that did business with the Arellano brothers. Some wanted to take the brothers' place. Others ran away from Tijuana, to start up their production again on another, less populated section of the U.S.–Mexican border.

Scrambling. Tekún Umán did not scramble. That was not his style.

"Where have you been all these years?" I said to the computer.

I checked to make sure the door was closed. Then I called up the Ten Most Wanted page. There he was, right between Richard Goldberg, wanted for child rape and porn, and Donald Webb, bank heist. Unlike the others, his was a fine photo. He was wearing a suit, no doubt receiving an award from a service organization some years back. This was the man both the DEA and the FBI sought with a vengeance.

He had kissed me once. Or perhaps I had kissed him. I'm still not sure.

Dibbs called my cell phone a little before five, saying he'd had the workup done on Chip Pierce's autopsy. I drove on ahead, and did not get around to calling Agent Nancy about the M.E. finishing early.

Dibbs was a gringo; but he didn't talk much English.

"External investigation showed extensive soft-tissue injury, but there is no intracranial hemorrhaging, nor in the subdural, or subarachnoid regions. No skull fractures, though the cartilage of his nose tore. Anterior and posterior dissection of the neck was unremarkable."

I looked at the tall, young-looking Medical Examiner. "Meaning?"

"Meaning all that mess that was on his face when you found him? Nosebleed. There was puffiness in his eyes and his cheeks, apparently from the beating with the prosthetic. But that was not the physiological derangement that resulted in death."

It took a second to absorb his vocabulary, especially with Pierce's face peeled off and hanging over the top of his skull. "What did it?"

"Probably the heroin."

I'm sure I looked shocked, laced with a bit of anger. "Chip — Agent Pierce was not a user."

"I never said he was. I just said the heroin might have killed him."

"An overdose?"

"No. A combination with another substance, like cocaine, or alcohol."

I looked at Chip's arm, which was partially underneath a cloth. "He liked scotch, but he wasn't a heavy drinker, he was always watching out for that . . . but maybe lately . . ."

"Excuse me?"

"What?" I looked at Dibbs. We had just met, but he looked safe enough. And nothing would change the fact that Chip was dead. "His prosthetic, his eye and leg, mostly his leg. Sometimes he still felt pain, right at the stump. It would pinch him, the plastic sheath would bind up in the socket. And he got headaches, around his eye. But he was always careful about drinking, didn't want to rely on it as a painkiller." I stopped, wondering if I had revealed too much.

Dibbs's professionalism saved the conversation. "I don't think it was the scotch. Not enough alcohol in his bloodstream to indicate intoxication. But so far, the mechanism of death is pointing to some form of speedballing."

"Why do you say that?"

"Apparent high levels of cardio and neurotoxins, which brought on depolarization of his nerves and muscles. It was irreversible. His skeletal muscles lost the ability to relax. This brought on respiratory paralysis. His body suffocated itself. That's what killed him."

"That just doesn't make sense."

"You're right. Especially if you look at this." Dibbs showed me a report, with numbers and graphs on it that I did not understand. I waited for his explanation. "Your traditional way of speedballing is with cocaine and heroin. But I found no traces of cocaine in his blood."

"But you did find heroin?"

"Yes — well, no. I found morphine and monoacetylmorphine."

"What's that?"

"Once you inject heroin, it metabolizes almost immediately into monoacetylmorphine, which has a nine-minute half-life. It then hydrolyzes to morphine, with a half-life of thirty-eight minutes. I found both elements in the vitreous."

"What's that?"

"The vitreous humor. It's a transparent gel that sits right behind your lens. In your eye."

"Okay."

"So what I'm telling you is the victim did not die immediately. It takes some time for all this to happen. Speedballs kill you pretty quickly, and to find residuals of heroin in the vitreous means that death was not immediate."

"Then what was the cause of death?"

"I just told you. Paralysis of the respiratory system. His own body locked up, wouldn't let him breathe."

"No no, I mean, how was he killed?"

"Oh, you mean the *manner* of death."

Ay shit. "Yes. Yes, that's what I mean."

"Undetermined. It could have been the mix of heroin and alcohol, which could have been accidental, or suicidal."

"Come on. What about the beating?"

"As I said, that didn't kill him."

"Yeah, but somebody could have injected him with a toxin before beating him up, or afterward."

"Sure. But it could also be two separate instances: Someone beat him up, right after he had shot up with too much heroin, or a mix of drugs."

"Like whom?"

"I don't know. A fellow user? His supplier?"

This was pissing me off. But it seemed Dibbs didn't notice that. Too much time with dead people, you forget how to read the living. "Okay," I said, "so it wasn't the beating. What about the, the cut to his abdomen?"

"That is just about as 'cosmetic' as the trauma to the skull." He pulled at another file. All these files of his made up the "Pierce, Samuel" log. "I've already made the Y-Incision, so I had to cut through the word on his abdomen. But we have pictures." He showed me the pictures. I looked away, as if staring at the floor would give me the gumption to look back at the photos. "The cuts are fairly superficial, sometimes reaching the adipose tissue, but mostly cutting into the dermis. That did not kill him. What's it mean, anyway? 'Cabron.'"

He pronounced it *KA-brun*. I corrected him: "*Cabrón*. It's a Spanish word, means 'cuckolded.'"

"Really? You mean like a guy whose wife is sleeping around on him?"

Obviously Dibbs had no information on Pierce and me. "Yeah."

"Strange." He looked at the word again, so objectively. "So, that bashing into his face looks more like a rage-kill."

"You said this seemed like some form of speedballing," I said. "What did the heroin mix with?"

"That's what I don't understand. I couldn't find any other substance, besides a slight residue of alcohol, in his system. And there wasn't a high amount of morphine in him. You all right?"

"Yeah. Did you . . . did you find where he injected himself?"

"No needle tracks in his hands, or arms. I found one possible injection point between his toes. Which, to my mind, shows that this was a one-time experiment."

Which also placed the other syringes found in his house in doubt. "He wasn't a user."

Dibbs said nothing. Not because he disagreed; perhaps he began to sense that I was closer to the guy on his slab than he had presumed. Kudos to him, for sensing the vibes of the living.

I got objective, once again. "What if he had been drugged? You know, something slipped into his drink?"

"I've sent blood and urine samples to toxicology. I should hear back from them by late morning."

"Have you checked the rug cutting yet?"

"What rug cutting?"

"The glass fell, there was a slight stain on the carpet. I told evidence to take a cutting. I'll make sure it gets to you. Maybe you can check it for some residue from his drink."

"Yeah. Yeah I can do that."

"Anything else?"

"Just the splinter in his scalp."

"What splinter?"

"He must have been working on some wood or something. There was a tiny wood splinter just behind his ear."

"No. No, that's not from woodworking." I almost snarled at that. "Where is it?"

"Right here." He reached over, found the stoppered glass vial, and held it up. Inside, a tiny chip of wood, smaller than the broken tip of a pencil.

"You'll want to check it."

"For what?"

"Poison. A sedative. Some damned drug that makes your body freeze up." I headed toward the door. I could take only so much of dead Chip Pierce, Y-cut down the chest and his face gone and that glass eye sitting perfectly in the sliced muscle fiber. That, and this new information, Tekún's little blowgun toy. "You've got my cell. Soon as you can, give me a call, doesn't matter what time." My voice was rough; keeping it rough kept it from cracking.

Once at the door, he called, "Agent Chacón?"

"Yeah?"

"If it matters any, I'm sure he wasn't a user."

"What?"

"His lungs."

"What about them?"

"Well, they were in good shape. He was a light smoker. But other than that, the lungs showed no congestion. I didn't find any talc or cotton fibers."

He said no more, as if I understood what the hell he was saying. "What's that mean?"

"In users, you find foreign body granuloma in the lungs. Cotton comes from the 'strainer' that heroin addicts use to clean out any impurities when they're cooking it. Talc's a pretty common cutting agent. None of that was in Agent Pierce's lungs."

So. Dibbs *was* able to read the living. He may have had a stick up his ass trying to be the new number-one Chief Medical Examiner of L.A. County, but he was all right by me.

Still, my throat was tightening up, so I didn't thank him; I just shook my head in recognition of his little burst of kindness.

I wondered if my mother would have found me distant now.

I drove home. There, I would be alone for a couple of hours before Mamá finished helping Uncle Chepe with an evening catering gig in Long Beach. Sergio preferred staying with his cousins on Saturday nights. Nintendo was a much more fun way to spend the weekend rather than in our own house on Woolf Avenue in Van Nuys, where there were no Nintendo games, only filled bookshelves. Some would say I'm fighting a losing battle in a hopeless war, steeping my kid's head in books. I'd rather go down fighting.

Tonight I would rather be alone. In my usually loud Salvadoran-Russian neighborhood, I cocooned. I thought about a drink, and followed up on the thought. Mamá wasn't around to say anything. But it was her silence that was worse than her words, for it meant a full disapproval. She had worried about me through the years, my love of whiskey. I kept it in check, as best I could. I kept a lot of things in check these days, these years. I worked out regularly, watched my figure. That was important to me, still, even after living with this fucking scar on my neck. That's why Mamá shouldn't have worried too much about the Jack Daniel's or the Wild Turkey — I measured it. Three ounces, no kidding; two jiggers at night, just to take the edge off a day. I watched my diet; in a city like this, you have plenty of reminders to keep vigil on what you put in your mouth. Ran every other day, did the weights and the kickboxing and the upgraded defense classes at the Bureau's gym throughout the week. Still kept a size eight (six at Macy's), still kept Chip Pierce looking at me. I remember him slipping his mouth down me; he'd put his tongue in the curves of my abdomen. "Damn, how many situps you do a day?" I'd laugh, only because he was tickling the shit out of me.

He could get me to laugh. To yelp. He could keep me from feeling what I was feeling now: a need for more than the usual three ounces. A desire for a bath in the amber drink of Tennessee. A night of shit-facing while surfing the Net. It was the Internet connection that kept my phone from ringing. But not the cell.

It was a number I did not recognize, so I answered it. "Chacón."

"Why didn't you call me?"

Oh, boy. She was pissed. Didn't even salute me with my rank. But I did to her. "Hello, Agent Nancy Pearl." Did I slur?

"I got to the M.E., and you weren't there. I had to wait over an hour before some assistant came out and said you had already been there."

"Yeah, I checked in a little earlier. Sorry about that."

She had other things to say, but my e-mail was chirping. I opened it. And tried to get sober, real fast.

There was no *Mi vida*, no cutesy, high-class Spanish introduction to the note. Nor were there any lovely sign-offs in which he told me how much he thought about me, how his days were filled with the image of me. None of that bullshit.

        Romi: I thought you were mine.

Nancy Pearl was still expressing her anguish over being stood up at the Coroner's. I mumbled something to her while typing fast an inebriated, frenetic response:

        Whre th e fuck areyou?

"Nancy, listen, can I call you back here in a little while? Okay? Yeah, bye."

She was still talking, her voice rising with a certain exasperation that I've heard in white people who just don't get Latinos. I clicked her off and stared at my computer, waiting for the mailbox to pop up open again.

It didn't. I wrote, very carefully, my fingers punching the keys and the space bar one at a time:

```
Come on, Goddammit, come out,
        where are you?
```

His answer:

```
        Ojalá
```

And that was it. He cleaned himself out of cyberspace. As if he could be clean.

Your own self-confidence could break you, ahijado. But maybe, sometimes the best thing for a man is to be broken.

Pearls of wisdom from his godfather, the older, usually quiet, Rosario Belén, better known as Beads. Tekún Umán's godfather had gotten less quiet as of late, due to the changes in their business. It was Beads who had warned Tekún: dangerous to move to Tijuana and get involved with the Arellano brothers. Those boys and all the boys under them were nothing but trouble. Sure, they ran the strongest cartel in all of the Americas, were *the* shipping import company for coke into the United States. That didn't mean Tekún had to get in bed with them.

"My dear Beads," he had said, "I'm not getting in bed with the Arellanos. Bad metaphor. I'm joining my business with theirs."

He doesn't say My *dear* anymore. He says little these days.

Beads could have said a lot more: that they needed to keep this business small, keep under the radar, no need for other lines to see them as competition. The Arellano brothers, El Min and El Mon, as they were better known, were not ones to put up with competition. That fishing village El Suazal? Over on the eastern coast, in Baja? One Mr. Fermin Castro. Minor-league drug dealer. Always paid his dues to the Arellanos in full and on time, but Min and Mon got to wondering, maybe old Fermin was getting too big for his britches. So what do they do? Send their narco-juniors in the middle of the night, line up every man, woman, and child against a wall and shoot them. The whole village, except for a fifteen-year-old girl who got to live and tell the authorities all about it. Why get involved with that?

Beads did talk a lot. Enough to get on Tekún's nerves. Still, now, he misses all that talk, those warnings. He hates the silence.

Six months after watching Romilia Chacón take down her sister's killer, Tekún returned to Tennessee. A great risk, he knew; the last time he had tried to visit his mother, his own aunt had set him up, bringing him into her house right after making a quick call to the cell phone of a DEA agent who sat in constant vigilance outside the two-story home. A DEA that was still enraged with him over how he had sliced up one of their men in Guatemala. Tekún had had to take a dive, then — literally — through an open window in order to escape.

A year later he returned to bury his mother. He watched the priest say the final blessings through a telescopic lens while he and Beads stood on Lookout Mountain, over a mile away. Beads had his own binoculars. He kept an eye on the DEA agents planted all around the cemetery, while Tekún watched distant cousins and uncles and great-uncles lower his mother into the ground. The Alzheimer's had emptied her. Breath pushed over her larynx and her mouth moved, but as far as language went, the plaque had filled in between the folds of her brain and she was but a functioning body. As if the plaque had snuffed out her soul itself.

Tekún does not believe in souls. He knows too well what people are capable of to have any need for belief.

He said nothing to Beads as they left Lookout Mountain and drove to a private airstrip in Georgia and flew toward Mexico. Beads said a few words, like a stand-in priest, or a hired substitute for a wake party. "She was a fine woman, your mother. Spoke Q'eqchi' better than most Guatemalans. I'll miss her." And still, Tekún said nothing.

He wonders now if his mother's death has made him less careful. Or perhaps it has simply been the movement of the business: Expansion meant taking on more problems. Before, Tekún relied on local people who, not so much owed him, but wished to show their appreciation. The Q'eqchi' Indian women who had raised him in Poptún, in the heart of the Guatemalan jungle. They were more than happy to offer up the name of a nephew or a grandson as an *oreja* who would listen in, like a good ear, to the gringos who gathered around the tables of the local inns. Making sure that those gringos were really tourists, and not some CIA or DEA or FBI plants looking for him.

He had fewer such informants in the States, though a number of the homeless in his shelter in Nashville were happy to keep their ears low to the ground.

All that was about to change. Demand for his product had grown; he was worth more than his father had ever been. And his father: long dead from a spray of bullets while drinking coffee in a café. Dead, as Tekún has always said, because his father fretted about this business, never entered into it completely. Dead because he hesitated, rather than moving forward. Boldly.

Tekún had three hundred and fifty kilos delivered to Min and Mon. Nothing really, in comparison with the daily amount that filtered through Tijuana. But three hundred and fifty kilos *regalados*: given, as a gift. That was what caught the brothers' attention.

It wasn't easy, going through Chip's files and office. It never got easier; but it became more necessary. I read every file he had made since coming to Los Angeles. Chip had been the Special Agent in Charge of the Olive Street bombing, which had happened six weeks before he died. He had been the one to speak with the media about the attack, the first to call it a terrorist hit, one that had killed fifty-seven people, some of whom lived in the building, others who were just passing through it.

We all knew who the people passing through it were. I wondered if the bomb blast, though an obvious terrorist hit upon the city, would have drawn as much attention had not one undercover cop and three students from Blakely Academy High School died in the blast. Neighbors from Brentwood and Bel Air had gone to town on the Bureau, demanding that more information about the attack be given to the families, and that the Feds stop everything else, all other cases, to find out what had happened to their children. One of the parents had the *cojones* to ask why their children were in there in the first place. But the other parents must have hushed her up quick, as if trying to avoid the obvious.

No one wondered if people would do what they had done in Oklahoma City, where the names and faces of all the victims were put up on a fence as a reminder to the world of who we had lost. The explosion on Olive Street was still new; no one could get near it, with FBI and ATF all over the place. Some of the bodies, recovered, had yet to be identified. Everyone knew that the homeless used the back of the building as a squatter camp. But it was the women who had lived in the building who got the most attention, not just for their deaths: Were they, the prostitutes, the targets?

On the edge of the site, beyond the cordoned area, an older woman kept vigil. Her name was Amy Spencer, and her daughter Kim had died in the blast. In those first days, Amy Spencer stood near the site and held a large sign with numerous snapshots of her daughter, from babyhood to adulthood, stapled to the cardboard. MY DAUGHTER she had written with a wide marker over the top of the sign. A silent protest to the world, as if to beg us to quit calling her child a prostitute. It was no accident that Ms. Spencer stood before a wall on which someone had spray-painted, YOUR WHORES. The *Los Angeles Times* had caught it just like that: my daughter, your whores.

Chip had pictures of the graffiti-covered wall in the file. I was studying the photos when my boss walked in.

"How's it going?" Letty asked.

"I see pieces. But they don't assemble."

"How about Tekún Umán? Got anything new on him?"

I wanted to share with Fisher my confusion about Tekún; but in that moment I made a decision, one that my mother would have said came from the past and from the hip. "No. Not yet."

But all this was not why Fisher had come into my cubicle. "You and Agent Pearl. How is she?"

"Fine." I looked up, then looked back down. Perhaps too quickly.

"I don't see you two together much. And you know me: I like my agents to be real buddies." Fisher pressed her palms together tight, sarcastically tight. "You know why we hired Pearl here? She's one of the best in her class when it comes to computer hacking."

"Yeah?" I was about to say, *So?* But that may not have been wise.

"So I notice you're looking through all the hard copy files. When are you going to get into Chip's computer?"

"I know how to run a computer. I'm getting to it."

"When it comes to computers, Romilia, I noticed you're about ten years behind the rest of our flock here."

She barely gestured behind her, to the large room of agents, all working at their desks, all sliding their mouses and clicking through the Internet. And there sat Pearl, sliding quicker than them all.

"Why don't you have Pearl get in here and work on the computer while you riffle through the paper files? Who knows? That way, you two might even have a conversation."

Having given the order, Fisher walked out.

"What are we looking for?" Nancy asked. She sat at Chip's desk, moved the mouse to get the screen saver to disappear. She was nervous; and, I could hear in her voice, a little upset.

"I'm not really sure." Better to put her to work. "Look into Chip's computer files, pull up everything on the Olive Street bombing."

She got to work on it. In a few minutes she had numerous files opened, all of which I had hard copies of in Chip's paper file.

"What about all these Web sites?" said Nancy.

"Which ones?"

"In his Favorites file. He's got half a dozen Web sites that deal with terrorism, fundamentalist movements, articles on Timothy McVeigh, al Qa'ida. . ."

"Terrorist info from the Web. Do they look legitimate, or are they some fly-by-night Web sites of nut cases?"

"Look pretty legit to me. Articles from *The Guardian*, *FRONTLINE*, *Sojourners*, *Atlantic Monthly*. Here's a Web site for scotch, www.singlemalt.com."

I laughed.

"He like scotch?"

"Only the best."

She named off other sites, one on cigars (he did smoke one from time to time), another on the history of the canals off Venice Beach, another called Dendrobatidae.

"What in the world is that?"

She clicked on the site. "Oh. Frogs."

"Frogs?"

"Yeah. Look, aren't they pretty?"

They were pretty. There was a photo of a blue frog, shiny, with its name underneath: *Dendrobates azureus.*

"It's a page from the *National Geographic* Web site," said Nancy.

"Oh. Yeah. He was a subscriber."

"You knew him pretty well, didn't you?"

I could hear it: one woman working on another. I could tell, under that veneer of Midwest wholesomeness, she was like us all: looking for inroads, cracks into another person's head. She didn't say it kindly, she said it with a slice: *You knew him, didn't you?* So I thought it best to throw her off just a bit.

"Yeah. We were lovers."

"Oh. Oh, I wasn't sure, I mean I didn't know . . ."

"Well, now you do."

"Yes, well, I'll . . ."

"Yeah, why don't you keep working through the computer, make sure you pull up anything that looks pertinent?" I walked out of Chip's office, back to my desk. There I sat and worked through the history, everything that the FBI knew about the Olive Street bombing.

Six weeks ago, on March 12, a simple plastique bomb plugged with a metal fuse and connected to a wristwatch shattered the front wall of a crack house on Olive Street between Eleventh and Olympic, bringing down the first four floors. The blast left people dead on the fifth floor and everyone stranded from the sixth floor up. It was one of Los Angeles's older apartment buildings, constructed in the nineteen twenties and nicknamed The Hang. Though it had gone through two cosmetic refurbishments (once in the fifties, another in the seventies), the ebb and flow of the city's economy had abandoned it in the following decades. Along with the rest of Olive Street, the apartment house became a refuge for poor and homeless men and women, for heroin and crack dealers who stayed hidden behind triple-locked doors and traded rocks of meth for money through small cat-openings at the bottoms of their doors. Everyone knew that prostitutes worked there as well.

All that ended on March 12. At least for The Hang on Olive

Street. Barely a week after the explosion, business picked up once again in the streets around Olive, and the movement of crack cocaine and heroin and ecstasy flowed smoothly downtown and into the neighborhoods of West Hollywood, Beverly Hills, Santa Monica.

The Hang stayed cordoned off. No one could get in, not even the owner, until the FBI and the ATF had finished with their investigation. Once done, all the media would learn was that the weapon had indeed been a bomb, and that fifty-seven people had died from the blast, with one hundred and nine people injured. The press bit down hard on this one. They couldn't get enough of the irony, that this terrorist attack was not aimed at the usual targets in a big city: a tall office building, or a military headquarters; rather, the terrorists had hit a prostitute dive in the worst part of downtown L.A. Was this the work of al Qa'ida terrorists who meant to kill off the symbolic dregs of our U.S. society? Or was it some sort of vigilante group that meant to take out drug dealers at one of their distribution sources? *Neither the FBI nor the ATF is saying.*

As if we would say anything to them: the intellects of local nightly news.

What we did know, which Chip indeed had not shared with the media, was that the blast had originated from a room that was not there; at least, according to the old blueprints in Chip's file, the room did not exist. But it did exist; it was a holding tank for imported cocaine. One of the many distribution drop-off points throughout the city that the held thousands of kilos and hundreds of millions of dollars in powder brought across the border. Like most coke brought into L.A., Chip suspected it had originated in Tijuana.

The owner of the building was one Bradley Pack, who lived in Sherman Oaks. He now lived in the Van Nuys Municipal Jailhouse, pending trial.

Life, or death, had been catching up to Mr. Pack for a while. It turned out that one of the two dead men Chip and I had found on the beach below San Diego over a year ago was Mr. Pack's son, shot in the head, with a strange scrape on his lower back.

"Not much here."

Nancy stood at the opening of my cubicle. She leaned against the wall façade, trying to look casual. "Nothing?" I said.

"Just the same research that he printed out for his file." She motioned to the papers strewn across my desk. "And nothing in Agent Pierce's computer on that drug runner, Murillo."

"Oh. Yeah."

"You know anything about him?"

"More than I care to."

"I heard that he threatened to kill you once."

I looked at her, but did not respond.

"Why is Special Agent Fisher so sure Murillo did this?" she asked.

"The writing on the belly of the victim. That's an old death squad signature, from Central America. He trained with them."

"God. That's horrible."

"Yeah, it is." My mind was wandering a bit, and I answered her somewhat automatically.

"Those countries are so violent," she said.

My thoughts braked. "Excuse me?"

"Central America. All you hear about is the violence from there. I don't know how people can live that way."

"What way?"

"How they attack each other like that. Killing each other off. It's like Rwanda, you know? What makes some people so, I don't know, like savages?"

What was it that kept me from slapping her around? But I only said, "What about our own country?"

"Yeah, we've got problems. But nothing like those places." She chuckled. Then she walked away. Just when I could have torn her apart with some solid thoughts on how fucking racist she was.

I've kept my vision clear about Tekún Umán. From the time I first met him in Nashville, I knew of his ventures in the drug trade. He was not the largest, but he was a player, and as far as I knew, had played in the narcotics game for over a decade. He was dangerous; I had never known him to kill, but he left people wishing they were dead.

Ojalá.

Chip had used the word to propose to me. At the time I'd thought it was just that: He had looked up the word to ask me to marry him. But Tekún's e-mail, with the same word; it was too blatant.

Tekún Umán would certainly know what *ojalá* meant. His Spanish was impeccable.

What was the connection? Had he gotten involved with the Arellano brothers?

Over the past three years, working homicide for narcotics, I had learned that the Arellanos had their own way of doing business. The land between Baja California and southern California was a killing field. Bodies left ravaged in ways that would make the worst death squads of Central America proud. Or the CIA.

A point of view that I didn't express around my Bureau colleagues. It wouldn't be good, having a federal agent being so critical of another federal agency. Not out loud, at least. And not with Salvadoran blood running through her.

But it was easy to see those historic dots: death squads in El Salvador came out of the Special Forces of the Salvadoran military. And those special forces had received specific training from the Central Intelligence Agency.

Tekún Umán had been a Kaibil soldier. The Guatemalan Special Forces. The best of the best.

The CIA had helped make Tekún Umán.

He had held a knife to my neck once, as I lay in the grass in New Orleans, unable to move because he'd shot me with some damn poisoned wooden dart. He had spoken so clearly, standing over me, right next to the phone booth where I had called my bosses to report that I had found his hiding place. *You know how I feel about you. But don't ever narc on me, Romilia. You can't hand me over to the cops as some sort of sacrifice. They are not my gods. They should not be yours.*

All that, I remember. But I remember even more how he placed the knife against the skin of my neck, on the unharmed side. The side I showed the world. *You wouldn't want a matching set now, would you?*

The son of a bitch.

Dibbs's number was in our computer Rolodex database. Little Phil answered: "Dr. Dibbs is unavailable right now, Agent Chacón."

"This is pretty important. It's about the Pierce case."

"I'm sure it's important. Can I have him call you?"

"Do you have access to the Pierce autopsy file? I haven't gotten a copy yet."

"I do."

"Could you look up something for me?"

"No, not over the phone I can't."

His voice sounded aggressively whiney. "Look, Phil, all I need to know is about the wooden splinter found in his skin."

"You'll need to come down and check that out, Agent Chacón." Was he smiling on the other end of the line? Did bureaucracy actually make some people happy?

"Have Dibbs call me. Soon."

I hung up and called Nashville. If I could get my old friend and colleague Doc Callahan on the line, I'd have no problem getting some information.

"Romilia! My favorite L.A. girl! *¿Como te va?*"

"My, Doc, you've been practicing."

We talked casual Spanish for a good forty seconds. Then we caught up on my mother and son, on Doc's latest fling ("She's a little older than you, Romi, maybe thirty-one? But nowhere near as smart as you."). Then I asked him about my urine sample.

"You mean after New Orleans?"

"Yeah."

"It'll take me, oh, about half an hour to track that down. I'll call directly."

"Thanks Doc,"

"*Para ti, el mundo entero.*"

Now why couldn't Doc be out here? And twenty years younger? Or maybe just ten.

They'd checked what type of poison Tekún had used to paralyze me, to see if it was lethal, if it would have any residual effects on my body, and especially if it would lead us to him. At the time, all toxicology had told me was that they had found some crystalline residue in my urine, granulates that they had not seen before, but other than that, they could find no real trace of the poison's origins, nor of the poison, for that matter.

Doc called back before Dibbs did. "You remembered correctly. It says here, 'Small particles (granules) found.' Good God, I didn't write this up. That's all it says. Wait, here someone's scrawled, 'silica formation.' Sounds like you were ripe to form some kidney stones."

"Nothing about what it was made out of? The silica?"

"I'd reckon that it was mineral-based."

"Would it have come from that poison dart he shot into me?"

"Possibly. But I don't know. There would have to be a fair amount of it in the poison to have collected in your urine. It was just a dart, it wasn't like he poured it into a drink. This buildup could be from drinking water with too many minerals in it."

I had another phone call coming in, and was sure it was Dibbs. "I've got to go, Doc. Thanks."

"Nashville misses you."

"Is that your name now? Nashville?"

He laughed.

Dibbs said hello by saying, "You'll be happy to know I've changed the manner of death."

I should be happy to know. "Okay."

"It's gone from *undetermined* to *apparent homicide*."

"Why?"

"Both urine and blood had residue of Mellaril. Thioridazine hydrochloride. It's used to reduce symptoms of psychotic disorders, like schizophrenia. Mix it with alcohol, you've got one punch of a Mickey." He laughed at his own endeavor at dated street lingo. "And the carpet piece you brought in? The stain was forty percent alcohol content along with the Mellaril."

"So he was drugged. Did that kill him?"

"No. That wouldn't have caused depolarization of the nervous system. Something else did that."

"I'll put money on the dart."

"What dart?"

"The dart that left the splinter in his head."

"Wait a minute, that's just come back as well." He put the phone down, picked it back up a few seconds later. "Here we go, yes: 'Tests on the viscous solution of the mahogany chip resulted in the finding of a steroidal alkaloid toxin, specifically a nonprotein poison known as Batrachotoxin.' Yes, no doubt that's what killed him."

But why hadn't it killed me? I wanted to ask. "Where in the world does a poison like that come from?"

"Agent Chacón, you've forgotten your Greek."

"Never studied it."

"*Batrachia*, former name of the order Anura. The tailless amphibians. What you have here is a natural poison from a frog. That's amazing . . . Agent Chacón?"

I hardly heard him. I was yelling for my partner. "Agent . . . Nancy. Nancy! Chip's computer, get on it.

At first, Beads was nervous to meet the Arellano brothers. Later he commented on the brothers' amiable manner, how they were friendly and warm in the way only Mexicans are: a bit loud, sure, with a more raucous Spanish, but more than happy to do business. So happy were they to do business with what they jokingly referred to as "our new *chapín* connection" that Min and Mon gave Tekún Umán two of their own to work under his direction: Francisco Muñoz, from Tijuana, and Leonard Pack, a white kid from Sherman Oaks. "These are some of my finest Juniors," said Mon. "Frankie's from here, his family lives off Agua Caliente, near the club and the racetrack. His old man's part owner of the track, he gets me the best seats. Frankie knows Tijuana like the back of his hand. Lennie's from the San Fernando Valley. His father owns rental properties in central Los Angeles, great storage units. Lennie knows L.A. better than any of my guys. They'll treat you right. You just tell them what you want and they'll make sure it happens. And don't worry. Neither of them is the Crack Killer." Mon laughed a hearty laugh.

There was no discussion around this. Tekún now had two new employees.

He accepted this. The Arellano outfit in Tijuana relied heavily upon their Juniors: young men from the upper class of Tijuana and southern California who bored of life easily, who were always looking for new action in town, with the only real action being the trade. They were young, most of them in their late teens and early twenties. They needed no money, considering the families they were from; the thrill made it all worthwhile. Frankie was home-grown Tijuana aristocrat. Since middle school Lennie had spent most of his summers in Tijuana. He was fluent in Spanish. His father, living in Sherman Oaks, produced television commercials. The rentals in downtown L.A. were supplemental income; they had become the main income once the Arellano brothers entered the Pack family.

"They seem good," said Beads. "They're kids, but they act like they know what they're doing." Yet in his voice there was an uncertain acquiescence: It didn't really matter if they were good or not; the two Juniors were their new employees.

"This may have been a mistake," said Tekún. He smoked a cigar and drank a tiny cup of espresso. He and Beads sat on the balcony of their apartment, where they were a part of the broken, low skyline of Tijuana.

"A little late for that, don't you think?" said Beads.

"I don't like having workers pushed on me."

"Should have thought of that before all this. But I think it's okay. You know how pushy Mexicans can be, even with their generosity."

"Spoken like a true Guatemalan."

"It's true, *ahijado*. I've told you that before. Mexican men, well, they're just more voracious about life. Nothing wrong with that. Remember what Octavio Paz said: *El hombre mexicano, debido a la mezcla de las sangres españolas e indígenas, es necesariamente el hombre más jodido del mundo.* Something like that. He was right. And he was Mexican himself."

Tekún said nothing to that. He just smoked the *puro*. It had been years since he had read Paz; his godfather's reference made him consider picking up a copy of *Posdata* at a local bookstore. Though he was not sure it was true that the Mexican man, due to his mix of Spaniard and indigenous blood, was the most fucked-up man in the world. Tekún thought about home; he thought about the home of his past, the *Kaibiles*, how thorough that training was. Special Forces, forcing the living and the dead to obey. You can't get more fucked up than that.

"I'd like to put a watch on Frankie and Lennie," he said.

"Where are you going to find a tail who will watch them? We're a little out of our jurisdiction here."

"Come now, Beads, be creative. Where would you look for a little *chapín* colony?" He smiled at his godfather. Then Tekún turned his head toward their right, to the north, to the great border.

Nancy and I spent the afternoon learning about the Dendrobatidae family.

"They're more commonly known as 'poison-dart frogs,'" said Nancy. She had already clicked through the Web page that Chip had saved in his Favorites file, and had moved on to other pages for more information. "They're very colorful. Look at that one, the blue one? Then there are these lovely yellow ones . . . oh, and that one, with the red head . . . They all live in the tropical rain forests of Central and South America. Well. That points to Tekún Umán. It says the South American Indians used the frogs to poison their darts for hunting monkeys and other small animals."

I said nothing to that. "What about the specific toxin?"

"Batrachotoxin? Seems it's the most poisonous of them all. It works on the nerves, shuts down communication between the nerves and the muscles. Just a small amount can kill a large man."

"But it didn't kill me."

"Excuse me?" She looked up.

I told her about my encounter with Tekún in New Orleans.

"Well, it says here there are over one hundred and seventy-nine species of poison-dart frogs known. Maybe he used another frog on you. Like this one, the *Epipedobates tricolor*—it's this multi-colored frog from Ecuador."

"You say those words fairly easily."

"Yeah, my background's in chemistry, before I got into hacking computers." She clicked on the frog. "This one produces a toxin that's a nicotine derivative. Says here it has a strong analgesic activity. It's two hundred times more potent than morphine. Maybe it had a complete 'relaxing' effect on your body."

"Maybe."

"Seems like our perp knows his frogs."

"Yeah. Yeah, he does. But why was Chip researching them?"

"I don't know how much he learned. The National Geographic site is the only information on his computer about the frogs. I found all this other information on other sites."

I looked closer at the screen, right under a photo of one of the cutest damned frogs I'd ever seen; there, it said: *The bulk syntheses of many of their toxins are not an overwhelmingly difficult problem; consequently, it is not impossible to imagine the misuse of these toxins as terrorist weapons.*

"I need to talk with Fisher," I said. I walked out of the office. As I did, I surprised myself; I half-slapped Nancy on her shoulder and said, "Good work," then continued out, as if embarrassed by my own spontaneity; something that happens when you feel like you've made a breakthrough.

Chip was working on the Olive Street bombing full-time," I said to Fisher. "But as far as we can see, he wasn't investigating Tekún Umán."

"Of course not. We've been working under the assumption that Tekún came after him because of you."

Instead of responding to that directly, I said, "The logic's not kicking in."

"Why not?"

"The M.E. just concluded that it was a poisoned dart that brought Chip down. Dipped in a toxin that comes from frogs."

"Oh. Just like what happened to you." She raised her eyebrows as if to praise this connection, one that pointed, once again, to Tekún.

"Right, well, something like it. I called Nashville about the workup they did on me after Tekún shot me with the dart. Nothing solid, to verify if it was the same toxin. One thing, though: Tekún's dart knocked me out. This one killed Chip. But that's not the only inconsistency. Chip had information on his computer about poisonous frogs."

"Okay."

"Why would he have info on poisonous frogs, but nothing on Tekún Umán?"

"I don't see where you're going with this."

"It seems he didn't know anything about Tekún's whereabouts. But he had learned something about frogs. And it was frog poison that killed him."

"So you're wondering . . . if Chip *did* know something about Tekún."

I paused, then said, "Right. But also, maybe these poisonous frogs had something to do with the Olive Street bombing."

"Now you've lost me."

"It's scant, but there's a possibility that these frogs can be used in terrorist weapons."

She paused. She looked hard at me. "How?"

"I'm not sure. I don't even know how they get the poison out of the frog. I don't know . . . maybe they grind the frog up, mix it in a fine powder, spray it into the atmosphere."

"That's a really gross image, Romilia."

"Yeah, like I said, this is new shit to me." I was looking out her window and didn't notice for a minute that she was staring hard at me, an authoritative, reprimanding stare. "Sorry about that. I'm just trying to think out loud."

"Then you'll probably be thinking out loud how Tekún Umán fits in all this."

"I have. And I don't get it. Why would he get involved in terrorism?"

"Why would he kill a man because of his obsession with you? Because inherently he's a nutcase. A psychopath. Smooth in one moment, and carving up a guy in the next. Besides, we've known for years that terrorists have been using the drug trade in their plans. Coke brings in a good income, and terrorists need dollars. Don't doubt that Tekún is involved in that."

I didn't even want to touch that one. "Who was Chip's partner?"

"He didn't have a partner. He was the head of the squad. Worked mostly out of here."

"Okay, then who did he work most closely with in the squad? I'd like to talk with him."

"Jerry O'Brien. He was second in charge of the squad."

"O'Brien. Yeah, I know him."

Between our two countries there is a third country of tunnels and trucks and coyotes. *El país ambulante*, Tekún once wrote in an old journal, in days when he used to write. An ambulant land.

Some imagine the border as the place of the swarm: Mexicans, like brown bees, pushing into the United States. That is the error. There is no swarm one way; there is a life that moves, certainly. It dodges and ducks, it learns when to eat and not to eat, when to fast so as to go days in a truck or through a tunnel without having to shit. Sometimes it knows to abstain from the drink or the powder, to keep its head on straight, because those who don't, their bodies litter the border of fence and river between the two Americas.

Here, Tekún walked alone. This world was not for Beads; Tijuana was bad enough. Tekún saw that the moment he left the outskirts of the city and walked to the edge of a barrio that ran against the edge of a desert.

The gang was on him quickly, though he had seen them coming.

It was night, and the street had no lights on it. Still, the four young men, teenagers, could tell he was not from here, just by the way he walked. He was taller; and he ambled with a superiority that tagged him as an outsider and a fool.

"What you looking for?" said the first, their leader, who smoked.

"*Chapines*," he said. "I'm hiring."

"Why not hire us?"

"You're not Guatemalan."

"And who would want to be a cocksucking Indio from Guate?" The other boys rustled with a low laughter.

The laughter gave them away: chuckles that tried to be older, deeper. They were fourteen, no older than fifteen. A dangerous age: still children with strong bodies, short lives with too many experiences. Training helped him see this, helped him measure the voices within their laughter. Tekún braced appropriately.

They worked their way around him. The first one was just about to pull his gun and say, *Hand over your wallet you stupid chapín cunt,* when he saw his boys go down. His cigarette dangled from his lips. It made no sense, how his companions all crumpled like that. He felt a blade up against his neck. The boy froze. He became pure boy.

Tekún said nothing. He just started cutting.

One kid would need stitches on a nick in his lower intestine, only after it was tucked back in. Another, a simple set of staples across his chest. All of them were sliced, one way or another. But they would wake up the following day.

The reception in the desert faired better. He called out a few words in Mayan Q'eqchi', then in Q'aqchi'quel, and the few words he knew in Pocomóm. Someone finally answered. They were afraid, but after certain words were exchanged among them, words that sounded, after the long haul from Guatemala through Mexico, comforting, they welcomed him to the small fire and the tortillas. They were Q'aqchi'quel. They asked his name. He was a bit embarrassed, but then smiled and said, in their language, "You may not believe this, but they call me Tekún Umán." They all laughed kindly at that, yeah, hell of a nickname.

They were all men. No women here; the women, they said, would come later, once they had made it to the other side. This, Tekún preferred. He explained to them his job. It was simple, really, and they didn't need to speak any Spanish to accomplish it. "There are two men, called juniors, who are following me. They are working for Min and Mon. So I just want you to follow them for a while, and report back to me."

J erry O'Brien really liked coffee. But he was calm, which surprised me, with all that caffeine running through him. He had a beautiful voice, deep baritone, like a jazz musician. We met in the Starbucks just down the block from the Field Office. He was older than me, older than Chip by a good ten years. I would have thought that might have caused friction, that a younger man was the head of their squad. But after talking with O'Brien a few minutes, I saw quickly this wasn't the case. He was more than happy to have someone else in charge. "Especially Chip," he said. "Great guy. Smart as a whip." A mature voice here, with a sadness that recognizes all too well the dangers of the job. Best thing to do with the dead: praise them. "Chip knew how to keep a squad together. Best boss I ever had. But yeah, yeah he was talking frogs there, for a while."

"What did he say?"

"We'd been following up on some studies on bioterrorism, especially with the anthrax scare over in D.C. Los Angeles is ripe for something like that to happen. I can't talk about everything our squad covered, you understand. In fact, why don't we take a walk?"

I followed him outside the Starbucks, coffee in hand. It was a cooler day. O'Brien buttoned his suit jacket. He was old school; he still wore a black tie, white shirt, black suit. He looked good in it. His gray hair combed back with a little gel, his eyes, still sharp, like a wise eagle's. Years in the Bureau had not eaten him up with cynicism. I remember Chip talking about O'Brien: *He's a good guy. Really good guy. Homegrown Angelino; well, he was conceived on*

Catalina Island. Chip had laughed at that. *A straight arrow. Doesn't drink, doesn't smoke. Goes home to his wife every night.* I remember later, thinking Chip had spoken about O'Brien like this as yet another hint that he himself wanted to settle down.

We strolled down Wilshire, meandering past some gawking tourists. O'Brien glanced at them, then, when we'd moved a comfortable distance away, started talking.

"We had an ear in Tijuana for a while. Francisco Muñoz, they called him Frankie. One of the Juniors, who realized he was in over his head, and wanted to come clean. Especially when he started hearing in Tijuana about possible connections between terrorists and the drug world. I met with him in San Diego just before the Olive Street bombing. Then the kid ended up dead on the beach . . . Well, that's right, you knew about that. You went down there with Chip.

"Frankie had told me he had heard about a hit on Los Angeles. He wanted to talk to the main man about it." O'Brien stopped, as if not sure whether to say the next thing, whether it was appropriate or not. "He called Chip 'The Cyclops.' Anyway, he said he had some info on an extremist religious cult working out of Tijuana."

"Muslim?"

"Frankie didn't know. I don't know if Frankie could have told you the difference between radical Muslims and some fundamentalist Christians. Matter of fact, I have a hard time distinguishing them . . ." His voice trailed as some tourists passed. "Anyway, Frankie did give us a heads-up, but not much else. Then he was killed. Then The Hang blew up." We were alone, with no one around us. "Have you read the toxicology report from The Hang?"

"Not yet."

"Read it through. We found more than just cocaine and shrapnel from the blast. A toxin residue in the coke."

"Jesus. That coke flew into the air, all down Olive Street."

"Right. And no one died from it. That we know of."

"What, are you saying people could be infected with something, a virus, or a toxin, and they don't even know it?"

"You don't want to be talking too loudly, Romilia. This sort of thing will set the whole city in motion."

I took it he meant *panic*, not *motion*.

"No one's gotten sick yet," he said. "Not anyone on the squad, either. But once the first tests came back from toxicology, didn't you notice we were all wearing suits?"

I remembered that, on the news: all the Feds, walking around the demolished building with their yellow rubber antibiological suits, complete with enclosed helmets. They had also extended the cordoned-off area another hundred feet.

"Check the toxicology report. You'll see what they found, and why Chip was doing his frog study."

I had to ask, "What about you? How are you feeling?"

"Me? Fine. They washed us down, scrubbed us head to toe to between our toes. And I've been checked: bloodwork, urine, whole nine yards. All clean, supposedly. But every time I cough or sneeze, yeah, I get a little nervous. And my wife wonders why I won't touch her. Yeah. It's bad." But he said nothing else.

Tekún and Beads planned to be in Tijuana for at least two months, working out of a Colonial two-story house that they had bought, setting up their computers and network inside. There was much to do regarding banks and handlers and transport vehicles. Min and Mon's people handled the central distribution; it was up to Tekún to set up the artery of shipment from the Petén in Guatemala, all the way to Tijuana.

Lennie and Frankie were good workers. They were young, and did not mind dropping everything in order to take Tekún out to an old warehouse that looked completely abandoned. They showed him the five hundred square foot compartment hidden under the cement floor. A chain had been sealed into the floor, though it looked like a loose pile of links in the midst of a junk heap of metal and wood. "This is one of Min's old holding tanks," said Frankie. "Now, it's a little dated, and you've got to give it some extra polish to conceal it, but it still works really well." Frankie pushed away the garbage, then took a solid grip of the chain and pulled. A section of the floor popped up. Dust floated in the air, showed a perfect circular line in the cement. "If you pull it right, one guy can lift it." He grunted, then hauled the cement plug from the floor. The hole was large enough for a man to drop through.

"Here's how Min used to do it," said Frankie. "He'd have two guys drop down in there, then two or three guys up here. You set up a fire bucket brigade. Basic pass-and-toss. With strong workers, you could fill this baby in three hours. Leave the top three feet empty, cover the kilos with a tarp, then pour two feet of coffee grounds over it. That'll take care of the dogs. You need to buy new coffee each time you stock, otherwise it loses its smell. Once you fill and close the compartment, use this white sand to dust over the floor and fill the crack."

Beads looked at the hole. Then he looked at his godson. Then looked at the hole again.

Tekún spoke for them both: "That's labor intensive," he said.

Frankie smiled a large smile. "Yeah, well, maybe you can get those Indian boys to do it for you. You know, the ones you got tailing us?"

Tekún looked straight at Frankie.

Frankie laughed hard. "Hey, no offense taken, man. We're used to it. But uh, you might want to call them off now, don't you think? I mean, hey, we've been working together over a month now."

"I'll consider that."

"Listen, don't get down on them, man. They're good. They kept low, hey, I didn't know they were following us until, what Lennie, about two weeks ago? Yeah, that's about right. We've got as many Central Americans in town as we do Mexicans, so at first I didn't catch on. But I've gotten pretty good at distinguishing, *me entiendes*? And after a while, I see these same Indian faces hanging around me, well, you gotta stay suspicious to keep in the game."

Thus Tekún learned an important lesson about the business in Tijuana: It's good to change *orejas* from time to time. Every few days, if necessary. He took Frankie's advice: Beads had the Guatemalan men from the desert work in the warehouse. They were happy to take the job. The money they sent back home that first week, to Chilatenango, was more than they would have made in six months of cutting grass in West Hollywood. And Beads was kind enough to pay for the Gigante Express Overnight courier, to make sure the money got directly to the families back home.

Still, Tekún made sure one *oreja* stayed vigilant on the Juniors: a man named Chamba. He was twenty-five, and though sometimes he worked in the warehouse, slipping through the hole in the floor in order to pack the kilos tight one against another, he made extra money by tailing from a distance. Chamba was Guatemalan, but from the capital: a mestizo, he could pass for Mexican, maybe even gringo. Chamba was Tekún's insurance. It was Chamba who said to him, during one of their informal, quiet meetings, "They're going to San Diego this weekend. Lennie said he might drive up to Sherman Oaks, see his parents."

"What about Frankie?"

"He'll stay in San Diego. Said he's got a meeting." Chamba chewed on a tamal.

"With whom?"

"He didn't say. Lennie didn't ask."

"Wait here."

Two hours later, Tekún returned. Chamba was asleep on the wooden rocking chair. Tekún awoke him by dropping the document on his chest: a U.S. passport, complete with Chamba's photo. "Take the weekend in San Diego," he said.

Chamba did. He returned on Sunday night. He was excited. "They met this morning," he said, "Frankie and this gringo."

"Who's the gringo?"

"Don't know. But I bet you he's a Fed. White, graying hair. A little older. Wore sunglasses. And a J. Edgar Hoover suit. They were in Old Town, you know, where those chintzy-ass Mexican stores are? They sat near the circular fountain, drinking coffee. They talked about a hit."

"Against whom?" Tekún was drinking coffee.

"Los Angeles."

Tekún looked up. "What?"

"That's what I heard. A hit on L.A. Frankie was doing the talking, filling the gringo in. Yeah, I'm sure that old man was Fed. Min and Mon hired us a narc."

Tekún got quiet. He pondered awhile. "What else?" he finally said.

"Frankie said something about wanting to meet with *El Cíclope*," said Chamba. "What is that, anyway?"

"It means 'Cyclops.' Who in the world . . ."

"Yeah. What's a Cyclops?"

"He's a mythological character, Greek."

"He a *cojo*?" said Chamba.

"What?"

"In the myth. Does he have a limp?"

So.

"No," said Tekún. "Not in the myth, he doesn't."

I've got my hands way too full with all the other biochemical threats to be spending my time on poisonous frogs."

Pamela Huston was the head of our bioterrorist lab. She never stopped to talk; I had to follow her around her lab and watch her pick up beakers with gloved hands, then pick up different pads and write on them, only to move to more beakers and more notepads. She sighed, low, every few seconds.

"Look," she said, "BioWatch screens L.A. every day. But they're not with us. They work out of Homeland Security and report to the CDC in Atlanta. They're doing tests on the air for every possible poison that's on the black market now: anthrax, tularemia, smallpox, botulism, ricin. But frog juice is not on the list."

"Maybe it should be."

"Okay. What's up?" She stopped, finally. She brushed some of her long, oily hair to one side and looked straight at me.

"This is the toxicology report from the Olive Street bombing," I said. I handed her the report that her own office had written up. "You all found traces of Batrachotoxin in the environment."

"Yes, I remember that."

"Doesn't that worry you?"

"Not really. I'm never surprised anymore what we find in crack houses, or any drug-run environment. Exotic animals of all kinds, birds, snakes, frogs. Once, when we had to follow the agents in for a test on possible neurotoxins in a safe house in Long Beach, we detected fragments of tularemia in the air. It's highly infectious, but it also occurs naturally, and you'll find it in animals, like rabbits. And the drug runner in Long Beach had a certain affinity for rabbits. He had seven dozen in his walled-off, enclosed backyard. Rabbits, right next to sacks of coke. We've found macaw birds worth several hundred thousand dollars, holed up in a closet that's packed with heroin. Iguanas. Boa constrictors. You think these guys sell only drugs? They have numerous other hobbies, my dear."

She was older than me, so I supposed that allowed her to call me *dear*. "Yeah, but these frogs are deadly."

"So are infected bunnies! Besides, I know a little bit about Dentrobaditae," she said. She pushed her horn-rimmed glasses up her nose. "Their inherent toxins can kill you only if they enter your bloodstream. How do you think the native Indians of Latin America eat the prey they bring down with their poisonous darts? They can even handle the frogs. That is, if they don't have any cuts on their hands."

"So, it can be put in your food or drink and it won't harm you?"

"Well, I wouldn't want to risk it, especially when my ulcers are acting up. But yeah, theoretically, the toxins in these frogs have to enter your bloodstream."

"How do the Indians get the poison out of the frog?"

"It's pretty easy, really. They just scrape their darts across the backs of the frogs. The poison comes out of the frog's pores, and when the frog feels under threat, it releases more of the toxin. Like sweat. Scraping the dart across the frog's back yields more than enough poison to kill a large animal, or a human. And the poison will remain on the dart a good year."

"You *do* know a lot about them."

She smiled. "Hey, we all got to have our hobbies. Drug runners, chemists. But these poison-dart frogs are pretty popular. There are whole Sierra Club groups devoted to the little guys. Think about it: the frog gets the poison by eating certain poisonous ants in the jungle. But the ants' poison doesn't kill the frog. Over millions of years, the frog has adapted, and it absorbs the ant poison, making it into its own unique, and more powerful, toxin.

It's a fascinating example of evolutionary survival. Nut-case nerds go ape-shit for stuff like that."

A bomb blast in Los Angeles, that takes down a brothel/crack house.

A bomb that was apparently planted within the very room where the cocaine was stored; a closed-off, hidden room in a building owned by Bradley Pack.

A bomb that blew some strange organic, alkaloid toxin into the air. Specifically, a steroidal alkaloid nonprotein toxin. Much like the toxin found in the splinter plucked out of Chip Pierce's head.

Tekún Umán liked using darts. But he was also a stickler for language.

The story's pieces moved together, then they drifted apart. I could see possibilities, but then they would dissipate, almost completely. Unlike for my boss. Whenever Fisher imagined the killing, she could see it, all too clearly: the how, the who, and the why.

And why I didn't talk with her more about this, why I didn't give her the complete information, I'm still not sure. There was a chance they would pull me off the case if they found in me any doubt: doubt that Tekún had killed Chip, thus doubt over the fraternity of anger that sometimes holds law enforcement together. One of your own is killed; no matter how much infighting, no matter how many petty fights or hard corruption is going on among your own, you join ranks against the enemy that took your brother down.

And that's what it was like in the Bureau. This was a family of sorts. Like any family, there were disgruntled relatives, power plays, grumblings about certain authorities. But once one of our own got knocked out of the living, we were one big happy, angry family.

Tekún had already angered our family. The attack on that DEA agent, three years ago in Guatemala. Carl Spooner. The last I had heard about him, Spooner had retired with full benefits and had moved away somewhere to try to forget what Tekún had done to him. Eviscerated his manhood. All the while, Spooner could see but could not move. Tekún had shot him with the same tranquilizer he had used on me.

He was the first of three people who had gotten the dart. He and I had lived. Why had it killed Chip?

Different frog. That was Nancy's theory.

Nancy. That may have been a mistake, earlier, patting her on the back, literally. She now took it that I wanted to pick out curtains with her.

"What did they say up in the lab?" Nancy asked.

I was going through the case files that our CSI had gathered from Chip's dining room table. Here were the three piles of photos: one of the Olive Street bombing; and the other two, I saw, from other cities, Las Vegas and Montgomery. Nothing had happened in those cities, though you wouldn't have known it by the number of pictures taken. These were scenes of possible crimes; places that had been targeted for terrorism. Chip, as head of the Counterterrorism Squad, kept in touch with other agents in other cities regarding possible hits. They were looking for patterns, connections between terrorist threats. They were thorough: The photos showed the insides and outsides of buildings in both those cities — a large Planned Parenthood in Las Vegas, the Southern Poverty Law Center in Montgomery. Neither had been hit. But both, it was obvious from Chip's notes and files, had been threatened.

"Romilia?" said Nancy.

"What? Oh. Huston's not going for it. She thinks the frog poison was just some drug runner's hobby." I didn't look up.

"That's a bit strange."

"Yeah, but she's got a point. The batrachotoxin can't be spread except through blood. It's not an airborne toxin, can't do anything if released in the air. I should tell O'Brien that."

Something about the photos bothered me. Chip had piled them in an order that must have been significant to him. There were pictures of graffiti from each city. He had placed the graffiti photos together, one after the other.

I had lost the conversation with Nancy; she may as well have not been there. But she was. "Hey, thanks a lot," she said, and she simply beamed.

"What?"

"Oh, for just, recognizing me, earlier, you know . . . when you said 'good job'?" That was really nice." She bobbed her head up and down, agreeing with her own statement.

"Oh. Yeah." I turned away, looked at the photos. Lots of graffiti, everywhere.

A few seconds of beloved silence, in which I was hoping she was heading to her own cubicle. But she wasn't. "You're not one to work much with a partner, are you?"

"What? No, I guess I'm not."

"Rumor has it you've gone through quite a few here. At the Bureau."

I said nothing.

"Why is that?" she exhaled through her nose, a way of concealing nervousness.

Okay, I thought; *let's be a little more direct.* "Because working with a partner once almost got me killed."

"Sorry to hear that. But that was the past. And I'm a new partner."

"Look don't take it personally, Nancy. I'm just a wee more careful than your next agent. And besides," and though I paused to think out how to say it, it didn't matter; I knew it would come out blunt, "I'm just not into training people."

"Oh. I see. Well, I may be new to the field office, but I've already had my training, at Quantico." Her voice, for the first time since I had known her these past four days, turned a bit acidic.

"Fine. But you're new to this area, aren't you? And I wish that Special Agent Fisher had just, well, put you with someone else a little more ready for giving an orientation."

This was not going down well. I could tell by the way she screwed up her face. Still, I had to give her credit for how she moved the conversation back to the case. And though every word she uttered was laced with the silent screech of *bitch* toward me, she fed me some new information. "Bradley Pack is being transferred to a federal prison in northern California tomorrow. I thought you might want to know that, in case you wanted to talk with him before they took him away."

"Thanks," I said, and looked up. My gratitude was sincere. Talking with Pack was high on the list of priorities. But she had already left my cubicle.

"Why did you assign Pearl to me?"

Letty Fisher looked up from her desk. "Not getting along?"

"No, it's not that. She's fine. But I don't have time for relationship building. Touchy feely's too. . .touchy feely."

"That's too bad."

"So am I stuck with her?"

"Yes. You are. And she's stuck with you."

I may have cocked my head to one side. "What does that mean?"

"Well, it's my policy to assign new agents to the 'seasoned' ones such as yourself, so you may bequeath to them the wisdom of your experiences. I was going to have her walk with O'Brien, but before I could say anything, she requested to work with you."

"How nice."

"She may be regretting it now."

"Why's that?"

"Come on, Romi. You're as subtle as a brick when it comes to showing your dislikes."

"She'll have to deal with it."

"Fine. But you should take her willingness to work with you as a compliment. Actually, a number of younger agents have wanted to work with you. I've held them off, however, knowing you needed to make a little elbow room."

"Thanks."

"Yes, but elbow room–making is over now. And besides, Pearl is sharp. You might learn a thing or two from her as well." As if that weren't humbling enough, she added, "We work as teams in this field office, Romilia. You've been here long enough now to know that. Get used to it."

I called O'Brien. "Got a minute?" I said.

"Yeah. Come on over."

I walked to his office down the hall. It was bigger than my

cubicle, though not by much. O'Brien, having been here a number of years, had a whole closet for a desk and books.

"What's up?" he said. He turned away from his computer and stood from his chair. Old school: standing up when a woman walked through the door. I liked that.

"These photo piles, they were on Chip's table. CSI gathered them after they finished the scene."

"Not surprising. Chip couldn't leave work in the office."

"Yeah, he also was looking for something, I think." I showed him the smaller piles of graffiti. "This is from Montgomery, the Southern Poverty Law Center. See all the graffiti? And this." I put the first pile on O'Brien's desk. He was placing his thick black reading glasses on, studying the pictures as I pulled the second set of photos out of a manila envelope. "These are of Las Vegas, at a Planned Parenthood. More graffiti."

"These places were targets?" he said.

"Yes. No bomb threats reported. But FBI had undercovers in each place, both at the Law Center and the Planned Parenthood. Enough threats had accumulated on each to warrant special attention from the Bureau. Looks like the undercovers discovered some pretty sophisticated bombs in each building. Semtex, I believe. Not easy to come by. They rushed it, got the bombs out. Then they took these pictures."

"No doubt by the skin of their teeth."

"Now, these are the photos from Olive Street." I pulled them out of their own envelope. "More graffiti."

"Yes. And the arrogant message," he said, looking at YOUR WHORES.

"There's a pattern."

"What is it?"

"The tags, the marks left by gang members. Some of these look real, like the symbol for the Crips, and some other tags I've seen from local gangs. Also some angry graffiti . . . look here. At the Planned Parenthood, there's this '*Baby killers!*' tag. Probably sprayed there by antiabortion protestors. In Montgomery, there's this word, '*Miscegenists*'." No doubt an Aryan group wrote that. But some of the other graffiti looks, I don't know, faked. Like someone had added graffiti to make it look more 'busy.' In fact, Chip had a note here, about some of these symbols looking newer, sprayed on more recently. He was wondering if maybe just before the bombings were to take place."

"Were they some sort of marker?"

"Maybe."

"What about at Olive Street?" said O'Brien.

"'YOUR WHORES' was painted after the bombing. At night. Whoever did it wasn't caught." I looked hard at each photo to show O'Brien what I had brought him down for. "But the crazy thing is this: in each one, mixed in all the graffiti, there's this one word." I pointed it out.

He pronounced it slowly, then said, "That's Spanish. *Ojalá.*"

"It certainly is."

"Doesn't that mean 'I hope'?"

"Basically. A really strong hope."

"You think that's the marker?"

"Yeah, and I think Chip was onto it." I told him about my last conversation with Chip. "He had asked me what it meant. I thought he had looked it up or something, to use on me—you know, to ask me to, to marry him. But now, thinking back, that doesn't make sense. He would have just figured out how to say all that in Spanish if it was just about marriage."

"He never mentioned this to me," said O'Brien, "this word."

"He must have been studying the pictures that night, and putting something together: that each place had this word written at the bomb scenes."

"This is strange." Through the glasses O'Brien looked owl-like. "I've never heard of a Hispanic terrorist organization. Well, unless you're talking about the FARC in Colombia, of course. They're Latin terrorists."

I was about to, not necessarily disagree, but put in a specific point: The FARC and other guerrillas in Latin America, well, they had a cause they were fighting for. But instead, I said, "Me neither." I stared at the photos again. Ojalá in each place. Ojalá as some sort of marker. "You know, I hate to say this," I said.

"What?"

"A hunch. A really lousy one. *Ojalá* is a Spanish word, with Muslim roots."

"Really?"

"Yeah. It means, literally, *Oh, Allah*, or, *May Allah make it so.*"

"No shit."

That surprised me. In the short time I knew him, O'Brien didn't seem like the type to curse. "How in the world did that word get into your language?" he said.

"Long time ago. The Moors, when they took over Spain. Lots of their words got into the Spanish. *Ojalá* is one of the few that survived."

"You may have something here."

"Maybe."

"But, like you said, it'll be a media mess. The liberals will get ahold of us and scream that we're persecuting the Arabic community."

"Yeah. But not only that . . . something doesn't feel right. 'Miscegenists.' 'Baby killers.' Those are phrases that come more out of the Christian crazies."

"True." He studied a photo, then pinched his lower lip with two fingers.

"Christians, using a Muslim name. Seems a far stretch. You can't get more opposite than those two groups."

O'Brien took off his glasses. "Actually, that's not true." He looked at me. "They're very similar."

"How's that?"

He leaned against his desk. "You remember Mahmud Abouhalima?"

I was embarrassed to say no, so I said, "The name is familiar . . ."

"He's the young man alleged as the mastermind of the World Trade Center bombing. Not in 2001, but back in 1993. I've been in contact with a professor up in Santa Barbara who once interviewed the kid. They talked about the Oklahoma City bombing. Know what Abouhalima said? He actually understood Timothy McVeigh, almost like he had an affinity toward McVeigh. He said that McVeigh was sending a strong, specific message to the U.S. government: that he and others were not going to tolerate how the government dealt with our citizens. That's pretty much Abouhalima's message as well, only his was directed at how the U.S. deals with citizens of other countries." O'Brien laughed, but it wasn't meant to be funny. "Abouhalima even said once that the United States' idea of separation of church and state was ludicrous, and that we'd be a better nation if the Christians ran the country, because at least we'd have a sense of morals."

"I don't see any Christian groups ready to join Muslim outfits."

"Maybe not in religious beliefs," said O'Brien. "But when it comes to tactics, well, they all want to 'wake up' the world."

"So, what are you saying? There's a link between Christian right-wingers and extremist Muslims?"

"No. Not a link, per se. But when it comes to ideologies?" He shook his head.

"Agent O'Brien, that's one scary-ass thought."

"Think about it. What do Osama bin Laden and Christian militia groups have in common?"

I didn't want to think about it. "What?"

"A hatred and a fear of a 'new world order.' All the different groups: Christian Identity, Posse Comitatus, Aryan Nations, Hamas, al Qa'ida. Stranger bedfellows have been known." He looked behind me, out the door, again to see if anyone was in earshot. "And though it pains me to say this, well, some of our home-grown terrorists, like McVeigh and his ilk? They may actually celebrate what happened on September 11."

Min Arellano survived the ambush in Tijuana, but his brother Mon did not. The Mexican authorities locked Min in a maximum security prison.

Tekún needed to contact Min. He had words sent to Min directly, with information on Frankie and, no doubt, Lennie. Within the week, Frankie and Lennie were found where Mexican and U.S. sand meet, with bullets to their heads, scrapes on their backs, and Federal Agents standing over them.

The two had died around the time the word had hit the West Coast: The Crack Killer had come to California. First, a rumor; then, in true community fashion, the rumor festered into belief: The Crack Killer, he's in town. He's anywhere. Knocking out drug dealers across the country. No one in the business is safe.

The story had already become folklore. In an industry that relied upon subversion, stealth, that had more than enough cash to buy the best in surveillance; an industry that packed small, unmanned, nuclear-powered submarines with a thousand kilos of heroin and sent them on their merry, automatic-pilot way to the shores of Alabama, where trucks, parked on the beaches at night, picked them up; in this high-tech, multinational business, in which the drug traffickers, with their overwhelming sources of cash would always be ahead of the U.S. government's measly multi-million-dollar budget that drug czars like Carl Spooner used to pretend was enough to end the drug war; amidst all this sophistication among the drug lords, the folklore started to take root. The Crack Killer: the one who killed dealers and distributors, not to take over their business but to suck up their immediate revenues (what they had on their bodies, in cash, and in bags). A serial killer that, unlike the sniper killings in D.C., never made it to the nightly news because he had become a private legend, known only to those who had a reason to know about it. He was a ghost. A vigilante phantom.

The phantom Crack Killer had gotten the blame for the deaths of Frankie and Lennie.

"Whatever," said Chamba. "Some believe that crap. When I heard about the killings on my scanner, I got there before the Feds did."

"So, what did you see? And did they see you?"

"No. I blend nice with all the gringos. I kept enough beach between us. And it was Sunday, mostly Latinos all over the place. It was El Cíclope Cojo who they called in. He and his partner."

Tekún laughed. Such a nickname for poor Agent Chip Pierce. He drank from a glass of Australian Syrah.

"They checked the bodies, said something about scrapes on their backs. Then the two took off quick, and jumped each other." This time, Chamba laughed.

"What?" Tekún put the glass down. He suspected what was coming, though he had to hear it.

"Oh, the two of them, Cyclops and his partner. They fucked each other's brains out in a hotel in San Diego. Didn't get back to L.A. until late that night."

Tekún knew; but still he asked, "Who is his partner?"

Beads never asked, partly because he knew he wouldn't get a straight answer. Tekún Umán had never spoken of his love affairs, and he wasn't about to begin doing so with Romilia Chacón.

The incidents swirling around them kept Beads from asking anything. First there was the question of the hit on Frankie and Lennie. Tekún could make no sense of Frankie's information about an attack on L.A., until Beads did some rerouting of Internet signals to access the VICAP files of the FBI. Yet the Bureau had become more adept with their firewalls; Beads could only pick up ghosts of information, names and numbers that meant little to him. Still, he could surmise, "It must be a terrorist threat. Some group is planning to blow up LAX again, or take down the Getty Museum."

"Los Angeles is always under threat of attack," said Tekún. "But why would Frankie have known about it?"

"Because Min and Mon did?" said Beads.

"Okay. But why would they?"

"Maybe they're working with the terrorists," said Beads.

"You're as bad as the DEA."

"But it's true," said Beads. "Terrorists need money. What better place to find it than in the drug trade?"

The two had never spoken so openly to each other about the business. Yet another sign of joining the cartel, where such talk was commonplace, and not feared. Here, in Tijuana, all the world, whether they wanted it or not, was involved.

"Think about it, Beads. Why would the Arellanos want to get involved with terrorists?" He looked again at the computer screen. "Have you heard back from Min?"

"No."

"Contact him. Thank him for cleaning up Frankie and Lennie," said Tekún. "I want him to hear it from me."

Beads sent an e-mail to a Junior in Mexico City, who then copied Beads's note and sent it along to a cousin in Ensenada, who routed it to a business associate in Brussels. From there the note made it to a computer within the prison walls outside of Mexico City, where a Junior opened it, wrote it down, deleted and swiped the computer, then took the note to Min. It would not be long — the time it took Tekún to make a cappuccino — until the answer from Min arrived via another route. Tekún walked back into the computer room, stirring his coffee. Beads turned to him and, before deleting the e-mail, said, "Min doesn't know anything about it."

There was no reason for Min to deny the killings; to say he had not ordered the hit was a flag of warning, that someone was in the courtyard with them, killing then hiding; someone else had taken out Frankie and Lennie, leaving them dead on the other side of the border.

Months passed before Chamba was killed. Dead from a knife

puncture to his throat, tossed in front of Tekún Umán's apartment early one morning. Tekún smelled him before he saw him; he pulled his own knife, shed his robe and placed his coffee on a table, then made his way to the front door. The smell was there, hanging about the wooden door like a stagnant cloud. Tekún unlatched the door and leaped to one side, just as Chamba's head and shoulders pushed the door open. He did not hesitate: Tekún pulled Chamba's body in and called Beads down.

They checked the body. Nothing, no note, no hint of whose signature this was, just a simple puncture to the throat. No doubt Chamba walked around wherever he had been when it happened, spurting blood through fingers locked around his skin, unable to speak, and surely unable to scream. They rolled him over. On his back was a large scrape, almost perfect in symmetry: squared off, as if a rectangular blade had been pulled across his skin. The scrape looked too perfect, and too large, to have been caused when Chamba fell. It had been placed there after the killing.

"Get rid of him," said Tekún.

La voz corriente, the current of voice, ran through town. The Crack Killer had arrived in Tijuana. Tekún ignored the rumors; Beads wondered. Whoever had killed Chamba, Lennie, and Frankie appeared in the mail: Tekún received a handwritten note, saying only *I will scrape you soon.*

"He was at my door," said Tekún. "Why didn't he just come in and do it?"

"Who is it?" said Beads. "Who the hell's going to scrape you?"

"I have no idea."

"Maybe it's the guy . . ."

"Don't start with that Crack Killer crap."

"You never know, *ahijado*."

Neither of them had time to find out, what with all the world turning its attention to the building in central Los Angeles, whose front end blew apart. But this was no federal building; this was a housing unit for homeless women and heroin pushers, prostitutes and pimps and Bel Air teenagers looking for an afternoon fix. This was one of the buildings owned by a Mr. Bradley Pack, Lennie's father. The Los Angeles Fire Department tracked the source of the explosion to a large, hidden compartment on the second floor. And amidst the shattered rubble that fell over the cars and buses and pedestrians of Olive Street, in the cement dust that fell like an exhausted fog, there was another dust, a white powder that mixed with the gray of shattered mortar, several million dollars' worth, dusting that downtown street in Los Angeles.

Tekún had little time to wonder about that attack, beyond the fact that this was what Frankie had mentioned; though he did wonder about the world, what had become of it. Had the world itself decided to go amuck, or had his decisions to expand brought him to this?

This: his godfather found in the desert just outside of Tijuana, left in pieces, some pulled off by feral dogs. A skill saw leaning against a rock, next to tire tracks, where no doubt the man who had done this had brought along with him a generator. Then the scrape, across the whole of Beads's back, and the note left on a tiny dry spot of Beads's shredded shirt, *How does it feel, the scraping?*

B ack at my desk, my phone blinked with messages. One was from my mother, saying she just wanted to see how I was doing. I'd call her later. Another was from an agent at the DEA in Washington, a fellow named Blanton. He was returning my call, a follow-up to my inquiry about Carl Spooner. I called him back. "Any closer to catching the prick?" he said.

I knew he meant Tekún Umán. "We're still on it."

"I know I should be careful about talking like this on the phone," said Blanton, "but you realize how we all feel about this Murillo guy, don't you?"

I did. I remembered how the DEA had stormed Tekún's house in New Orleans. They'd found nothing of him, not even hair. But what I remembered was the rage. Though it was never on record, these men of the Drug Enforcement Agency, as individuals, meant to do more than just bring Tekún in. They meant to hunt him down. Treat him like game.

Blanton kept talking. "I mean, I'm sure you all feel the same way now, with Special Agent Pierce murdered by Tekún. I never knew him, but everyone said he was a good man. A good man. Hell of an agent as well."

"Yeah. He was a good man," I said.

"You know, some here think Murillo's the Crack Killer."

"Yeah. I've heard that."

"But I don't believe it," said Blanton.

"Really? Why?"

"Because I don't think there is any serial killer. I think those are just bullshit stories floating through the drug trade, either for the dealers to entertain themselves or to throw us off."

The conversation was getting longer than I cared for; and I was ruminating still on my conversation with O'Brien on a possible al Qa'ida–Evangelical tent-show. "So, did you find the information regarding the tranquilizer used on Agent Spooner?"

"No, I'm afraid I didn't find anything. At the time, we weren't thinking about tranquilizers. Carl was bleeding to death. We just had to get him out of that damn jungle."

"Were you close to Agent Spooner?"

"Yeah. Yeah I was." Blanton cleared his throat. "I was there, in Guate, when Murillo took him down."

"Oh, God. I'm sorry."

"Yeah." He got silent for a while, longer than I was comfortable with. But I said nothing, knowing he wanted to talk more. Sometimes that's what we need, from one agency to another. Talk about what we can, even though we know all our phones are tapped by our own. We still talk; and those listening in, they know.

"Carl had come down to Guate with the specific order of bringing in Murillo. I was in the other room, playing cards with some of the guys. We never even heard anything going on in his bedroom. Didn't hear him hit the floor, of course, didn't even hear anything like a dart shooting into him. There we were, drinking coffee and playing five card stud, and Carl was getting carved up in the other room."

"You sure you want to be talking about this?" I said, referring to the tapped lines.

"It's all on file. It's known. The Agency didn't blame us, didn't put a stain on our record. But I guess I still got a stain in my head, huh?" A laugh chucked out of him.

"Wasn't your fault," I said.

"That's what my wife tells me."

This was getting uncomfortable. Still, I tried. "Listen, you can't blame yourself for what happened to Carl." And that was as far as I could go; I had never been good at playing therapist, with anybody—not even my mother. Something she had brought up more than once, how I wasn't the best listener when it came to hardships. I'm a good listener; I just listen for facts. "How is he now, by the way? Didn't he have a family?"

"Oh, Jesus, that's the horror of all this," said Blanton. He almost choked on the irony: "Carl goes into this deep depression, you know, he couldn't . . . function. As a man. Here he's got this beautiful wife, Sarah, man she was gorgeous. And three kids, cute, wonderful kids. But he goes down, really down. They were afraid he was suicidal, you know? They took care of him, best they could, gave him an office job here in D.C. But he can hardly put it together. So his wife surprises him with this trip down to Florida, take the kids to Disneyland, then they were going to fly out to one of the islands in the Gulf. So what happens? They take a commuter plane from St. Petersburg to the island, one of those hoppers, and it's caught in headwinds or something. Goes down somewhere in the Gulf."

"Jesus," I said. I meant it, too.

"Yeah. Fucked-up world, huh?"

"Yeah. Yeah it is, Agent Blanton."

We started saying our good-byes around then, after some more stumbling, in which he realized he had said more than he had planned. "Listen, sorry to take up so much of your time. You'll keep us apprised if anything new comes up?"

"You'll hear from me first, Agent Blanton."

"Thanks. Thanks for listening." He hung up.

Ironies.

I looked for my partner, to go see Bradley Pack in the Van Nuys jail. I considered trying to be a little more tactful with her, cut her some slack. "You want to drive?" I asked.

Bradley Pack was a man you could truly call penitent. He wasn't on his knees when we met with him in his jail cell in Van Nuys. But he may as well have been. Regret had written deep lines into his face.

He wasn't very old, maybe in his mid-forties. Waspish looking, except for a once-nice tan that was beginning to recede in jail. Good shape: He looked like a guy who worked out at Ballys or LA Fitness or one of the other legion of spas in southern California. Only a little bit of softness around those muscles, probably due to a Manhattan or two every night with his (no doubt) lovely, BOTOX-ed wife. All that warm, comfortable, relaxed southern Cal persona was breaking away from his body, now that his kid, Lennie Pack, was in the ground. That, and his building blown all to hell by terrorists who may have targeted the drugs that he housed. No wonder he looked a bit haggard, poor thing.

He looked at Pearl and me as if we were safe, especially once we showed him our credentials. He had more safety with us than anybody else he had been working with the past few years, including the Arellano brothers. When we said their names, he actually trembled.

"We're here to talk with you about the murder of a federal agent, Mr. Pack," I said. "Special Agent Samuel Pierce was investigating the bombing in your building downtown. He is now dead. We need to know if you had any contact with him."

"Was he the one with an eye patch? Fake leg?"

"A prosthetic. Yes. That's the man."

"Yeah. He had me arrested. He brought me in."

Nancy spoke up, "So, would you have any information on how he was killed?"

"Are you kidding? I've been in here since my building got blown up."

"Did you have contact with anyone outside who would be interested in seeing Agent Pierce dead?" asked Nancy. I looked at her; she was decent at this.

"No way. Look, they've pinned me with drug smuggling, okay . . . but I had nothing to do with that explosion, I have no idea what happened. You think I'd want to blow up my own building?"

"We're not here to talk about the case against you," I said. "We're on a murder investigation."

"Good luck." He chortled, like a man who thought there were enemies in the cell with him. "You never found the sons a bitches who killed my son. You think you'll figure out who killed your agent?"

Pearl said, "Mr. Pack, did your son ever talk about a possible 'hit' on Los Angeles?"

"Yeah. Yeah, he did. My son had warned me about a terrorist attack. Never told me who it was, but it shook him up. That's part of why he wanted to get out. And he was with a group that was pressuring him. Some religious outfit. He wanted me to get out of it, too, but you know how it is: You don't just stop doing business with the Arellanos. Shit, they'll kill you. They'll take the skin right off your back, like they did to my son. We were in way too deep. My whole family would be dead now, if the brothers hadn't gotten caught. But the Arellanos, they've got their cousins and uncles and, jeez, even their mother's probably in on it. They're all killers, every damn one of them. I doubt I'll even be safe in prison. They're everywhere."

"Mr. Pack, do you know anything about a group called the Ojalá?"

"The what? What's that?"

Nancy looked at me, wondering where the hell that came from.

"Never heard of it?" I said.

"I only speak one language, Agent Chacón. And nowadays, I'd like to keep it that way. No more work with Mexicans, or anybody from out of town."

What was that all about, that word?" Pearl asked.

I explained to her my conversation with O'Brien, the graffiti. What the word meant. How it came from Moorish sources.

"That's a strong lead," she said.

"Maybe."

Silence for a few moments, then she asked, "What do you make of that, taking the skin off Leonard Pack's back? Think it's some sort of signature?" We were in the car, driving out of the Valley back to the offices.

"I remember that, from the forensic report. Chip and I identified the bodies on the beach below San Diego." My mind drifted slightly, to that wondrous afternoon in the Holiday Inn Express. I remembered how long, and how hard, he could stiffen his tongue.

"Did the fellow, Umán, did he ever do that to people? Skin them?"

"No. He's cut them up. Once I saw his work on a teenage boy in Nashville. He had hauled the kid over a barbwire fence for an afternoon."

"God. That's horrible."

I said nothing to that. But it *was* horrible. That kid was still alive. I wondered where he was; was he still in Nashville? And how did that incident work on him psychologically? The boy—Gato Negro was his nickname—had lost an eye to one of the barbs in the fence. That was four years ago. He must have reached age twenty by now, if he had reached it; if he had lived. No doubt he had scars all over his body from the fence. No doubt he could read that one scar on his stomach, *soplón*, tattletale. Narc. Tekún made his messages clear. Unlike these scrapes over dead people's backs.

What did that do to a kid? The operation Tekún had performed on Carl Spooner had driven Spooner to near suicide. What would it drive a teenage boy to do?

I thought about my boy, Sergio. I'd hardly seen him the past two days. Hadn't talked with my mother, either. I was about to return her call on my cell, but decided that would be rude, especially talking with her in Spanish while my English-only partner drove us back to the office.

Instead I actually started a conversation with Pearl. I told her about my earlier phone call with the DEA agent, Blanton, ending with the fact that the Spooner family had died in a plane crash.

"God, that's horrible. It's like Spooner's family was destined for — no, that's just wrong," she said. "Crazy to think that way."

"What, destiny?"

"Yeah. Yeah, because Spooner was just doing his job, and here he gets attacked by a drug dealer, left all cut like that, and his life is ruined. So his wife decides to help him out, make him happy again, with a surprise trip, only to have them all die. If Tekún Umán knew what he had started, I wonder how he would feel about it all?" She said it with a baited tone, as if, had Tekún been in the car, she would have whipped around and slapped him.

"Yeah. Good question." I was looking out the window. How would he be feeling about this? Was it just business? Would he even care, all the broken lives he'd left behind him?

"Then Agent Pierce . . ."

"Yeah." How many times had that been said in the past twenty-four hours? Connecting Carl Spooner's attack with Chip's murder, always in that tone, *Then Agent Pierce*. Especially when the *then* made no sense.

"Agent Chacón, may I ask you a blunt question?"

I looked at her. She watched the road through stylish sunglasses, staring at the traffic that moved briskly through the Mulholland Pass on the 405 Freeway. "That's a hell of a setup. Okay. Ask."

She hesitated, as if gaining some quiet composure, then said, "Do you believe Tekún might be innocent of killing Special Agent Pierce?"

It was my turn to hesitate. "Why?"

She fell into a stumble of an explanation, obviously embarrassed. "Well, I've noticed you've never actually said you think he's a suspect."

I straightened myself up in the passenger seat. "Gosh, Agent Pearl, that's true." I could hear the defensiveness in my voice; Pearl was more perceptive than I had given her credit.

Pearl went on. "The fact is, he's a dangerous man. A drug runner. He's attacked and maimed another federal agent with the DEA. And everyone in the office is out for him now, with Agent Pierce dead. I'm just a bit, I don't know, surprised that you might have your doubts."

I sighed heavily, angrily.

"I'm sorry, Agent Chacón, I don't mean to question you. I'm just trying to figure things out myself."

"Look, okay. I'll be straight with you. Ready? Yeah, I do have my doubts, Nancy. Just slightly, but there are some things that point away from Tekún Umán."

"Like what?"

"Well, like the bludgeoning."

"What, beating Agent Pierce in the head?"

"Yes. That's not his style. That would seem, well, brutish. It looks too much like rage, and Tekún is not one to show his rage like that."

"Yeah, but wasn't he in love with you?"

"Okay, so you're one of the many who put their faith in that."

"Wasn't he?"

"He had shown . . . overtures . . . once. Or twice." I may have blushed.

"So, maybe his feelings over you got the best of him. Maybe that's why he beat in Agent Pierce's face."

"Well, maybe. But I doubt it."

"And then there's the word carved into Agent Pierce's stomach."

"Well, that's another reason I have my doubts."

She pulled into a section of the FBI parking lot where there were few cars, as if to give us some space to talk. A large SUV sat to my right. She had taken off her sunglasses, held them up to study some stains on the lens, then placed them on the dashboard. "Agent Chacón, you yourself said the carving points to someone trained in the death squads."

"Right. But whoever did this made a mistake."

"What?"

"They forgot to accent the *o*."

"*What?*"

I knew she'd be thrown by that. So I explained it to her. "The word '*cabrón*'. It's spelled with an accented *ó*. It wasn't accented on Chip, on his abdomen."

"You're kidding." She shook her head, opened her purse, and pulled out her sunglasses case. "Just because of a missing accent, you think this wasn't Tekún Umán?"

That pissed me off. There's nothing like the narrow-mindedness of a person who speaks only one language. And Nancy was beyond provincial; she was *über*-cracker. I had to explain everything to her about my Latino world, which was starting to piss me off. *Ojalá*. The importance of accents. While she pulled out her little cloth hanky to clean the stain off her brand-name sunglasses, I began a little diatribe on how the accent in Spanish is more than a decoration, it's an intrinsic part of the language, but of course a monolingual person from the United States wouldn't understand that. I was just a fourth of the way into this little speech when I smelled it. Too late. Agent Nancy Pearl pushed the ether-soaked cloth over my face. She was strong. Even when I shot my fist into her chest, she didn't flinch much. She held the cloth over my mouth and nose in a practiced fashion, while her other hand slipped around the back of my neck. She pressed. I reached for my holster, but it seemed far away. I quit kicking. And then I was gone.

Though still heavy-headed, I did not doubt where I was. Somewhere inside that huge SUV that we had parked beside. A Suburban of some sort. Maybe a Cherokee. It was black, I remembered that; I remembered her lifting me, placing me. That was about it.

Nancy was stronger than she looked. She was a lot more than what she appeared to be. And she had been hired by someone else, no doubt about that.

This was the SUV, but I was sure the Cherokee company had not built the section that she laid me out in. A hidden compartment somewhere underneath the back passenger seats. Wide and long, but not too deep, maybe a foot, gauging from how close my nose was to the roof of the compartment. She had placed something soft on its floor, mats or cushions, so that the ride wouldn't shake the teeth out of my mouth. That wouldn't have been possible either, not with the duct tape over my face. And my wrists, stretched out and tied to something in the upper corners of the compartment, my ankles tied to the lower portions. And the odor in the air meant a thick wad of cloth somewhere, soaked in ether or some other gas, no doubt to keep me from panicking, from slamming my skull against the compartment door.

All well planned; that, I could say to myself, as my head meandered in and out of sleep, in and out of consciousness. All planned, a thought that flowed right next to images of my son and my mother, and shit I hadn't called her, like I had meant to do, had had the chance to earlier in the day but had decided to take the call from that DEA agent. Always the job, always having to do the damn job, while my mother wondered how I was doing.

Sometimes I could hear Pearl. Her voice was muffled, but these compartments were not made for soundproofing, no need for that; hidden coke doesn't make a noise. Though it does make a smell: Usually these stash holds were air tight, with a rubber casing around the top door. Which explained the dot of light that pierced through. She must have drilled airholes. Again, all thought out well ahead of time.

It was a long drive. Long enough for the ether-soaked rag to dry, for the wind rushing underneath the SUV to push through the holes and suck the vapors out of the tank. I started to wake. I pushed my face toward one of the airholes, got my nostrils as near the airflow as possible. It woke me more, enough to feel the binds around my wrist and ankles, which made me think of Chip, and how he had hated playing with handcuffs.

Enough to let me hear her, talking with someone through the driver's side window. And I cursed her, underneath the duct tape: bitch, tagging along with me like she had, pretending to be incredulous about an accented *o*; and here she was, her head halfway out the window, talking to the border patrol in perfectly groomed Spanish. Giving her credentials, *Agente del FBI*, no doubt showing her badge (Was it real? Must have been; Fisher authorized all badges. Was Fisher in on this? Who else was?), and her Spanish, *Estaré en Tijuana solamente por el día es que hay una reunión con una agencia de la migra que tiene que ver con asuntos del gobierno* . . . and a slew of other bullshit. I could hear how the guy started flirting with her, and she laughed and said, *Maybe on the way back, tequila sounds good, but without the worm, Mister*, in perfect Spanish, and they both had a good laugh.

Bitch.

No doubt she had my gun. But I had time to think about how to pop her, once she opened this tank. We drove beyond Tijuana; I could tell that by the speed, no doubt going around a bypass. But then we left that as well, and from the potholes bashing up through the thick blankets and into my pelvis and thighs, I knew we were on the real roads of Mexico.

I had to think it out: In the dim light I could see the hinges of the compartment, not above my head, but below me, just over my waist. Which meant she had stuffed me in here headfirst, and that my legs were at the hind end of the SUV. The door wouldn't open up completely, but rather halfway. Which meant the sun would not hit my eyes, and I would not have to squint, and I could pretend to be unconscious.

Pearl was, however, a chemistry major, or so she had said; so maybe she would know the ether was gone. Then again, she had said a lot of things. By now, I was beginning to doubt her Missouri roots.

She parked and shut down the motor. It was quiet, too quiet for a city. No radios, no people walking around. But there was a bird, chirping nearby. Which meant, more than likely, countryside. Footsteps joined her. But only she spoke. "No problems," she said. "And your blankets probably kept her from bruising up." She opened the back door. I heard the movement of packages, then the tearing of Velcro from its foundation, as a carpet was pulled up. Then a key sliding into the lock of the hidden hatch and then sunlight; but I did not move. I kept my eyes closed, even though they could not see my face.

Pearl undid the tie from my left ankle, then started working on my right. "That ether really did her in," she said, which meant the little bitch *wasn't* a chemist. She untied my right ankle; she would need to bend in enough to reach the plastic straps around my wrists, which made it easy to lift my legs and wrap them around her back and pull. Hard. I slammed her head against the compartment door.

"Shit!" She tried to pull away. But, oh, I had her. I went for another hearty tug; her face popped against the metal. Then I heard his voice, for the first time, actually a bit panicky, "For God's sake, Romilia, let her go." He grabbed one of my legs to pry it off Pearl, so I went with his pull and popped the side of his head with my shin, which hurt like hell, which meant it hurt him like hell, too.

"All right, all right," he said, and pulled Pearl away from me. Then Rafael Murillo, a.k.a. Tekún Umán, lowered his head and looked at me through the thin gap. "*Mi Vida*," he said, "you're going to need to calm down to let us let you free."

I kicked again, impotently, toward him. That wasn't enough, so I kicked even harder. Pearl backed farther away, as if from some feral mammal.

"Have it your way, Romi," said Tekún. He motioned for Pearl to follow him.

Something about that bothered me even more; not that they would leave me, I knew it was a game. They would wait until I was exhausted, then they'd come around and cut the plastic off my wrists. No, it was the fact that he motioned silently for Pearl to follow him, and that that blond, tall glass of water who spoke perfect Chilango Spanish obeyed; and the thought, of her, with him, inside a house out here in the Mexican *campo* . . . I belted out a high-pitch set of hums through the duct tape.

He approached again. "You promise to keep calm?"

I looked through the gap, straight into his eyes. I nodded.

He reached in, pulled the tape off my face, undid the ties, gave me a hand to help me out of the holding tank. I rubbed one wrist, then the other, shook my head, leaned against the fender of the car. Then I reached for my holster but of course merely slapped my thigh; but my eyes had gone up to Pearl and the new cut on her forehead. She knew then, had she not taken the gun, she would have taken the *balazo*.

Tekún simply said, "Would you like something to drink?"

Things had changed. He looked older. He was, of course; he must have been forty. Maybe already in his mid-forties; perhaps that's what accounted for the look, the way he took in a room. In this room, this house, there was not much to take in. It was clean, well kept, but there was very little furniture, and the paintings on the walls were too realistic for Tekún's taste. I always figured him more of a Pollock lover. Still, the music was his: A small CD player filled the room with Bach. The Partitas. I saw the CD case, with Glenn Gould's young face on the cover.

The small stack of books was also his. Three of them, piled haphazardly together. The memoir *Vivir para contarla*, by Gabriel García Márquez (I had yet to read that; Mamá had told me to hold off for Christmas); a novel by T. C. Boyle; a book of poetry by David St. John. And a small black notebook, a Moleskine, with its famous little black rubber band slipped around it. His journal?

A small collection of books. No doubt carried quickly from another home. This was not his home, it was his hideout.

I watched him as he pulled glasses from the kitchen shelves. He was still himself; but something had shaded his eyes, and I should have guessed what that was, not so much in where we were, or what was in the room; but rather, who was not in the room. Beads was not here. And in the small, short span of time that I had known Beads, I could tell there had been an affinity between them. Beads was his *padrino*. That is no light relationship, to be some-one's godfather. And he was not here.

He dismissed Pearl, and that appeased something in me. It

pleased me that he said to her, "That's all for now," in a way that showed her to be an employee, and perhaps nothing more.

She did not look at me when she left the room, but her head was held high.

"So. What's the deal with Pearl?" I said. By the tone of my voice, I may just as well have said, *What's the deal with your gran puta de la madre jodida?*

He glanced at me. "Her name's not Pearl, if that's what you mean."

"I figured that."

"But let's call her Pearl."

He handed me a glass of water. I drank it down at once. "Where's Beads?" I said, and knew, immediately.

"He's dead." He walked to a bar. This was a small room, in a plain, though well kept, adobe house; still, he walked as if the bar stood far away.

Back in Nashville, he wore Versace suits. Here, he wore Latino formal wear. A white guayabera with two simply adorned stripes running down the front. Four pockets, with nothing in them. Black pants. Leather shoes. His black hair combed back, just a bit of pomade. Older; but he was still so very handsome.

"I'm sorry."

He said nothing.

"So, where did you meet . . . your Pearl?"

"I caught up with her in New York. She was a student in the Studio. She loved the acting but not the hustle. And all that emphasis on Hollywood instead of the stage. So I hired her to get herself hired by the FBI. She's a hard worker. Made her way through Quantico, passed all the tests with flying colors. I might have lost her to your crew if it hadn't been for my payroll. Now, of course, starting today, she's said good-bye to almost two years of building her career in the Bureau."

"What happened to Beads?"

He told me. Then he told me about other men: a guy named Chamba. The two boys I had stood over on the San Diego beach, Lennie and Frankie. In my head, I couldn't help but add Chip to the list.

But I had questions. "So you think someone's framed you. And they're out to kill you. Any ideas?"

"No."

"Not the Arellano brothers?"

"Maybe. But I haven't done anything to them to have something like this come back to me. Unless the Arellano family thought I was connected to Frankie being a narc. But that makes little sense. They hired him, and Lennie, for me." He drank from a glass of clear whiskey. It was the first time I had ever seen Tekún Umán take a drink of alcohol. "So you know I didn't kill Agent Pierce?" he said.

"I know."

"Pearl told me why. I'm glad whoever did spells poorly."

He sat down, almost heavily.

I did not sit down. I poured more water from the pitcher on the bar, drank it. I looked at him; something was all wrong. "You haven't written me, either, have you?" I said.

"No, of course not. Why?"

"I received an e-mail. Someone was trying to make it sound like you. Someone who wanted me to believe that you killed Pierce, like you were some jealous lover."

"Well, on the latter thought, they may have been correct."

"You knew about Chip and me?"

He said nothing.

"Look, who I hang out with, or whoever I go to bed with, that's none of your business." I wasn't thirsty anymore, so I poured a shot of the tequila, as if to shut myself up. When I turned and looked at him, he had his eyebrows raised; and he smiled, as if this was the first real sense of joy that he had had in a while.

"So," he said, "the e-mail. Did you write him back?"

"Yes."

"Why?"

"He baited me. I wasn't sure at first—it *could* have been you. But I was still thinking about the *o* without the accent, which didn't make sense. I wrote back, just to see if he'd say anything more."

"Well, it wasn't me. It was the guy who's hunting me."

Something I knew Tekún hated. And not in the usual, human way. Tekún had a rabid side to him when it came to getting trapped. That's what made him able to do the things he did: cut up a teenager; slice up the genitals of a federal agent; and put a knife to my neck. I had to wonder about that. It was more than a fear of getting caught. I wondered if his reaction to entrapment came from a darker part of his past.

"Whoever he is," I said, "I think he's part of a larger group."

"Yes? What group?"

I told him all about Ojalá.

He listened, but he didn't seem that interested. Something was blurring his vision. It took a while to see that it was me: worry, sliding off his face, revealing a relief. But I was still pissed. "So, what, you kidnap me and bring me here, for me to protect you?"

And he: "Mi *amor*. I brought you here to protect *you*."

He took me to a bedroom, opened the door, and turned on the light. "You can stay here. Pearl has some clothes for you. Her jeans might be a bit snug, but I think they'll still fit."

I turned to him, my mouth open, ready to blurt out a *fuck you*. But he was already down the hall.

Then he appeared in the door again. "By the way, I wouldn't advise trying to leave. We're far from any town. No one's out here. The cars are all locked up. Pearl has your gun."

"What's your plan, Rafael?"

He turned his head as if knowing that I, using his proper name, was reprimanding him, like a mother. "I'm going to make us some dinner." He drummed the doorstop with his fingers, then walked away.

There were pajamas on the bed. And there were jeans and a T-shirt and a jacket. I threw the pajamas on the floor.

The jeans were not that snug. I wanted to tell him that. I wanted to tell him a hell of a lot more: that I didn't need him protecting me. That I had to talk to my mother, find out how my boy was doing. No one pulls me out of my life like that with some fake FBI partner—and don't get me started on fucking partners.

I looked out the window of the bedroom. That was pure countryside out there. No telling which way Tijuana was, much less the border.

Not much else to do but try to calm down. And that shot of tequila made me hungry.

* * *

Tekún was roasting red peppers and onions on a thin, flat stone. The odors made my stomach leap. He gestured to a mountain of freshly made tortillas, which were piled and wrapped inside a thick towel. I opened the towel; the steam rose and ran right up my nostrils. I ate two tortillas without saying anything. They were delicious, as good as the ones my uncle Chepe made. I checked the pants again, lifting one leg to feel the tight cloth around the curve of my ass, then ate another tortilla. "These are good," I said.

"Thicker," he said. "Just like from El Salvador."

However I was going to say it, I knew it would sound silly, so I just said it. "I'd like to call my mother."

"I thought you might. Pearl has your cell phone, and I'd prefer you not use it. I know the Bureau has serviced your cellulars with those satellite locators, and I wouldn't want you to be tempted to use yours. Use the one in the office. She'll show you where it is. She'll dial for you."

So I couldn't surreptitiously punch in another number, such as that of my boss, Lettie Fisher.

"By the way, Romi, careful with Pearl. She's very, capable."

Pearl was in the office, sitting at a desk. She had my unlisted home number. "I've already dialed it. Please don't say anything you shouldn't, or I'll have to disconnect the line. Just tell her you've been called to head out of town for a while, on assignment. She'll get it. She knows you can't say too much on the phone."

"You've studied up, haven't you?"

Pearl smiled. "I'm still Bureau trained."

And there was no regret in her voice. Could money have that effect on someone like that? Or was it more than money? Was it loyalty . . . and were they lovers? Shit.

Mamá was not home. So I said into the message machine, as pleasantly as possible, what Pearl told me to say. All in Spanish, of course: "Can't say where I'm going, but it's pretty routine, don't worry. I'll call from the road. I'll probably stop at a *pupusería* stand near the office, pick up some *revueltas* before I leave. Love you, and love my little *cipote!*" and I hung up.

"Good."

"So. What's the deal between you and Tekún?"

The question had sat on my tongue from the moment I had seen them together, ready to spring out of my mouth, like a panther.

She smiled. "You think the worst in people, don't you?" she said.

"Only with the ones who give me reason to."

"And does Tekún Umán give you reason?"

I did not answer that.

She had been sitting at the desk, right beside me, ready to shut the line down if I said something wrong to my mother. She stood now and walked toward the door, motioning for me to follow her, no doubt to get me out of their office. We walked down the hallway to the bedroom. "I used to live in Atlanta, when I was a kid. You know where? My address was between 136 and 138 Peach Tree. An alleyway. My mother and I lived there for five weeks. We had come down from Cincinnati. Trying to get out of the cold. But Atlanta gets cold, too."

In the bedroom she saw the pajamas on the floor, picked them up, refolded them, and put them on a dresser. "He found us. Or rather, some of his sellers found us. They took us to his shelter downtown. My mother never wanted to go to one of those shelters. Here we were, living in cardboard, and my mother had too much pride to ask for help. She'd been in one before, run by some evangelicals. You had to listen to their preaching for two hours before you could eat, or sleep. That was enough for her. But we were hungry, and I was just, I don't know, seven. So she took the boys up on the shelter. And she was glad she did. Have you ever been into one of his places? I think it was the first time my mother had felt respect from someone in a long while."

"Wait a minute, Tekún told me he met you in New York. At the Actors Studio."

"He did. That was later, after he had sent me to college. We lost touch for a while. You know how it is with fathers, surrogate or real. He caught up with me at the Studio. I knew about his past, his business. He offered me a job. It sounded more intriguing than the Hollywood life. So I took it."

"You think it's okay to work for a man who runs his own drug cartel? Who uses homeless shelters as fronts for drug-running?"

"Yeah. Yeah, I do," she said. "But I must admit, my attitude's a little subjective."

"So, living out of Dumpsters makes you get in bed with a cartel." I knew that was mean, but at this point I didn't care.

"That, and almost getting raped."

"What?"

She hesitated; but then she barreled right into it, as if she had done the major psychological work years ago. "Some guy, he was abusing my mother in the shelter. He started coming after me. That was too much for Mom. Word got to Tekún. He took care of it."

"What's that mean?"

"He was gone." She paused. "Tekún has a real bad time with child abusers."

Okay—*that* was new information for me. "And now what, he owns you? Your mother had to give you up to become one of Tekún's lackeys?"

"My mother runs a tourist shop in Guadalajara now. She sells Indian wares to gringos. I see her whenever I want."

"So, you volunteered for this?" I was getting edgy.

"Yes. Well, he pays me."

"And you're lovers."

She laughed. "Hmm. Don't think I haven't thought about it," she said. "I've always had a crush on him. But, no. He's like a father to me. And I'm not the incestuous type." She walked to the bedroom door. "Look, I'm sorry we had to do this." She gestured to the room, my comfortable kidnapping hideaway. "But he's telling the truth. He doesn't want you hurt. And you shouldn't be jealous, Agent Chacón. You're the only woman he thinks about."

She left me. That stung, though in a different way. She wasn't hesitant at all in giving me the upper hand, in letting me know I had no reason to see her as a threat. Which meant she knew something of how I felt about things. Had he told her about the last time we were together, how we had kissed? A kiss that, despite all the moves that Chip and I had practiced on each other, still overshadowed all that sex? Or was it just obvious, whenever she and I had talked in Los Angeles, that perhaps there was a tinge in my voice whenever his name came up? A confused tinge: I never knew what to think about him. And now, with her being so honest, I had a regret: I wished I hadn't told my mother about picking up the *pupusas revueltas* on the way out of town. Everyone knows I can't stand *revueltas*.

Tell me where you got that poison-dart collection of yours."

"Why?"

"Because it was poison from a dart that killed Chip."

He had made us breakfast. Pearl was not around. Tekún was dressed formally again, today with a dark blue guayabera shirt. The house smelled of coffee; the very air bloomed with the odor of freshly roasted beans. Before preparing the eggs and chorizo and refried black beans and rice, he had thrown green coffee beans into an old cast-iron skillet and shook them for a good ten minutes. Our coffee was truly, freshly roasted.

"The hunting elixir of the Guaranee does not kill the prey. It merely paralyzes it." He sounded almost disgruntled, as if I had personally insulted the entire Guaranee tribe.

"Look, I'm not saying it was your poison. But somebody's out there using a similar poison, from frogs. One that kills people. And they found the same poison at the Olive Street bombing."

"Frogs?"

"They're from jungle regions in South America."

"I know about them. Dart frogs. So what's your point?"

"Whoever killed Chip no doubt had something to do with that terrorist attack six months ago."

"Oh. So some terrorists killed Chip. With frogs."

"You make it sound far fetched."

He looked at me.

"Okay. Okay, so maybe it is stretching. All I know is, there's a connection." I looked down at the plate, now clean of one of the better breakfasts I'd had; my mother would have been either pleased or jealous. Or maybe pampered, having a man cook for her. "Whoever killed Chip is out to get you. They used poison from a frog. The same poison found in the Olive Street bombing, apparently near the coke that was stored in the building. And the coke came from here, through the Tijuana cartel."

"I see similarities. But no connection."

"Neither do I."

"So what do you think you're looking for?"

"Extremists."

"We're in Tijuana. What kind would you like?"

"Are there terrorist organizations here?"

"Organizations? You mean like with a Board of Trustees? Not the kind you're thinking about. Of course, I don't know if anybody in the U.S. really understands an outfit that uses terror as a weapon."

"What's to understand about them?"

"One simple thing: They believe in something. And they're desperate."

"Please," I said. "They're zealot nutcases."

"Emphasis on 'zealot.' They have zeal. Something you should recognize, the woman who hunted down her sister's killer." He drank more coffee, and let that soak in. "And besides, what's the difference between the terrorists of today and the guerrilla movement in your beloved El Salvador? My understanding is that your own mother had some sympathy toward the Salvadoran FMLN."

"Keep my mother out of this." Yet I remembered how, years ago, dear Mamá had fallen under Tekún's spell; she had thought, at the time, that he would have been a good mate for me. That was before all the drug busts, of course. Still, she had a way of singing his name. "There are no similarities between the Farabundo Martí National Liberation Front of El Salvador and people who run planes into towers, or blow up old crack houses." And then, of course, I thought about my conversation with O'Brien, about guerrillas and terrorists, and how I had been about to say the exact same thing Tekún had just said.

"I disagree."

"Yeah, you would. You were trained by the Guatemalan army."

He looked at me hard. It was a look meant to toss a stony caveat at me: *Don't go there.*

But I went there: "You were a Kaibil. You were trained to bring down the guerrilla movement."

"Unlike some of my . . . brothers in the force, I also had an education. I could still see who the guerrillas were, why they formed. They had a purpose."

"Yes? And what was it?"

"A rhetorical question."

"Yeah, but I just want you to answer it."

"Their purpose was to fight for the rights of the poor."

"Yeah. Kind of like people who help out the homeless."

"Is that a compliment, or a jab?"

"Just an observation." But I crossed my arms over my chest, as if getting close to winning something: an understanding of a man who until now had been adept at slipping away from definitions. "Of all the different money-laundering fronts you could have created, why make it homeless shelters?"

"For the record, I have no idea what you're talking about. Regarding my shelters, I have my reasons."

"Pearl certainly appreciates your reasons."

He said nothing, but he looked at me. Without judgment. "The point is," he finally said, "every zealot group, or fundamentalist group, or guerrilla group has at least one thing in common: They believe in something. They get corrupted along the way, like any other band of human beings. But at their core, there's a basic belief in something that got them started, that moved them to act." He said this as if in passing, while raising his cup of coffee to his lips.

"So what would bring together a group that wants to blow up prostitutes, abortion clinics, civil rights buildings, and call themselves Ojalá?"

Just as I said that, a clarity rang through me, wrapped with an insult: *Are you really so dense?* And another image, from the Olive Street bombing. That woman, what was her name? Holding up the sign with photos of one of the victims. My *daughter.* That's what *she* had written. But someone out in the world had written on the wall behind her, had scrawled angrily, the words *Your whores*. The women in the building who had died in the explosion: the women with their clients. Our whores. According to them, whoever they were, the prostitutes were ours.

"Are there any Christian fundamentalist churches in Tijuana?" I had asked it so quickly that I had not noticed how my fingers had gone to his forearm and rested there.

He looked down at my fingers first, and smiled, then looked at me. "It's Tijuana, *mi vida*. We've got everything."

We drove into Tijuana in his Land Rover, with Pearl at the wheel. Tekún sat in the front passenger seat. He sported the crispest Panama hat I've ever seen on a man. I was in the back. At a red light, where the traffic slowed and turned congested, I took my index finger to the door handle and carefully, quietly pulled it. Locked. Not with the top button, but inside; this SUV was either equipped with child security locks, or he had rigged it just in case he needed to transport someone who didn't want transporting.

That was not a fun image to keep in my head.

Neither Tekún nor Pearl looked back to check on me. As if they knew I couldn't get out. Of course they knew.

"There's one church that I've had some association with," said Tekún. He had been quiet for most of the drive. He seemed more quiet than all the other times we had been together. Was he still thinking about Beads? Was he in mourning, or depressed?

"*La Palabra del Señor*," he said. "It's evangelical. That's the closest I can get you to extremist."

"It's a start," I said. I moved my hand away from the door handle.

"Why are we looking at churches?" said Pearl. "They're public gathering places. I don't think fundamentalist groups would use a church as a front. And especially, well, Muslims."

"I'm not looking for Muslims," I said. "I think this is a domestic group. Homegrown, in the U.S. And not necessarily extremist Islamic. Most of the proposed hits were things that extremist Christian groups would target."

"Why's that?" she asked.

"The graffiti on the building next to the bombing, it said 'Your whores.' That rings of Christian right-wing fundamentalists. And the places that were targeted in Montgomery and Las Vegas: abortion clinics, civil rights. That's not like the hits on New York and Washington. It's more like Waco, or Oklahoma City."

"Good point," she looked back at me in the rear-view mirror. I looked up at her. I couldn't see her eyes, as she wore her nice sunglasses. But she could see mine.

"You're still pissed at me, aren't you, Agent Chacón?"

"Getting abducted just ruins my day."

"Even if it's for the right reasons?"

"The right reasons? Maybe you're right, what would I know about right reasons? I've been taken away from my family, I can't get on with my investigation of who killed Chip, and maybe I just don't completely believe you when you say you're trying to protect me. Maybe you're just trying to keep the killer from getting to you. You're just protecting yourself."

Tekún said nothing.

"May I ask how long you are planning to hold me?"

Pearl looked at her boss. Tekún barely glanced back at me. "Once I find the one who's after me, you'll make your way back home."

"No offense, Tekún, but I've never known you for having skills of deductive reasoning."

He looked back at me, through his own wire-frame sunglasses. He smiled, as if having to agree.

"No, you're right," he said. "But I shoot well from the hip."

Then he got quiet. I could only see the back of his head. He had his right hand hooked to the bar above the window, to steady himself on the rough road. He looked out at Tijuana, at the women who sold tamales and colas from small kiosks, at the young men hanging out on busy street corners, wearing *cholo* gear: baggy pants, baseball caps, new tattoos on their adolescent arms. The youngest of the trade, the fledglings. They were buying and selling, you could see this from the way they passed other people who passed them, how they did not look at the passerby, but their hand moved easily to the other's waistline, and something was exchanged, and no good-byes were said. Tekún watched this as Pearl drove slowly down the cobblestone street. He saw other kids doing the same hustle. A young girl, maybe thirteen, was dressed like a woman. She stood at the corner like a woman who knew how to give messages: She smiled at some white college boy in a USC T-shirt.

Did Tekún regret this? Tijuana was not his world, as far as I knew. The Arellano association may have been his neighborhood for the past several months, but was he comfortable here? And then I wondered, was any dealer in this business ever, really, comfortable, at any point in their days?

It was simple to see: Tekún was not cut from this border-town world. It should have been no surprise that he had found a house way out in the countryside, away from all this. Perhaps it was a hideaway, yes; but also, perhaps it was an endeavor to get away from all that Tijuana meant. Perhaps, even for Tekún Umán, Tijuana was too much of a recognition of the business he was involved in.

"His name is Hermano Javier," said Tekún. "Don't forget to use the 'hermano' with him. The evangelicals of this church are very formal in that way."

We parked outside what looked to be a grocery store, or at least, once a market of some sort. The large open windows had no glass in them, and the large shelves underneath were now stacked with papers rather than groceries. A woman could put all sorts of produce out there for the day and sell through the window, then simply lean over and fill the shelves up again. Now there was no fruit or any vegetables; the wooden shelves held small, neat piles of papers, with pictures of Jesus on the front, his arms out, and a photocopy glow emanating from his body as he smiled down on a crowd of happy people. Words about El Señor de nuestros corazones, and Alaba al Señor, Dios es nuestro Salvador, all over the page. But that didn't bother me as much as the singing that I heard the moment Tekún opened the back door of the SUV for me:

Demos gracias al Señor, demos gracias,
Demos gracias al Señor.

I've never been one for religion, any religion. Not my own Catholicism, and certainly not anything that's going to shove Jesus down my throat. I looked up and down the street, with a dwindling hope: I started to doubt the phone call to my mother. Perhaps she hadn't caught it, that I had used our little code phrase, one made up in Atlanta long ago in case I got caught in a compromised situation. Maybe she had forgotten that I hated mixed *pupusas*; no. No that wasn't possible, the way I, as a kid, had pitched a fit whenever I bit into one of them accidentally, thinking it was pure cheese or pure meat. I threatened to gag. "Mommy, it's a *revuelta!*" I was known to scream, as if I had eaten someone else's mixed vomit. No, she'd know now I was in trouble. . . .

And she would have called Special Agent Fisher, who would have taken my mother seriously; and by now, Fisher would wonder where Pearl and I were. But then, where would Fisher send her agents? Where would they look? I thought it out: Yes, they'd check the borders, one of the first things they'd check; and I hoped they would get hold of that one fellow who had flirted with Pearl. That was one mistake she had made, showing off her Spanish too readily; I knew other gringas who had done that, showing the world how slick they were with the Latino ways. They'd find Mr. Macho at the border, who would say he had seen Pearl, but no, no one was with her; which would get Fisher thinking, of course: If Pearl had been at the border, where the hell was Chacón?

Or maybe not.

I looked up and down the street in front of the church. All I saw were a boy playing with a Bionicle figure, two teenage girls wearing Catholic uniforms and talking about their math test, an old man who wore an old fedora; cars passing by, with families in them, or a *cholo* at the wheel, his fingers covered in rings, sunglasses on, a CD pushing an old ballad of Los Tigres del Norte through the open windows.

And here I was, walking into Praise-the-Lord Hell, where Fisher would never find me.

We walked by the singing chorus of women who told everyone in earshot to give thanks to the Lord, give thanks, give thanks to the Lord ad nauseum. We walked through a main room that had been turned into a small sanctuary of sorts, through a side door and into the backyard of the building.

It was small, but well kept. The children who played there looked happy enough: a good twenty of them, skipping rope or shooting into a low hoop or kicking a soccer ball. Not all Mexican; or, at least, a couple of them were from the southern part of Mexico, more Indian looking, maybe from Chiapas or Oaxaca. Or maybe Guatemala. Twenty kids, with four women taking care of them. This facility had nice, clean toys, a swing set made of thick plastic, and a climb-along, the type Sergio used to crawl up in when he was a toddler.

Sergio would have liked this a few years ago. It was simple, but it had everything a kid would want. And, I figured, especially a kid whose parents were either dead or had abandoned them. Yet I saw no building that could have housed all these kids, no orphanage, no set of dorms.

"It's a day care," said Tekún, noticing how I checked the place out. "Women drop their kids off early in the morning, pick them up at the end of the day. They work it on a sliding scale. It's one of the cheapest places to keep your child."

"Where do the women work?"

"Some of them cross the border. Clean houses in San Diego. Others work in the *maquiladoras*, just outside of town."

I looked at the nice climb-along. "You pay for all this?" I asked. That may have sounded snotty, but it was a legitimate question, I thought.

"No. Hermano Javier takes no funds from any businesses. All this comes from nonprofits."

"So why do you know him?"

Tekún looked at me, incredulity in his gaze. "Romi, I know a lot of people who may surprise you."

Brother Javier was a bit older than either Tekún or me. He had a rugged look to him, though a smile cut through that worn face. The eyes, for lack of better word, were piercing; and yet, his smile, if not mollifying the gaze, put something in check. He was shorter than me by an inch, and darker. His words were eloquent, from an old schooling; I thought Catholic, at first, and didn't doubt that perhaps he, like many in Latin America, had been born in the Catholic tradition but somewhere along the way had gone Protestant. A change I never really trusted: not that I trusted Catholicism in the first place.

He called me *Hermana Romilia*. That didn't set well at all, as if he were trying to usurp my soul without permission. But it seemed more a habit. "Sister Romilia, a pleasure," he said, shaking my hand. "Romilia . . . my, you don't hear that name much anymore, do you, Brother Rafael? That's a name from olden days." He chuckled politely. "How can I help you?" He put his hands behind his back. Like Tekún, he wore a guayabera. His was a beautiful light cream shirt that hung comfortably on him, not tucked in; as nicely pressed as Tekún's, the four pockets crisp, the ornate stripes in a pure white thread. He was looking at me, kindly, with that smile; but he was also studying me.

Tekún tried to rouse a credible story, but I heard in his voice, for the first time, a faltering, as if he didn't want to lie to this guy. "Sister Romilia is doing some research of a kind . . . she works for an office in Los Angeles . . ."

"Yes. DEA or FBI, Sister Romilia?" Brother Javier smiled. "Let's go back to my office. Would you like a soda?"

Pearl stayed outside, talking with the women who had taken a break from their choral practice. She was chatting lightly with them, and they were enjoying her company; but I knew she was really keeping her eye on the door, to see who might come in, looking for her boss, with a gun in their hand. Her right hand was draped over her crossed legs, dangling fairly near the cuff of her jeans, where I saw the ankle holster.

It took only our short, half-hour conversation to learn that Brother Javier was a zealot. A fundamentalist. But in a way that made me both uncomfortable and somewhat thrilled.

"So, Brother Rafael, have you decided to get out of your business and follow the path of the Lord?" He smiled but did not laugh; for this was not a joke.

"I'm doing fine, Brother Javier."

"I do hope so. Please consider your options." Again, a blatant smile.

Tekún looked at me. He was smiling too, but no doubt he was uncomfortable, like a child whose father has scolded him before visitors. "This is a little game that we play each time we get together," Tekún explained to me, in English, which surprised the hell out of me. Tekún was never one to be rude like that, to speak English before a non-English speaker.

"Yes," said Javier in his own crisp English, "each time he visits, I remind Brother Rafael of the corruption and the evils of the drug business. And he tells me one or another form of a lie. Is that why I don't see you much anymore?" He turned to Tekún and laughed. Tekún chuckled as well and shifted in his seat, as if the seat were too small for his tall, lithe body; a man in a child's class desk.

"Besides, Brother Rafael, especially these days, after your loss." Which must have meant Beads.

I joined in. "Do you do that, Brother Javier, with every drug runner you meet?"

"Oh, of course. That is our charism here."

"Charism?"

"Our call."

"Forgive my bluntness, but I'm surprised that hasn't gotten you killed."

"Sometimes I'm surprised as well, if I think about it too much.

Once I could have papered these walls with death threats had I kept them. Of course, with Min and Mon out of the picture, my wallpaper project has been held off."

"So let me get this straight," I said. "You're here to try to evangelize the drug traffickers?"

"I'm here to spread the word of Jesus Christ. And dealing in drugs is not exactly on Christ's list of 'to do' activities."

"What about doing drugs?"

"Nor that, Sister Romilia. That is the vicious vortex of the relationship: The great consumption in the U.S. makes Tijuana what it is today."

Tekún interjected: "The women who use the day care for their kids have dried out, gotten off drugs. They're working and providing for their families."

"In the *maquiladoras*," I said.

"Honest work," said Javier.

"For the women. Dishonest . . . no, damned wrong, on the side of the factories. The pay is lousy, they treat the women like shit."

"Another injustice," said Javier, "that we're working on." And he did not reprimand me for my cursing. I liked him. "I've got an ecumenical meeting later this afternoon. A consortium of local churches wants to organize a campaign to deal with the owners of the *maquiladoras*."

"So, you're organizing the people?" I said.

He laughed. "Big word, that."

"Aren't you ever afraid? Death threats from drug lords, taking on *maquiladora* bosses. That sounds dangerous."

"Jesus once said, 'Don't be afraid.' I try to heed that advice."

"It must be overwhelming," I said.

"Of course it is."

"And you keep smiling."

He laughed.

"No, really, it seems like an impossible job, Brother Javier. Don't take this wrong, but it seems almost ludicrous."

"Oh, it is. As ludicrous as your job is."

We were weaving between Spanish and English, all of us fluent in both. It was something I had to get more accustomed to now, living on the West Coast, where people wove their conversations between the two tongues as commonly as if they were one. My mother had raised me in a more conservative manner: One or the other, make up your mind, but stick with it for the duration of the conversation. But that was a rule she used in Georgia and Tennessee, where the world had a hard go of it following Spanish. Here, people ruled both tongues.

Javier said, "And as ludicrous as our work is, we've opened franchises, in both San Francisco and Los Angeles."

"More churches?" I asked.

"Yes. In the Mission District in San Francisco, and in Compton. Doing the same work we're doing here."

"So they're like drug rehab churches."

He laughed. "That's a nice, what do you call it, 'sound bite.' Now, obviously you're not here to join my church," Javier said. He smiled again. "How can I be of service to you?"

Without telling him everything, especially about the poisoned frogs, I referred to the Olive Street bombing in Los Angeles, and the harsh graffiti painted the day after, next to the blown-out building: *Your whores*. Then I told him my suspicions about the Ojalá connection. "I'm wondering, to be honest, if this was some domestic fundamentalist organization, maybe Christian in origin. You know, like the same people who shoot abortion doctors, or beat gay men to death? And there's the possibility of a link to the drug trade coming out of Tijuana. I know it's a long shot, but . . ."

It took a second to register the fact that he wasn't smiling anymore. Brother Javier was looking directly at me. "You all right?" I asked.

"I said before that I'm not afraid." He looked down at his desk, at a rosary that lay piled to one side of the blotter. "But some things on this earth do scare me. And leave me very, very angry."

While Tekún and I were saying our good-byes, Pearl met us at the front. I shook hands with Javier. He wished me well. He said nothing more, not here on the street, not about what we had dis-cussed in the back room.

Pearl drove us through Tijuana. She stopped at an outdoor market, pulled up in front and got out. "We need more masa," she said. "Anything else?"

"Red peppers," said Tekún. "Oh, and cilantro."

She left us there. Tekún still sat in front, looking out at the world, making sure I didn't escape. He stayed quiet, as if he knew I was thinking.

Javier knew about Ojalá. At first what he was saying didn't make sense. And then, gradually, inevitably, it did make sense. That there was a movement growing in the city surprised me enough, for I had thought of Tijuana as foremost and perhaps sole-ly a city of drug traffickers. But such a vision both blinded me and limited Tijuana. Yes, Tijuana was a cocaine port into the United States; the Arellano brothers had built up the business through the years. No one could ignore that. But it was a complicated city, with a population of some of the most diverse Latin Americans anyone could find in one place. A city that attracted over five thousand gringos from across the border every Friday night. They came to party: drink at cheap bars, buy cheap marijuana, score heroin or cocaine. It was the party town for college students, whole football teams and cheerleaders looking for a place to let go, away from the constraints of North America. Here, treating Mexico in the way

Mexico found the most insulting: as the *patio trasero*, the backyard playground of the United States. A place where a boy from UCLA could hope to bed a little Mexican girl, maybe somebody eighteen, maybe less, without thinking of the traps awaiting him, a Mexican cop behind the bedroom door, a Mexican judge behind the cop, the Mexican jail cell waiting, just waiting, until little UCLA-dude called up Daddy for bail. All that made little horny boy go home and talk about the wicked ways of the Tijuanans, how they waited to prey upon the poor gringos who came to the city to fuck it, from one Friday night to the next. Why should I be surprised that Tijuana, with so much human traffic, so much white powder traffic, a city with so many faces sitting on a border, could be a place where a movement was born?

And *movimiento* was the word Javier had used. Not *organización*. He corrected me on this. "My people? We're evangelical, yes. You could even call us 'fundamentalists,' in a way. But not in the way you're thinking. I'm a church. Not a movement."

"So, what about Ojalá?"

"It was just a little group for a long time. But now, they seem to have gotten funding. Lots of funding. I first heard about it from my brothers in San Francisco. At the church there, in the Mission. Ojalá has been proselytizing there."

"Whom do they proselytize?" asked Tekún.

"Mostly the poor. Homeless. Drugged-out kids. Some kids at colleges, who look lost. You know: the desperate souls. They're the most ripe for such a group."

"So, it's a church?"

"No. I wouldn't call it that."

I needed more clarity, and was getting impatient. "Okay, Brother Javier. What would you call them? What is it they do that's so bad?"

"Their new, seemingly endless supply of cash, for one thing. Before, they used to try to coax people into their temples, or whatever they called them. Just like street preachers yelling through megaphones. But now they buy people. Go out in the street, hand money out, twenty-dollar bills, fifty, to street people. They keep doing this, day after day, hitting different places on a weekly basis.

Before long, the junkie who needs money for more smack? He's seeing this Ojalá representative as a really good source of income. So he starts getting closer to the group. Their 'congregation,' if that's what you want to call it, has gotten bigger in the past two years."

"Where's the money coming from?"

"I'm not sure. But it's cash. And there's only one production company I know that deals mostly in cash."

He looked at Tekún. Tekún looked down at the floor. I liked that, how Brother Javier could pin him so quickly.

"Okay," I said, "so they pay people to believe. What's the harm in that?" Though I didn't believe my own statement, or question; all those places, with the graffiti, told me there was much harm involved.

"I was curious," said Javier. "So I went to one of their meetings, here in town. They pay people to go to their prayer groups. But this prayer group, it was nothing about prayer. It was a hate group."

"Who were they hating?"

"Abortionists."

"Oh." The Planned Parenthood in Las Vegas came to mind.

"Don't get me wrong. I'm against abortion as well. I don't believe in taking life, any life," said Javier. "But the way this woman was talking, it was frightening."

"What, was she advocating violence?" said Tekún. "Shooting abortion doctors and such?"

"That's where she started. Then she started on women who have abortions done. Starting with the women here. It was like a witch hunt. Women started to disappear."

"What do you mean, disappear?"

"Just that, Sister Romilia. Gone. Pregnant women who looked for help in the local clinics, who asked about termination of their pregnancies. Gone."

"Who was this woman doing the preaching?"

"She was a gringa. From California."

"She the head of the church?"

Javier shrugged his shoulders.

"I'd like to meet her."

"Be careful," said Javier.

"I just want to talk with her. Where's her church?"

He told me where: The meeting had been held in a nice apart-ment building just off the northeast corner of the main plaza. "But please, don't mention me. After that night, I knew I didn't want much to do with her."

I don't mean to interrupt your ruminations," Tekún said from the front of the SUV, "but are you coming up with anything?"

"Maybe." I stared out the back passenger window. "Funny. Javier deals with drug runners all the time. But this woman shook him up."

"He doesn't deal with drug runners, Romi," said Tekún. "He works with the poor, and along the way, he takes Jesus-shots at anyone he suspects is in the trade."

"I see. So you're saying that facility of his wasn't bought with coke cash?"

"Exactly. Javier's clean."

"You're so sure."

"About some things, yes." Tekún turned to me. "Javier's taken no handouts from anyone big or small. No small town crack head dealer has given him money to build his day care. And certainly no money's come from the Arellano brothers, though I'm sure they tried to pay him off a time or two. Javier manages with a few grants from nonprofits. And he's cultivated a growing congregation."

"You've got a lot of respect for him, don't you?"

"Yes." Tekún got silent for a minute, then said, "He buried Beads for me."

Enough said there. He had to explain no more.

That was too much memory for him. He moved the conversation another way. "So. You hungry? There are some decent restaurants on the Boulevard."

I was hungry, but I also wanted to work. He talked like I was on vacation and we had all the time in the world, like I could stay happily kidnapped. "Let's go home. . .I mean, you're place. Ah, shit."

He just laughed. The loudest I've ever heard him laugh.

At dinner I said to him, "Let's meet Miss Antiabortionist."

He did not act surprised. Though he did say, "So. You're not holding it against me, that I'm holding you?"

"Yes, of course I am."

"Oh."

"*Ojalá.* Written at every target place. Now here's a woman in Tijuana, handing out cash in its name. And pregnant women considering abortion have disappeared."

"Forgive me for saying this, Romilia, but she'll sniff you out before you knock on her door."

"I'm not talking about going undercover, like your little friend Pearl. I just want to ask her some questions. I've got that right."

"Fine. But I'll just be your driver. I refuse to apostatize."

"Tekún. What in the world would you apostatize *from?*"

On the third day of my "holding," as he preferred to call it, Tekún dropped me off a block away from the Ojalá Church, with the promise he'd circle the building every three minutes.

A holding for my protection. Something I believed in less and less. Even with Beads's death still in Tekún's air, and even with the series of murders that had led to Beads's death, and even with Chip's death still fresh in Venice, I was hard put to believe I was the next in line.

Or perhaps I was just getting more involved in this nutcase notion of a group called Ojalá.

Or, my mother may have said, I was just getting involved.

I would have agreed with her, those moments I almost blurted out to him about my phone call message to Mamá. Something wanted me to do that; something wanted me to believe him. But I couldn't. The bastard had taken me by force.

Still, he had lost someone significant. And even though he was not about to show how much that hurt him, it revealed itself, in the way he drew quiet, and how he handled me: not as a prisoner, but as a fellow traveler of sorts. This was not his home; we were both out of our environment. Still, he had the advantage: my gun, my license and credit cards, my badge, any items that I had carried on me before Pearl knocked me out—he had them. So I still didn't believe him.

And so I told him nothing.

"I'll come from the different streets, in a counterclockwise fashion, starting with the northeast street," Tekún explained, and pointed across the plaza to that street. "Over there is the address that Brother Javier gave me. Let's say twenty minutes?"

He drove off. I walked toward the address, a building in the middle of the street. It was handsome, newly painted an off-white, eggshell tone. I waited until three minutes had passed. There was Tekún, entering the plaza. He smiled at me, then drove on.

I went in. The place was still being refurbished. Walls were being taken out. In the back, men worked on drywall, prepping the stark, dry area with putty in order to smooth on an adobe veneer. Another crew worked the landscaping of an inside garden. A third moved plumbing through a corridor. They spoke to one another, all in Spanish, saying "*con permiso*," as they passed me. Busy workers, no doubt well paid.

The only thing that revealed this as a church was the small sign in the foyer, IGLESIA DE OJALÁ.

The Church of Oh How I Wish.

A damn strange world.

A young woman, white, with long black hair, and green eyes that meant to look nice but had a hard time of it — perhaps due to her strong eyebrows — smiled at me. "May I help you?" She said it in a broken Spanish.

"Yes, I'd like to speak with the person in charge of the church," I said in English.

She didn't look relieved at my English, but actually hesitant. "Yes? May I ask who's calling?" Her voice was California clean, maybe somewhere from Orange County.

I introduced myself, my name, my Bureau. This, of course, was embarrassing, due to the fact that I had none of my credentials on me. Tekún hadn't allowed that. "No, no," he had said in the car. "I give you your badge, then you could be tempted to give it to them and have them call your headquarters. And I'm not one to want to lead you into temptation, *mi vida*."

But this was no problem for the woman. She believed me. "Oh . . . How do you do, Agent Chacón? I'm Virginia Roberts. I'm the administrator. It's a real pleasure to meet you."

We shook hands. "Sorry," she said, "I didn't mean to be standoffish. But starting a church in Tijuana, well, you get some really interesting crazies coming through the door."

"Oh, I understand." I followed her back to her office. "Really nice place you've got here."

"We've still got a lot to do. But it's coming along." She let me pass her by, then she closed the door to her office. After that, she closed the windows.

So I kept talking. "It's a lot nicer than most of the buildings around here."

"Yes, well, we mean to bring some dignity and upright workmanship to our community. A sense of pride in the American spirit." She sat behind her desk. "What can I help you with, Agent Chacón?"

"I'm on an investigation. A colleague of mine was murdered."

"I'm sorry to hear that."

"Yes. He was one of the agents in charge of investigating the Olive Street bombing in Los Angeles."

"Yes."

"And I'd just like to know more about your church base."

"Oh, would it help in your investigation?"

"Yes. It would."

"Very well, then." She sat back slightly, as if to clear her throat and deliver to me a well-rote monologue. "We are the church of Ojalá. I'm sure you know what that means."

"Yes, I do." Though I didn't remember ever speaking any Spanish to her. Six minutes had passed since I had entered the building. Tekún had circled the plaza twice. He had four more times to circle before coming in here, making sure I was okay.

"So," I said, "why pick that word?"

"It's really a simple matter of veneration, to the ones who inspire us."

"I'm sorry?"

"Agent Chacón, I'm sure you wouldn't be too surprised that we're involved in a holy crusade here, in this church. Throughout the world, really. But mostly directed north of the border."

Nine minutes had not yet passed. This was happening too quickly.

"Are you saying you're connected with certain terrorist groups?"

"What, like with al Qa'ida?" She laughed. "Now what would give you that idea?"

"Maybe the name of your group? 'Ojalá.' A word with Arabic roots."

She said nothing.

"Ms. Roberts, are you or any of your . . . congregation, involved with any radical Muslim group?"

"Only in the hope we all have for our world."

"Excuse me?"

"Come now, Romilia. You're from the States. You know how bastardized our society has become. For them it's *jihad*. For us, Crusade. Because our nation is a freak show. Not at all what it was supposed to be. Take the abortionist doctors as an example. Satan dressed in white jackets and stethoscopes. And people cry out because they're murdered by snipers. But I tell you, there are more people applauding their deaths than there are those who mourn them."

"You're an antiabortion group?"

"That's my part of the coalition."

"'Coalition?'"

"Sometimes people of many different ideas find they share the same fundamental principles. I, for instance, have a hard time with my own government sponsoring the slaughter of innocent babies while putting good Christians in jail for stopping the slaughter by killing the doctors. And my anger toward that government really dovetails with the beliefs of the Branch Davidians in Waco who were murdered by your own FBI. It's no wonder Timothy McVeigh did what he did. The U.S. government has become a traitor to the people."

Did I shake in front of her? I was prepared for insidiousness; I got that all the time, from suspects. But not this arrogance. "Do you really believe all that?"

"Believe?" She laughed. "Hard for you, isn't it? That's the world, blinding you. Once you see, Romilia, through eyes of faith, then you know what the truth is. You see the seamless garment

that weaves among all our crusades. You see that the Israeli con-
quering of the Middle East is but a step toward the Jews accepting
Christ in their hearts, and how that divine plan has everything to
do with the basic blending of true Christians and true Muslims
who mean to stop the New World Order, and how *that* crusade has
everything to do with ending the depredation of society by the
homosexuals on the West Coast, particularly in San Francisco. It
all makes simple sense, really."

"Ms. Roberts, why are you telling me all this?"

She smiled. "Because you can't stand *pupusas revueltas*."

"What?"

She waited, for all the significance of her statement to sink in.

"What have you done?" I demanded.

"They're fine. But if I were you, I'd listen very closely to what
I'm about to say."

"You bitch."

"Ah ah ah ah *ah*!" She waved a finger at me. "Not in my
church, now."

"What do you want?"

"You need to go out the door, and find your friend, Mr. Tekún
Umán. And you're to deliver him to our sponsor."

"Who is that?"

"That's not important. You just need to get Mr. Umán across
the border. Into the United States."

"And how do you expect me to do that?"

"Why, with the truth, of course!" She did not laugh. "The
truth shall set your family free."

It took everything I had not to reach over and choke her. And
I could have. I could have easily taken her down right there. As far
as I saw, there were no other church people around, only those
construction workers, who would not hear her as I shoved my
elbow into her mouth and snapped her jaw open. All of which
would mean a complete disconnection from my mother, from
Sergio. This Virginia Roberts was but one person; yet so sure she
was of her position, she could stay in one room with me and tell
me that she had my family captive. Which meant there were
others.

"Just go on out there and tell Tekún Umán that your lovely child and mother are being held. You have to get back home. And he'll do it, he'll take you there."

"How do you know that? He might just let me go back, and he'll stay here."

To which she finally laughed. "Now what's the word in Spanish? *Ingenuo?* Yes. Naïve. Everyone knows Tekún Umán would move the world for you."

"Why are you doing this?"

"Because these are drastic times."

"No, why are you going after Tekún Umán? What's he got to do with abortion doctors?"

She sighed, as if almost sorry to have to explain the obvious. "Believe me, this isn't my way of handling things. But sometimes you have to do favors for those who support you. And to be frank, Romilia," her voice turned in tone, from lofty Christian to street smart, "our sponsor simply has a real hard-on for your boyfriend."

In her private world, there is a simplicity: Romilia has her mother, her son, and a home. She lives in a neighborhood that few people outside of Van Nuys covet. Some call Van Nuys the armpit of the Valley. Others remember it as the porn capital of the world. For Romilia, when she first moved to Los Angeles, Van Nuys meant cheaper real estate. She could buy a home.

Which she did, with a little help from her Uncle Chepe, who has done so well in the catering industry. Chepe helped her with the down payment, so now she pays the mortgage to the bank and the personal loan to him. Romilia sits down on the first of every month, cuts a check to the bank that machetes her salary, then writes another check for sixty-five dollars to Chepe, in the hopes of paying him off in the next twenty years. It's all very simple, as is the house: thirteen hundred square feet, three bedrooms, one and a half baths. Romilia and her mother made the large middle room into their library, for they have a tendency to spend too much on books, mostly novels, many in Spanish. Books are piled on coffee tables and on one end of the dining table, while the three of them eat on the other end. Books cover the top of both toilets and are stacked on the floor. Sometimes they spill. Celia or Romilia always repile them where they were, and walk on, with a book in hand. Because they read, the house is quiet much of the time. Her boy Sergio gets one hour of television a day. If he knew the word "fascistic," Sergio would use this on the two women in his life, when it comes to sitcoms.

But it is because of such rules that Sergio, while playing in the park that sits just across the street from the Chacón home, always brings a book with him. He's eight, so he's making his way through the Harry Potter books. His grandmother watches him from the low window of their library, though she has her eyes on the pages of the newest García Márquez book. Sergio is reading about Harry's godfather Sirius Black when Sergio's neighbor, Raymond, walks into the park with a large rubber ball. "Hey, Sergio," says Raymond, who does not speak Spanish and says Sergio's name with a "j" instead of a breathy Spanish "g." "Harry Potter. You seen the latest movie?"

"Not yet."

"Want to play some handball?"

"Sure. But no skippies this time, all right?"

"Yeah yeah."

They're not three minutes into the game when Sergio accuses Raymond of a skippy. "It ain't a skippy if it goes over your head, dawg," says Raymond. Raymond likes saying "dawg." He says it a lot, both because his older brother says it and because Raymond watches reruns of *The Fresh Prince of Bel Air*. Neither he nor Sergio notices the white man who has just walked into the park from a car parked on the far side.

There are two mothers on a bench, watching their toddlers play in a sandbox; sometimes Celia looks up and sees if the mothers are still there, as there is safety in such numbers. Then she returns to Gabo.

"I wish the city would get us some new swing sets," says one of the mothers. Her name is Raven. Miss Raven, Sergio calls her. The other mother, named Connie, says something about the mayor not giving a rat's ass about the Valley, much less the people living in Van Nuys.

"Don't you be doing the skippies, dawg," says Raymond.

"All right. Hit it."

The white man is carrying a rope.

The women on the bench are deep into conversation. They have much to talk about: Miss Raven's boyfriend has a new job at a Circuit City nearby. "He's good at those computer games, and says he can get us one of them new PlayStations when they come out, for Julia, yeah right," Miss Raven glances at little Julia, three, pouring sand all over her dress. "You know David, he'll be up past midnight playing those damn games."

"I know it. Can't get my son off it to do a thing around the house."

The white man lifts the rope up. He whistles. It is not a rope, but a leash. He calls for Smokey. Smokey, here Smokey, come here.

He's made his way around the two mothers, nearer to the wall where the two boys play handball and accuse each other of skippies and roundies.

Those certain words: "Smokey," and "Home," and "Where are you?" Lost. Words that echo into eight-year-old boys' souls. He doesn't need to ask them first. Raymond is more than ready to help. "Lost your dog, Mister?"

"Yeah, I, I usually walk over on Cedros Avenue, but I think the clip was weak, look." He holds up the leash. Sure enough, the clip is loose, open. "Smokey took off running after a squirrel."

"What's he look like?" asks Sergio.

"He's got some Lab in him, but he's mostly terrier. Black dog, real thin, real friendly, wouldn't hurt a fly, just likes squirrels — darn it, Smokey, where are you?"

Sergio looks around, and he calls out, "Smokey! Smokey!"

"What's the matter?" says Miss Raven.

"Man's lost his dog."

"Oh, that's a shame." Both mothers look around to help. But they are mothers, always on guard, so they pick up their toddlers before walking about the park. "What's the dog's name?" asks Connie.

"Smokey," says the man. He then walks up to the two boys. "Do you all live around here?" he asks. Both boys say yes. Then Sergio shifts, as if something his mother taught him, long ago, pushes through. He pulls at his hair, a nervous tick. "What's your names?" asks the man.

"Raymond."

". . . Sergio."

Celia looks up and sees the women on one end of the park and the two boys talking with a stranger that has a leash and no dog. She stands up from her chair, drops the book.

"Is that your house, Sergio?" says the man.

Sergio looks back. He sees his grandmother. He sees his grandmother's face.

"Let's go ask your grandma if she's seen my dog."

The man puts his hand on Sergio's shoulder and leads him home.

"Can I come, too?" asks Raymond.

The man presses hard on Sergio's shoulders to keep him from veering.

"No, you keep looking here, Raymond. We'll be right back. I'll let you pet Smokey when we find him!"

There is no dog. Sergio knows this by the way his *granmamá* holds him to her while the man sits in the seat in front of them. Granmamá has to obey this man, because the man has a gun and holds it limp in his hand, like he's used to having a gun. Just like Mamá is used to having a gun.

The phone rings.

"Don't answer it," says the man. "Let the message machine take it."

Some are friends. Uncle Chepe, who's hoping Celia will help with a big catering job for the new Russell Crowe movie shooting in San Diego. Then Romilia calls. She speaks quietly, in Spanish, but she says something that makes Celia shift, ever so slightly.

"What did she say?" says the man.

Celia sits on the sofa, still holding Sergio. "She's going out of town. She'll be gone a few days."

"Okay," says the man. "And what else?"

"Not much more than that."

"Oh, no. The message was longer than your translation. What else did she say?"

"She's going to get something to eat."

"Oh. Anything else?"

"No. That's all she said."

The man raises the gun, leans forward slightly, and pushes the cold metal barrel into the skin of the boy's forehead, enough to leave a little red circle. A grandmother behind him, holding him. A gun barrel to his head. Sergio does not move.

"Anything else?" says the man.

Sometimes the man talks with a woman named Virginia, who is in Tijuana. The man says "Tijuana" like gringos tend to do —somehow managing four syllables.

"You need to find her. Romilia Chacón. She's there in Tijuana . . . I know because I had one of your boys camped out near the FBI offices. Yeah. He got into the parking ramp when the two agents drove in. Says Nancy Pearl kidnapped Chacón. Nancy Pearl, she's a Fed but she must be working for Murillo, yeah . . . never mind that, you just need to get to Chacón. Tell her I've got her family. That simple. Think you can do something so simple? Because I've got my doubts, Virginia. Ever since Olive Street, I've got my doubts. Don't say it wasn't your fault, Virginia, because it was. You need to keep a tight reign on your zealot friends. They destroyed some very precious belongings of mine that I had stored in that building. Yes, they did . . . they were frogs, if you must know.

"No Virginia, I don't want to hear about the problems with your group. They're not my problems. Ojalá was just a rinky dink little evangelical tent show before I came along, so you should never complain to me or make excuses or especially lie, because when you do that, you're nipping the hand that feeds you. Do you want me to keep feeding you? Do you, Virginia? Deliver me Murillo, then. That's why I funded you all in the first place: tit for tat, remember? But now your group is getting out of hand. Tell them to straighten up or Daddy here will close the wallet. And *you*, Virginia . . . well, never mind."

Sergio and Celia hear his next phone call with Virginia through the locked door of Celia's walk-in closet. "So. You found them. Oh, she found you? Really? . . ."

He unlocks the closet door and kneels down to Sergio. "Your mother is a very smart woman. She connects the dots better than your average agent."

The man's face then turns strange. "Sergio. How old are you?"

"Eight."

"Eight. I had a daughter, your age, once.

"I miss her."

He looks sad, then worried, as if his concern for his daughter turns into a worry for Sergio's future. "Come here, son," he says. He takes Sergio's hand, shepherds him out of the closet. Celia whimpers, but he says, "You can come on out, too, Mrs. Chacón. I just kept you there so you wouldn't run off. Why don't you make us some coffee, and get a soda for the boy?"

She obeys. She watches from the kitchen counter as the man takes her grandson and sets him on his lap. "Sergio, has your mother ever talked to you about drugs?"

"Yes." Sergio's voice cracks. "Yes," he says again, without cracking.

"Oh. That's good. What has she said?"

"How bad they are for you."

"That's true. What else has she talked about, about drugs?"

Sergio believes that placating this façade of a conversation may save him, save his grandmother. "She's told me how many people use drugs. They use coke, and meth, and, and there's crack, yeah, and ice, which is like meth, just more in little rocks that look like crystals? Yeah, and she's showed me what they look like."

"Really? She's shown you? How?"

He looks at the man's face, so close to his own. "Down at her office? They have a room, where they keep stuff that they've found."

"Oh. I see. Yes. Go on."

"And, well, one Saturday she took me down there, just to show me what all the different drugs look like. Because, well, she wants me to, you know, recognize them if I ever see them. At school."

"Wow. That's good, that's really good, Sergio. You've got a good mom. A really good mom. Wow." He looks over at Celia, who's now pouring the coffee into two cups. "Ready for the world, this grandson of yours." He looks back at Sergio. "Now, what has your mother told you about the people who sell these drugs?"

". . . That they're bad."

"Oh, yes. They're very bad. Very bad. You see, the men who sell these drugs, they don't care how much the drugs hurt you, or me. No, they just want to make a lot of money. And they do. Lord, they do!" The man laughs. "I wish I could take you into some rooms, where the drugs are stored. Just like your mom did. Only, in these rooms, where I've been? They've also got the money, see. Cash. Piles and piles of it! Can you imagine?"

Sergio's eyes widen, like a child who is in awe of such an image; but it is an awe weighed with the fear of sitting on this stranger's lap. A blond man who is not that old, who looks like he was once kind of handsome, but he's got a constant wince of pain in his eyes.

"Yeah, all this money, and these drug guys, they don't know what to do with all of it. So they start buying things. All sorts of things. You know why? It's like if you came home with a hundred-dollar bill in your pocket. Your mom, she'd ask you where you got it, right? And you'd have to have a good explanation, I mean, you're a kid with a wad of cash. It's the same thing with drug dealers, see, they have all this money, and somebody's going to find them with it. So they spend it. On stupid things. You won't believe what I've found in their warehouses, jeez! Pet iguanas, and, and whole sets of blown glass. Once there was this guy, in Memphis, he bought up every single painting from a twenty-four-year-old artist who sold her stuff on Bourbon Street. Anything, just to get rid of all that cash. And they can't. It's too much. So they get scared, they buy more stuff, a thousand old vinyl records, three old Mercedes right off the lot. They buy boa constrictors, elephant tusks, monkeys. One guy had an entire Mayan altar shipped to his house in New Orleans. Another guy had a cage of panthers, he was in Ohio. I found an entire Koala family in a home in Birmingham. Oh, and frogs. Frogs! This guy in Houston had poisoned frogs, now *that* was something!"

The man nods his head, smiles at his own little story. It takes him a moment to see how the boy on his lap is hardly breathing. The man calms, just barely.

"Now what do you think about guys like that, Sergio? Sergio?"

". . . They're . . . bad?"

"Yeah. Yeah, they're really really bad. Really bad. Hey, what do you think should happen to them?"

"They should go to jail."

"Oh, jail's too good for them. Way too good. No, Sergio. They should die. They should all die."

Celia stands with two cups in her hands. She has gotten as close as possible to her grandson.

The man speaks to her, as if coming out of a dream. "You got any travel mugs, Mrs. Chacón?"

"Where are you taking us?"

"You'll want your coats."

Outside Virginia Roberts's church, I tried not to shake while leaning against a pillar, waiting for Tekún to come around.

I had lost count of the time. Had it been another three minutes? I looked up and down the street. Older cars, rusted on their lower edges; new cars, a Mercedes, and a Jaguar. I could see that. Could see that there was money unequally distributed in this town. I could see all that, even as the image of my empty home dug into my stomach like a large rodent.

They weren't in the house, nor in my uncle Chepe's house. They were gone.

Desaparecidos. A hated, feared word among Salvadorans. The Disappeared.

Tekún pulled around, just as I slid down the side of the pillar and landed on my knees and retched. He leaped out of the SUV, grabbed me before I fell completely over. I had forgotten how strong he was, how he could sweep me up without a thought. He let me empty my stomach, then lifted me and placed me in the passenger side. I told him, in sentence fragments, what had happened. He drove us off fast, calling Pearl on his cell as he spun the roads of Tijuana under the tires.

Pearl handed me a shot of whiskey. I didn't want it; I wanted only one thing, followed by another: find my family, then take down the man who took them. But I drank it, to steady . . . something in me. I wasn't sure what. You can't steady anything, not with your son, your mother, gone.

Pearl rubbed my shoulder. "What are you supposed to do?" she said.

I jerked away from her.

"Romilia . . ."

"I don't need that from you." My entire body tensed, my bones turning metallic. And then a spew of anger, toward her, Tekún, blaming them for what had happened up to now, blaming them for taking me away from my family.

Tekún waited. Just stood there and waited, like some Zen Buddhist monk, until my tantrum passed. He repeated Pearl's question: "What did she tell you to do?"

"I'm supposed to deliver you."

He didn't flinch. "To whom?" he said.

"Whoever's been coming after you."

"Where?"

"She just said for me to go home. I'll find instructions there."

Pearl looked at the floor, then up at Tekún, who had his hands in his pockets, his blue guayabera shirt ruffled up around his wrists.

"What should we do?" she said.

He looked hard at me. "We need to put a call in to Special Agent Fisher. Tell her to search Romilia's home."

"No," I said. "The bitch was explicit about that. We call in my Bureau, he'll kill them both."

And then I felt it: The rodent of anxiety tore right though me. If we have souls, that's what he ate. An evisceration of any hope, for I knew I could not call my Bureau, and there was no way I could control Tekún.

He and Pearl were talking, lowly. "What do we do?" she said. It did not sound desperate, but strategic.

"Mule train number four," he said.

"It's clean?"

"I took it off Min's hands, right after Mon was executed. We've not used it yet."

"I'll get everything ready," said Pearl. She walked to a back room.

Then Tekún did what she had tried to do. He put his palm on my shoulder, carefully, as if not wanting to set me off. Under his hand I felt the internal shake, a quaking that rattled through me. "What was that all about?" I said.

"Just clearing the road," he said. "We'll be at your house before morning."

"How?" I said. I was sniffling before him, which I hated, but then I didn't. I didn't care, all I cared about were my son, my mother. "You're on the list. Your face, plastered in every border guard post. They'll pick you up the moment you cross the border."

He smiled. "No, they won't." Then he looked down, as if gathering something from the floor, and looked back at me. "You know, your mother and I have always gotten along."

I smiled, but the smile became a wedge and split me.

He handed me my gun. "They're going to be all right," he said.

Mule train number four was an hour's drive from his house. We didn't have to pass back through Tijuana, but rather drove northeast, straddling the border with barely a mile between us and the U.S.

"It's a small village, called El Macizo," Tekún said to me. Again, he sat in the passenger seat, with me in the back. Pearl drove.

"Is it easier to cross the border there?" I asked.

"Yes."

"No patrol?"

"Not where we're going, no."

"Oh. So we're going *mojados*, right?"

He laughed. "Well, considering we're all U.S. citizens, I wouldn't say we're illegal immigrants."

"Yeah, but this is the way they do it, right? Crossing the border at night, so *La Migra* doesn't find them?"

"No, not quite. Our immigrant brethren don't know about mule train four."

Half an hour later, we entered the village of El Macizo. It was small, with hardly a semblance of a center, and certainly no plaza. The buildings stood haphazardly, strewn along one dirt road that ran through the middle of what Tekún called a town. Just a few small homes, and little stores that had already boarded themselves closed for the night. Music played through windows. Young men — boys, really — leaned against a low rider. They stared at us through the night air, checking out who we were. There were no streetlights. Tekún called out to the boys. They recognized him, called his name, waved. Pearl drove the SUV up to an old building that had a sign above it, which I could see in the vehicle's headlights: REFRESCOS. I doubted that whoever lived there made their money off juice drinks.

Her name was Ricarda Guerra. She was in her sixties, but she still had a look about her that had not let go of youth. Sexy, to say the least. She carried her body, round all over, as if ready to dance. *"Hola Tekúncito, ¿cómo te va?"* she greeted Tekún.

Tekuncito. Little Tekún. The loving diminutive. What thoughts had she entertained about him? Or were they thoughts?

And how long would we have to be here? They greeted each other with a strong hug, somewhat like mother to son; but then she grabbed his face and kissed him on his lips and he smiled at her and they whispered to each other.

I thought only of my mother and son; here, now, there was no room in my head or my heart for jealousy.

Ricarda hugged me like she knew me. She said in north Mexican Spanish, "So this is the lovely Salvadoran bloom who we're always wondering about! Oh, my goodness, you *are* everything they say about you. Look at you, just *look* at you!"

Tekún and she moved to the kitchen while Pearl pulled the SUV into the dusty backyard of Ricarda's home. I was alone for a moment in her den. But I could hear them: Tekún explaining, and she responding: *"Ay no, y ¿quién es el pendejo que te quiere matar? Y ¿ese tiene a su hijo, y su mamá? Un sinverguenza hijo de la gran chingada."* Tekún spoke in between Ricarda's loving curses. Again, the mule train, and some clarifications: Had there been any traffic through town? And she: No. No DEA, no Migra, and certainly none of the Arellanos.

"We need to go tonight," he told her.

"You want me to pack some tortillas? Beans?"

"Thank you, *mi bella*, but we're fine."

Ricarda was his *bella*. I, supposedly, was his *vida*. I wonder if he had any other women dangling from metaphors?

Pearl came into the den. "You ready?" she said.

"Yeah."

"It's a two-mile walk, but there are no obstacles. There won't be any traffic now."

"Okay. But what about light? What do we do, just travel by moonlight?"

She looked at me, surprised, as if she thought I would have figured all this out by now. Then her expression shifted to sympathy, not only for my family, but for my naïveté. "No. We'll turn on the lights." She grinned. "Come on, partner." She patted my shoulder.

We walked outside, past the SUV, and toward a set of flowers that stood on the edge of Ricarda's dirt backyard.

A cross protruded from the flowers, small, with a name on it. With the moon I could just make out the words:

JUAN JR. VILLALOBOS.

Somebody's grave?

Tekún explained, as if he knew I would ask. "Ricarda lost a son, long ago. A baby, maybe three years old. He was once buried here."

Once buried.

Tekún turned toward Ricarda, who was standing by the fence. She then crossed the backyard, looked to the other side. A last check, before turning to Tekún and whispering hard, "*Ya, vayanse.*"

Tekún turned to the cross, grabbed it in the middle, just below the cross's arms, and pulled. Something metallic popped. A suck of air into the edges of earth. The cross lifted up and back and, with it, a chunk of ground. Ground sealed with thick metal, which opened up a hole large enough for a person to fit through.

Mule train number four.

"*Vayanse, vayan,*" said Ricarda, shooing us away. We obeyed: Pearl went first, tossing a filled backpack over her shoulder. She gestured to me. No lights, no flashlights; Pearl reached up and took my fingers and led me down into a cold, moist-aired corridor. I looked up. In the moonlight, and in the frame of the opening in the earth, I saw Tekún turn to Ricarda. They gave each other a quick, tight hug. She told him to be careful, to take care of me, that she knew how much I meant to him, that it would be okay, just keep your head low. He patted her on the back, thanking her, maybe wanting her to hush up a bit. Once he was down in the corridor with us, she waved, said something about sweeping up, which I took to mean cleaning the area around the hidden man-hole and making sure the pretty flowers were once again arranged. She reached above the plug of dirt, grabbing the cross; the door closed with a clunking of metal upon thick, hard rubber. Complete darkness.

Then complete light, right after I heard the click. And there stood Pearl, right next to a light switch, which protruded from a concrete wall. She motioned to the long hallway ahead of us, all lit up with lamps that hung from a concrete ceiling.

"I told you we'd leave the lights on for you."

We walked through the long corridor, which was cemented on all sides. After five minutes the cement ended, leaving only dirt walls and floors. There were fewer lights, with longer stretches between each lamp. Sometimes we walked in darkness, with only the light ahead to beckon us.

"I can't believe this," I said.

Neither of my companions responded.

"So, mind telling me how you came across this little under-ground highway?"

Pearl walked to my left, Tekún to my right. He had changed clothes before we left, donning jeans, hiking boots, a denim shirt, and a leather jacket. A small backpack, smaller than Pearl's, less filled, hung from his left shoulder. He had his hands in his pockets as we walked, as if knowing there was a security here, that he could relax a moment. "They abandoned this a while back."

"The Arellano brothers," I said.

He did not verify or deny. "I offered to wipe down the facility and take it off their hands. They were happy to oblige, considering the pressure they were living under."

"I take it, if this is mule train number four, there are mule trains one, two and three as well?"

Pearl laughed.

"What?"

"Why stop at the single digits?" she said.

"Now, Pearl," said Tekún. He smiled.

"But how the hell do you move cocaine through here?" I said. "You carry it? Do you hire people to pass it through, like a fire bucket brigade?"

Pearl chuckled.

Tekún said, "I suppose, for something like this to work, you'd have machinery down here. Perhaps electric cars, ones that don't emit exhaust, and that can pull carts behind them. The tunnel is wide enough for two lanes, don't you think?"

"Where are the electric cars?" I asked.

"Maybe Min and Mon sold them to a golf club," he said.

And that was about as close as they were going to get to telling me about their trade. I may have been someone they cared for, but I was still a federal agent.

We walked in silence a while. I had questions, but I didn't want to ask them; for asking them meant giving them permission to answer. Such as Pearl: What was going to happen to her now, once our boss Fisher found out she was a mole working for Tekún Umán? Once she had abducted me, she had blown her cover. It would have been better for her to keep heading south, away from the United States, perhaps join up with her mother in Guadalajara, color her hair, get a tan and go Latina. But to go back to the States meant possibly getting caught, arrested, and tried for a number of crimes. The Bureau was not one to be lenient on a spy. And that's basically what she was: a spy for a *narcotraficante*. Spies who worked for a federal agency were tried as traitors and executed.

She walked beside me with an assurance, a sense of calm and purpose. I did not understand this, except to remind myself that, all these years, not only had she been trained by the FBI, she had also been trained by her godfather here, a man who had in turn trained with the best in Guatemalan Special Forces.

We passed an area where someone had painted a thick white line over the hard dirt of the tunnel, like an arch. Some of the line was cracking, sloughing off the wall. There was a small wooden sign to one side of the line, written in a formal, official font. I leaned over and read it.

WELCOME TO THE UNITED STATES OF AMERICA.
PLEASE HAVE YOUR PASSPORT READY FOR INSPECTION.

Tekún smiled at me as I walked away from the sign. "One must have a sense of humor in this business," he said.

On the other side of the border stood a manhole made to look like something else: this time, a cabinet into a kitchen. A kitchen in a home where no one lived. In a village that looked much like El Macizo, which stood two miles south of us; this village was in the United States.

Yet another SUV was waiting, parked in a tight shed. Pearl found the keys somewhere, hidden in a rafter. She disengaged the alarm; the Land Rover chirped at us.

It was past midnight. Pearl drove fast. These roads were like those in Mexico: dirt, gravel. It would be a while before we hit pavement.

"How many SUVs do you own?" I said to Tekún. "And I thought you were a Jaguar driver."

"Oh, I am. No other car like the Jaguar. But these days, it's best for us to look like any other soccer mom."

He smiled. And I tried to laugh. But "soccer mom" made me think of Sergio. And the last time I had seen my son, he was still wearing his soccer uniform from practice. He had taken his cleats off, just like his grandmother had told him to do, before going into Chepe's house. Sergio had a tendency to forget such things at home, stomping around in his black cleats, leaving clods of dried mud on the carpet and making dimples in the wood floor.

Images that rattled through me. Like a metal pole beating the insides of a wooden drum. Breaking the interior walls. Ready to break me.

I breathed. Who was this bastard who had kidnapped my

family and had killed Chip? A man who had a hard-on for Tekún. *Your boyfriend.* That's what Little Miss Terrorist, Virginia Roberts, had said. A terrorist. A real-live terrorist. A woman who was ready to kill off abortion doctors, and who didn't mind evoking the name of al Qa'ida or utilizing the money of drug runners to support her cause. At any other time, this would have made me think about our state of affairs, of our America, and what the hell we were doing, and what we were allowing to happen to us. Fundamentalists of opposing religions, joining together with *narcotraficantes* in order to attack the U.S. from the inside and from the out. Along the way, kidnapping a grandmother, a son, all for the sake of a cause.

Whenever the rattle did not make my breath shallow, I made vows. I had made such vows before, when a man killed my sister. A promise, to take him down. A promise I had kept, though not in ways I had meant. And that door to my past had closed; I had done the closing. This, now, was not my issue, had not been my issue until Tekún's hunter decided to bring me into this. Bring my family into this. Killing Chip. Making this mine. Making me take vows again.

Pearl was speeding. Still, from the back, I said, "Floor it."

An hour later we were in Los Angeles. It would be another ten minutes before we made it to my house in the San Fernando Valley. From the back of the Land Rover I gave instructions, "You take the Victory Street exit, it's right after Burbank, and from there you take —"

"We got it," said Pearl.

I said nothing; I was about to say, *You know where I live?* And then the question seemed very stupid. Tekún simply looked back at me.

No more talk now. We had talked along the way, in shards of analyses, of what needed to be done, who was this guy, why was he hunting Tekún? Tekún went through a list of possible enemies, names of people I had not heard of, other names I was familiar with. "Too Bits. He's way too small to do anything to us, and he's still stuck in Nashville. Cowboy's dead. The Crack Killer got him in Texas. Nathan Bayback's moved to Ecuador . . . Carl Spooner, poor fellow, dead in a plane crash —"

"Wait a minute, you believe in that shit?" I said.

He looked at me. I knew he hated it when I cursed. Too bad.

"What, the Crack Killer? Romilia, I believe in rumors much more than I do the news."

A public knowledge, born in rumor; and, as my mother has so often said, rumors, in our Latino worlds, are more valid than newscasts.

"A serial killer in the drug world? That's ludicrous."

"No, it's not. There's someone out there, killing people off. To be honest, I think that's who's after me." He looked out at the Los Angeles that we passed, so quickly, with little traffic on the freeway. This was amazing; it was the closest Tekún had ever gotten to admitting his involvement in the business. "There's someone out there who's done his homework, tracking associates down. I don't doubt that's who's doing this."

"Then what's his motive?" I asked.

"Motive?" Tekún looked at me. "Do you know what the Crack Killer has done? He's slaughtered some of the major players. Then he takes their money, all the cash. He doesn't take their supplies, he leaves the product behind. But he's ruthless. When the Crack Killer found Cowboy, do you know what he did? Killed him with a butter knife."

"Oh, God." I had images, a blunt edge, how that could mutilate. "That's horrible."

"No, no, not with the knife itself. Cowboy was poisoned. The Crack Killer dipped the knife in some poison and just stuck Cowboy under the neck with it. And that was all."

"What kind of poison?"

"I don't know."

He said nothing more. He sounded worried, but it was not just for himself. There was a current within his voice: He was concerned, not for his own life, but for me. For my mother and son.

There are those who have wondered if the feelings Tekún has shown, publicly, for me, are real or a façade, yet another tactic he uses to keep eluding the authorities. The police in Nashville, the

Bureau, both in Quantico and out here on the West Coast: Many have said, either under their breath or overtly, that Tekún has used me. He's played with words, on e-mail, in letters, in conversations: I am his *vida*. Words and phrases that I have said, just as publicly, are nothing more than a string of bullshit.

And yet I have to confess—if to no one else, then at least to myself—that hearing Ricarda Guerra's words back in that shithole of a village in Mexico moved me. How, just as in the world of law enforcement, so too in the world of drug traffickers, it was well known how he felt about me. That he, one of the kingpins, was in love with a federal agent: Romilia Chacón.

And I have been so careful, so good, in hiding how I feel about him.

Yet his love was so public. A public knowledge that had now gotten us both in trouble. It had dragged my family into the line of fire.

The day he had kissed me, when he had helped me bring Minos down, I knew then that he did love me, that it wasn't just some façade. That day I instinctively reached for my pistol and almost told him to stop, almost told him once more that he was under arrest, but didn't. A silent agreement between us: I would never hunt him again. Not out of fear, but rather, something more.

Which is why I had believed, for a scant moment, while lifting Chip's bloody shirt off his stomach, that Tekún might have killed him. Then I had seen the missing accent, and knew that he hadn't.

A clue that left me feeling at first confused—he did not kill Chip out of jealousy. I can't say I should have felt bad, or that I had wanted it to be that way, for that wouldn't be right. But I did feel so alone.

I have known, since the day Tekún helped me bring down Minos, that I have been in love with him.

Not a good thing to share with my law enforcement brethren.

Dead Chip. Hunted Tekún. My mother, my son.

"Get me home," I said, from the backseat. My teeth popped with the grinding.

It was still dark when we reached my home on Woolf Avenue. No lights on anywhere, except for the lamps above the street. Pearl did not park in front of the house; she drove by first. We all looked out through the SUV's tinted windows for what we needed to look for: federal agents on watch. Cars parked in ways that did not show a nightly parking habit, but surveillance. "Know these cars?" Pearl said to me.

"That's my neighbor's, Don, his truck. Daniel and Ariel, that's their Honda, that Hybrid. I don't see . . . check out that Mercury, over there." I pointed to the white car down from Don's house.

Pearl drove past the car slowly. "It's empty," she said.

Still, Pearl drove around the corner and took in two blocks before coming back. She parked on Livermore, a street above mine, underneath one of my neighbor's jacaranda trees.

We had talked this out: It was my house, so I was to go through the front door, like I always did. Hit the alarm code, if it was still on, and then head to the back door, where Tekún and Pearl would enter after crossing a couple of my neighbors' walls and fences. I had given Pearl the key to the back door. Just in case.

Just in case someone was inside, and, I, though with my pistol raised, could not stop him in time.

All this felt clumsy. But it seemed the safest bet to get in. "Watch your fire," I said, "just in case he's there with my family."

"You all right?" said Tekún.

"Yeah, I'm fine, fine. Let's do it."

I got out of the Rover, closed the door with both hands to

cushion it; the clean *click* of the door was easy, and showed how new the SUV was. I walked down the sidewalk, past my Vietnamese neighbors' home, and through my front yard, under the lemon and grapefruit trees, neither of which I have eaten from, as I hate both fruits.

I unlocked the door with my right hand, held my gun straight out in my left. Pushed the door open; the alarm didn't sound. I didn't stop to look at it, but walked quickly to the corner of the front room, our small library, where we kept the shelves filled. I hid behind the corner, listened for any sound, then pulled around and headed to the corner of the kitchen.

Nothing.

The key turned in the back door. The door swung open fast. I raised my gun. Tekún and Pearl stepped into the light.

We checked the entire house. It was empty.

My message machine blinked, showing two messages that had yet to be heard. I hit the button. In Spanish, my uncle Chepe spoke, his voice a rattle of anger and worry. "Sister! Where in God's name are you? Where's Romilia? I called her office, but they said she wasn't available. What's going on, Celia? I'm worried. You call me the moment you get in." It went on like this for over a minute.

Message two said only, "You need to call (714) 555–4886. Use a cell phone." Then he hung up.

I listened again, wrote the number down. "That's him," I said. "Got to be." I looked at Pearl first, then Tekún; his mouth had opened, his jaw gone slightly slack.

"I know that voice," he said.

"Who is it?"

"I'm not sure . . ."

"I'm calling."

"Wait," said Tekún. He raised his hand, looked at me; but then he snapped out of something. He nodded.

I dialed. Someone answered. "You are Romilia Chacón?" he said.

"Yes. Where are—"

"They're fine, I assure you. Let me speak with him."

"Let me speak with my mother you son of a bitch."

"Please. Go over to your computer."

A moment's hesitation, and then I obeyed. The computer on our desk was off, as was the printer. But there was a sheet of paper sticking out of the printer's tray, with "MapQuest" printed over the top, and below that, a map of California, and a thick blue streak going through the Central Valley.

"If you follow that, you should get to us in five and a half hours. You could speed, all you'd have to do is show your badge, the police would let you through. But I wouldn't advise that. You don't want anyone picking up on your whereabouts. It's now three thirty. If you leave in the next five minutes, you'll be at the destination point around nine a.m., though I'll give you another forty-five minutes or so, for traffic."

"What's going to happen?"

"If you do everything right, you'll get your mother and son back. If not, they will die like all the others."

"What all others?"

And there, he began to list names: Cowboy. Blaster. Mary Jane Pollock, a.k.a. "Green." Lennie. Frankie. And twelve other names, not all of which I had heard before, but I recognized enough of them to realize that certain folklore is based in too much truth.

They were all drug lords — minor, major, but all in the business. And he listed them off, with no hesitation. He had no fear of killing. And he had my family.

"Please let me speak with him," he said to me.

I had no chance to curse him; and from Quantico training, I had learned not to curse the one who had power over you. I wanted to curse the training, for teaching me too much. I handed the phone to Tekún.

"I'm here," said Tekún.

He stood there for a long minute. Listening. His face did not register reaction, though I thought I saw a certain surprise streak across his vision. Just a flash, as if his own special military training had taught him to stay as still as possible. Even when there were surprises.

He hung up.

"What did he say?" said Pearl.

"He gave me a list of the various times he could have killed me but didn't."

"Do you know who he is?" I asked.

"No. I thought I knew the voice. But, no."

A look came over his face, as if the truth of what was happening finally reached him. But it wasn't that. He glanced behind me, at a front window. Outside, a car drove by.

"Just a neighbor, or some teenage kids," I said.

But he didn't relax. I had seen that look before, and it had frightened me then, though I had been paralyzed seconds earlier, not by fear, but by his damn dart. The look of a man who hates to be hunted.

I studied the map. "It's to San Francisco," I said. The computerized trail showed us exactly where to go: follow the 405 north to the 5. Take the 5 up north, then all the various routes into San Francisco. Straight into the middle of the city. Below, the killer had typed his own note: GO TO THE SOUTHWEST CORNER OF 20TH AND MISSION. PARK. THERE WILL BE A SPACE FOR YOU. GET OUT OF THE CAR AND HEAD SLOWLY TOWARD THE VIDEO STORE. That was it.

"He's going to jump us there," I said. "But right out in public? What in the world does he think he can . . ."

But then I got quiet. For I heard what Tekún had already heard, for a good ten, fifteen seconds. The whipping sound of an approaching helicopter. And, no doubt, it was coming our way.

"How did they know . . ." I said. Then thought about my alarm. I opened its plastic casing. A thin green wire ran behind the casing, spliced into the computer chips of the control board. Someone, no doubt my boss Fisher or one of our dependable computer geeks, had rigged it to go off but to give no sound here, in the house. Pearl and I had been missing three days. Our colleagues were looking for us, in a full-out hunt.

I looked at Tekún. He just turned to Pearl and said, "Nancy dear, you just may be able to hang on to your career as a federal agent."

No room for thought or movement, except for his: Tekún's arm shot back behind him, lifted his leather jacket. There it was: that damn jade knife of his, out and in his hand. But he flipped it, caught the knife below the shank. He held it like a miniature club and slammed the handle against Pearl's forehead, right next to the bruise I had given her. She went down. He flipped the knife again and turned to me. "Give me your gun," he said. And I obeyed.

BI and LAPD usually coordinated together fairly well. Still, I was glad to see it was a cop car skidding to a stop in front of my house and not one of our Bureau vehicles. The screech of tires was way too loud to let my neighbors sleep. Don and his wife, Ramona, walked out of their front door, but a cop pushed them back inside. Daniel across the street stuck his head out with a *What-the-hell?* look on his face. Another cop pushed him back as well. But that didn't keep my neighbors from gawking out their windows at the organized scramble of gun-toting authorities on their street, or the apparently crazed drug runner who held a gun to my head and, with his forearm locked around my neck, walked out my front door. And then the blowhorns and Tekún yelling, almost screaming, like a man in the worst of panic attacks. Swearing to God that he'd kill me, that he had left my partner alive, inside the house, and if they ever wanted to find Romilia Chacón alive again, they'd do what he said.

The cops backed off.

He whispered straight into my ear, "See?"

"This is crazy." Still, I pretended to look terrified, as if Tekún might kill me at any second; I was afraid that they would kill *him*. He looked like Pacino in *Dog Day Afternoon*.

"Come on, *mi vida*. A little more fervor. 'Else the sniper shooter behind your neighbor's Hybrid will get a good laser bead on my forehead." Then he started screaming again.

This is how we walked, all the way to the SUV: him behind me, the gun to my head. Using my neighbors' houses as a shield, so none of the cops could sneak up from behind and try to take him out.

In the SUV he handed me the keys, which he had pulled from Pearl's backpack. "You drive."

I started the motor while he dug in his backpack. Actually, it was Pearl's backpack. The once-heavier one. Now looking lighter. He was working fast, looking for something, while my fellow agents moved into position around the SUV, in perfect formation. They were good, I could see that. Which was why Tekún almost looked slightly, just slightly, panicky. Until he found his little device.

"You'll have to forgive me," he said.

"What?"

"Don't worry. It'll be intact. But you'll want to hire a house cleaner for a day or two." He hit the button. In the night, my house lit up with one-two-three explosions. All the cops before us, and the agents alongside them, caught off-guard, turned their heads to my home.

"Drive, *mi vida.*"

I punched the accelerator. The powdery explosion had caused a psychological rift in the formation of the agents. The ones I drove toward fell back slightly, enough for us to escape.

Past Albertsons and the Krispy Kreme. Beyond the train station. Into a neighborhood that I did not know, though it was only half a mile from my own. Behind us, three helicopters now swarmed my house. But that would not last long; they would quickly learn Tekún's sleight of hand, that it was nothing but loose, multicolored powder and talc burning against the windows. Their formation would no longer remain tight: It would open up wide, and seek us out.

Which was why Tekún did not wait long. "That one," he said.

"What, that Honda?"

"Yes. Accord. Very reliable."

He was out. Jimmied the lock. Popped out the alarm, broke open the transmission. The motor turned over.

"Great. Now you're in it for carjacking."

"No, it's a trade-in," he said, motioning to his SUV. He tossed the Land Rover's keys into the front seat. "I think they've come out ahead."

He drove up Van Nuys Boulevard. I looked behind us, at the widening net of police helicopters and their beams of light, all circling my home. Their net fell over my tiny corner of Los Angeles, hoping to catch Tekún, and save me.

Outside of the city, he asked me to drive. "In case we get pulled over. Your badge will keep a police officer from asking too many questions."

I stayed close to the speed limit through the Central Valley, all the way to Oakland. There, I slowed with the traffic, though my chest snapped with a speed all its own.

Tekún looked ahead of us, at the long line of commuters crossing the Bay Bridge into San Francisco. "We're on time," he finally said. He turned to me. "We'll have them soon."

"How do you know?" I stared hard at the traffic in front of me, wanting to burst through it. "How do you know they're not already dead?" We had hardly spoken during the long trip. As if we were afraid where the conversation would take us.

"I need to hand myself over to him. I believe he will keep to his word."

I didn't want him to see me. I turned, looked slightly to the left of the windshield, tried to wipe my eyes, to keep the little mascara left from running, to keep him from knowing. As if I could keep that from him.

Tekún looked at me. Then he looked back out the front window. He spoke that way, out to San Francisco. "He told me of seven occasions when he could have killed me. The last was when he dumped my worker's body — Chamba, that was my worker's name, good fellow — this guy just dropped him at my front door. He claims to have been right there. Right there."

Tekún was lost in that memory, studying it, trying to figure out where this killer had been. Also trying to figure out why he had not seen the killer, why he had not been more aware.

"He says he was there at my mother's funeral," said Tekún. "He saw me, on the mountain, looking down. He had a sniper's rifle. But he didn't take me out."

I couldn't tell if Tekún sounded sad, or just confused, that he could have slipped up so much. That he had allowed an enemy to get so close to him.

"Do you think it's the Crack Killer?" I asked.

"Of that, I have no doubt."

Then there was a silence as he collected his thoughts, ones that meant to form an answer to his questions regarding his slip-ups, the near-misses.

"Once, my godfather told me that it's good for a man to get broken. I wasn't sure what he meant by that. But I think I do now. He was warning me about hubris."

I kept quiet.

"It is difficult to recognize that you have regrets."

"Do you regret?" I asked.

"I regret my godfather's death. I regret what has happened to your mother, and to Sergio. This has gone way too far."

These were words of emotion; and yet Tekún Umán had a way of holding his face solid. Not tight, but quiet, near-stoic. I couldn't tell anymore if he was planning, or simply caught up in a dark rumination.

"Look," I said. "I just need to know how we're going to do this."

"What is the address?"

"Corner of Twentieth and Mission."

"Right in the heart of the Mission District."

"You know it?"

"A little. A friend of mine's from there. A writer. He used to live on Capp Street. It's a very busy area. Just like all of San Francisco: tight. All the buildings close to one another, everything jammed up together. Bad place for a confrontation. Especially if he's planning to shoot me. He's also planning for you to shoot, as well. Which is why he picked it."

"You talk like you work for the Bureau."

"Pearl taught me a thing or two."

Half an hour later we were in the Mission. Tekún was right: San Francisco was tight, as if some giant had crammed the entire city upon this little bay. Not like my Los Angeles: sprawling wide. Here, the world of the Mission—obviously Salvadoran, Guatemalan, Mexican—hunkered together in thin streets and tiny alleyways.

"Turn here," he said. I did, onto Twentieth Street. Numerous tiny shops and restaurants stood on the edge of the sidewalks. A Guatemalan woman stood outside her establishment, with a fake quetzal bird roosting above her.

Tekún turned and took in everything while I drove. It was hard, dodging men who cut across the small road; the parked cars felt stuffed alongside me. "Slow down," he said. I did. He opened the window and spoke with the Guatemalan woman, in a language I did not understand. Indigenous. No doubt Mayan.

She looked at him, confused, and said in Spanish, "I'm sorry, what do you want?"

"My mistake," he said. He closed the window. "Ay. Damn mestizos. Can't speak their own languages, don't know a thing about their own culture, though they're happy to sell it."

It was the first time I had ever heard disgust from him. And a curse word. His words were laced with a silent alarm.

"Where to?" I said.

"Go to where he told you. To the corner of Twentieth and Mission."

I took right turns, back to Mission, then one more right and to the corner, where three large young men stood in front of a clothing store. Cholos, all: no doubt gang members. The three were part of a team of seven who walked in small circles on the corner, looking up and down Mission. When people passed, words were exchanged, and the Cholos reached into their pockets and pulled items out: tiny plastic bags, drivers' licenses. Money was pushed into palms. They worked fast.

Three of their *carnales* held a spot right at the corner of

Mission and Twentieth, not allowing anyone to park there. Some white guy in a mauve Volvo tried to get in. One of the large boys leaned up against the Volvo, said something. The white guy had his face halfway out his window, taking on the boy. Then the other two came around the Volvo, and the man quietly drove off.

"What's your name?" said the first Cholo, when Tekún lowered his window.

"Tekún Umán."

The Cholo turned, whistled to his two friends. They opened up the area.

I parked.

Tekún was out first. He stood up, his hands at his sides, looking almost calm. He spoke to the Cholos; but the boys looked confused, as if their jobs were done, and they had already been paid. One said, "Don't know, *cuate*, he just paid us to hold your space." But the boys performed one final act of obedience: They moved away. Quickly.

Tekún turned, took in the entire city block. Latinos all around, in groups of three, couples, or individuals looking into shops or hurrying off to work. A couple of Mexican business women with Starbucks coffees in hand, pulling their jackets closer to their necks, heading to an office somewhere. The Salvadoran-American Cholos, who now dispersed, in a way that was not haphazard: It was a formation. A way of spreading out across a blank area of the sidewalk, where Tekún stood and I entered and the man wearing a tank — what I first thought was a backpack — strapped to his back opened his long trench coat and pulled out a weapon.

A large water pistol.

That's what it looked like: one of those Super Soaker squirter guns that my mother had bought Sergio for his birthday once. Shoots water a good thirty feet after you pump the hell out of it, storing the pressurized water in a rubber bladder. Sergio had shot me more than a few times before I ran after him in the backyard, threatening bruises.

This guy: His Super Soaker was all black. It had a hose, which ran under his arm and connected, obviously, to that tank. He did not enter the opening made by the Cholos; he stood to one edge of it, the far edge, from Tekún and me. He opened fire. Just as Tekún, in trained fashion, reached behind his leather jacket and unsheathed his blade. Tekún flung it, as a thick thread of water hit him in the chest.

It was not water. It was a bolt of clear, liquid lightning. Tekún looked as if his body wanted to shatter. He vibrated, as if hit by a Taser gun. Another shot, another direct hit at his lower back, and Tekún went down.

Three men stepped out of the everyday patterns of the Mission District, like background actors breaking out of their roles. They were on Tekún, picking him up. Just as I aimed my pistol at one of them and shouted my rank, my Bureau, I got soaked in electricity. My body turned against me. Jesus, it was like being turned into metal and getting rattled. It was killing me, I knew it. I'd have a bruise on my forehead, from where I hit the car door's edge. But I wouldn't feel it for a while, just like I didn't feel the hard, cold asphalt of Mission Street.

These must have been dreams; for there was my mother, kneeling over me, loving me in the ways that only Celia Chacón can love. Holding me, begging me to wake up. Behind her are people, all worried, with that look of strangers, wondering if they should help, wondering if they should just leave the scene. And there, there is my son, standing to one side of my mother. He's so afraid, and he's about to cry because he knows that Mommy just might be dead, and you can't get too close to that.

W here are you?" said Pearl.

"San Francisco. Mount Zion Hospital. I can't talk long. They've got an agent standing at the door."

"Tekún?"

"They got him. A group of people, men, the one shooter, two others carried him away."

She paused, breathed. But then quickly said, "Your mother, Sergio?"

"Right here. With me."

"Gracias a Dios."

"I'm sorry," I said. I gave a quick rundown of how it happened: the Cholos, the liquid stun gun, the men in the crowd who took Tekún away. "The Cholos are still being held. But I could tell, they knew nothing about it. They were just paid to hold the parking space, then told to move the crowd out of the way."

"What about the guy with the stun gun?"

"I've never seen him before. White, brown hair, scruffy beard. He looked like a professional." I didn't want to ask the following, but I did: "How's Fisher?"

"She's just glad you're all right. The SAC in San Francisco called her first thing, said they had picked you up the moment SFPD called in the downing of a Federal Agent. She's expecting a call from you."

Pearl was also telling me: We were taking a chance, talking like this. Fisher would want to know why I had called my partner first, rather than her. Then again, she could have read it differently: Pearl was my partner, and I was concerned for her well-being after the pseudo kidnapping at my house. And Fisher would have been right. And she might have even been happy with my developing relationship with Pearl.

"What are you going to do?" I said.

"Me? I've been given orders. Rest. Dear Tekún did give me a concussion."

"You all right with that?"

"What?" She said it as if she didn't understand the question; as if she and Tekún had thought it out, as one of many possible scenarios.

"She expects you back soon, you know," said Pearl.

"Yeah. To put me on sick leave. Which I'll take them up on. I might just tour the Bay Area."

Not a complete lie. My stomach felt like a knot. The doctor and the SAC of the FBI's field office in San Francisco both confirmed it: I had received an electrical shock. Not enough to harm me, not even enough to burn my skin. Just enough to mess up the natural electronic impulses in my body and throw me to the floor.

"It was a liquid stun gun," said the SAC, a warm gentleman in his mid-fifties whose name was MacGunther. "New on the market. Much better than a Taser gun, though a little bulky to carry around. Tasers shoot the prods with the wires trailing around them. They can go maybe twenty feet. Liquid stun guns, they can hit you from a good thirty, forty feet. No wires to mess with. They're great for crowd control."

I wasn't sure whether to say *thank-you* for that lesson in technology. "It looked like my kid's super water pistol."

"It might have been. Same basic concept."

"Where is my son?"

"They're outside. Want me to send them back in?"

Hardly a need to answer that.

They came through the door. We did what families do when families realize they've almost lost one another.

Sergio, he looked normal. But then I reminded myself, children who have been sexually abused, who have been beaten and stripped and had pictures taken of them for kid-porn magazines, look normal after they are rescued. There is that time, that immediate moment after trauma, when we can all look normal, for we believe ourselves to be safe, at home, away from those who had taken us away and had done all those dark, blunt things to us.

I asked him what had happened. He said he was fine. The man had kept Sergio and Mamá together, had never separated them. He had bought them ice creams, after they had eaten hamburgers from the drive-in window of Jack in the Box. Whenever Sergio had to use the bathroom, the man took him, but did not go in with him. It was a small bathroom, in a small apartment. "So I peed by myself. He left me alone, Mamá, he didn't bother me."

Federal agents who are mothers cry.

There was the fact that the nice man who had respected my boy's privacy in the bathroom had also pushed a gun to Sergio's head. Sergio told me that, as well, before my mother could hush him—not with censorship, but with worry; no need to bring up those images, she meant to say. "We're all right," said Mamá. "He, he didn't hurt us in any way. We ate fine." But, for a moment, I couldn't hear her. I just saw the picture: a gun at my son's head.

But I would have to hear her. My mother had spent two days with the man. She would know something. No doubt the field office had already questioned her. They would also want to question me; I was surprised they hadn't already. I was willing to tell them what they needed to hear, but I couldn't tell them everything. I wouldn't tell them of Pearl's connection with Tekún . . .

Which meant I had to match my story with Pearl's. No doubt Fisher had already interviewed my partner. What story had she told? "Shit," I muttered; we should have talked about that. Too much to think about.

Mamá stayed in the hospital room with me. I was still dressed, had not needed to put on one of those gowns. I would be able to check out soon, right into the hands of the San Francisco Field Office, right into questioning. I couldn't afford that. I had to talk with my mother, who had not left my side since the moment the man had let her go, when he had let her run out of the clothing store on Mission Street and to my side. She and Sergio had been with me in the ambulance, and had stayed with me all this time. There was safety in being together, we all wanted to believe.

"Tell me everything you can remember," I said.

Mamá had not recognized the man. He was white, fairly tall, brown hair. No scars showing on his face. Bluish eyes. She told the story, from the moment the man had entered the house, how he had tricked Sergio into letting him in. They had taken the same drive he had mapped out for me. They had stayed in a small apartment in the Mission District, near where they had grabbed Tekún, right on Twentieth Street. Sergio had spent time watching television, and the man had given him a Game Boy to play with. "He even had some videos, though Sergio had already seen them. But Sergio still watched them, which made me glad. It kept him occupied."

She was nervous as she talked to me. It was a shaking that would not go away anytime soon.

"Did he talk with you? Did he mention anything out of the ordinary?" I said.

"No. We talked little. He kept quiet all the time, unless he was on the phone. Then he would go into the kitchen and talk."

"Who was he talking to?"

"I don't know. But he kept getting them to promise not to go through with it, until he gave the signal."

"Go through with what? Mamá, couldn't you understand him?"

Wrong thing to say to Mother Celia. Even in her nervousness, she could remind me, "*Hija*, I've spoken English for more years than you. I understood the man. He said 'Don't go through with it,' until he told them to. That he had some matters to take care of, then they could get on with their own work."

MacGunther was kind enough to offer my mother and son a flight back to Los Angeles. But we had decided to stay together; too much forced time apart, we just did not want to be in separate cities. MacGunther had to have me interviewed by his agents. We chose to stay until that was over with.

Again, I was on the phone to Pearl. "What did you tell Fisher?"

"That Tekún had kidnapped us both, had taken us blindfolded to an undisclosed location. Remember he used red and black blindfolds."

"What, red for you, black for me, or the other —"

"No, no. Red and black, in the same cloth."

"Like flannel?"

"Good grief, Romilia. Just remember, red and black. It's a good detail. He separated us once we got to the destination. Use the house we were in—I pretty much described it like that, only that he kept you in one room, me in another. He hardly spoke with me. Spent more time with you."

"Could I hear you?"

"Not a peep. Nor I you."

"You're good at this."

She said nothing.

When my time came to be interviewed, I followed suit: We were kidnapped by Tekún. He held us for three days, after using these black and red bandannas to blind us, keep us from seeing where we were going. He separated us. No, he didn't violate me in any way. Yes, he did show overtures to me. But no physical or sexual abuse.

MacGunther was my interviewer. He seemed confused by this. No doubt he had heard the rumors. But a mistrust also flipped into his eye. "Why do you think he abducted you?"

I told a truth, "He wanted to protect me. From whoever has him now."

"I see. What about your family? Have any idea who took them?"

"I think it was the Crack Killer."

MacGunther looked at me. He smiled. "The Crack . . . you mean that guy the whole drug world is . . . isn't that just folklore?"

"I don't think so, sir."

"I thought he only killed dealers. Why would he kill Chip?"

"To bring Tekún out, into the light. To hunt Tekún Umán down."

"I see. So you're telling me this Crack Killer, whom no one has ever seen, goes around killing drug dealers. But then he decided to kill a Federal Agent, Pierce, in a way that looks like Murillo did it. Because, as rumor has it, Murillo was jealous about you and Pierce. Right?"

"That, yes, that's right."

MacGunther looked at me. He glanced over at the digital camera that was recording this interview. Then he looked at me again. "Okay. I think that'll do it for now, Agent Chacón."

"Wait, sir."

"Yes?"

"I think there's something else you should know."

I told him all I could about Ojalá, and Chip's incipient investigation of that group, about the graffiti, the word found in every photo, including the photos taken after Olive Street.

"What does this have to do with Tekún?" he said.

"I don't know if it does. But when I talked with the woman at the Ojalá Church, she was very, blatant about it."

"What Ojalá Church?"

Whoops.

But it was too late. So I worked around the time line. "The one in Tijuana. Her name is Virginia Roberts."

"You were assigned to Tijuana?"

"Yes."

"When?"

"Sometime last week. No, week before last, I think. I've lost track of time," I said, and I chuckled with that, hoping he would put together some dots, *Kidnapped, held for three days, she's addled*.

He was writing this down. He did not flinch, which I thought was a good sign. "So you're saying to me that Chip Pierce was onto this Ojalá fundamentalist organization. Then he was murdered by the Crack Killer. Because . . .?"

"Because I think the Crack Killer is working with Ojalá."

"I see. Why?"

"He's funding them."

"With what money?"

"Drug money."

MacGunther scratched his bald head and decided to be honest. "I don't get it."

"The Crack Killer takes down drug dealers. He steals all their cash. He gives the money to Ojalá. This Ojalá movement was just a small group of nutcases before the Crack Killer started funding them. Now they've got money. They're more organized."

"And why would this Crack Killer want to give money to a terrorist organization?"

"Because he needs henchmen."

MacGunther looked at me straight on. Again, he didn't get it.

"The Crack Killer had several opportunities to kill Tekún Umán, but didn't, like he was playing with Tekún. I don't think he could have done all that cat-and-mouse without help. Those men who came out of the crowd, the guy who shot us with that electric water pistol, I'll bet they were members of Ojalá. And what's more, I bet that's why the Crack Killer murdered Pierce, because Chip was getting close to exposing the Ojalá organization. The Crack Killer couldn't have that, because he'd lose his crew."

"Wow, Agent Chacón," said MacGunther. "That's a lot to chew on."

He said nothing for a moment, just finished writing a note. His cell phone rang. He took the call, said, "Let's take a break, meet here in half an hour," and walked out of the room.

I walked out of the building to a coffee shop next door and called Pearl. "Your friend in Tijuana, the evangelical preacher . . ."

"Hermano Javier," said Pearl. Our phone connection was crackly.

"Right. Javier. He said something about having a church up here in San Francisco. And that they knew something about Ojalá."

"Right. What about it?"

"Know their address?"

"Who, the Ojalá nutcases?"

"No, no. Javier's people. That church."

"Hang on a second." She turned, either to her computer or to an address book. "It's downtown. On Howard, between Fourth and Fifth. Down from the Moscone Center."

"Thanks."

"Romilia? I think they're catching up."

Meaning Fisher. Meaning MacGunther had talked with my boss in the past thirty minutes or so. Maybe that's who he was talking with now. "What's going on?"

"Fisher just asked me if I knew when you were down in Tijuana."

Shit. "What did you say?"

"I said I didn't know about that. I said maybe you had gone before we started working together, sometime last week."

Last week. A lot had happened in, what? Five, six days.

"Good. Keep it like that. Do me a favor, look into Chip's files, anything about Ojalá. I know he had pictures of places that Ojalá had targeted. See if there's anything on Ojalá and possible attacks on San Francisco."

"Why San Francisco?"

"I don't know, but according to my mother, the Crack Killer's barely keeping them from going through with some new plans. I'm sure it's an attack of some sort, here in the city."

We hung up. I walked out of the coffee shop. MacGunther would expect me in ten minutes, which gave me a moment to stand on the sidewalk and think before I went in for the rest of his debriefing.

It was cold in San Francisco, though the sun had broken through clouds. People wrapped up in jackets and sweaters talked on their cell phones with one hand and buried the other in their coat pockets. It was windy as well; a colder, windier town than Los Angeles. Different in many ways. Of course, I was in a nice part of town, with a Civic Center across the street, office buildings around me, coffee shops and restaurants that made the bulk of their money off the business-lunch crowds. Like that couple, just down from me, coming out of the coffee bar. One guy had just hung up a phone. The other fellow kissed him, and they parted from each other.

Attacks. I thought of attacks. On cities.

In Las Vegas, a Planned Parenthood. Semtex found on the premises, plastique bombs ready to go off. In Montgomery, a similar bomb found on the premises of the Southern Poverty Law Center. In Los Angeles, the home of prostitutes, blown up.

Hatred, aimed at people who defended a woman's right to choose; hatred toward those who fought for civil rights, for racial rights—specifically, for those who advocated mixed marriages, or miscegenation. Hatred, for prostitutes.

Three different issues. All the same hate.

San Francisco. Where men hold hands, safely. Where they give each other good-bye kisses for the day.

Back in the building I looked for MacGunther, found him talking with an agent outside his office. The other agent excused himself and left.

"Okay, Agent Chacón. Let's continue." He ushered me back into our room.

I asked, "Agent MacGunther, is there a human rights group of some sort in San Francisco?"

"I'm sure there are several. What, do you mean like Amnesty International?"

"No, more local. You know, a group that would advocate the rights of homosexuals. Gay rights groups?"

He grinned, and it almost became a laugh; but he restrained himself. "Romilia, you do know what town you're in, don't you?"

"I know. But I was just wondering, is there like a focal point for the gay community? You know, a place that could be a target?"

He understood. "Castro Street historically has always been the place. It's where the gay rights movement really took off, then it became a place to organize around the AIDS epidemic. Lots of shops, nonprofit organizations there."

"Could they be possible hits?"

"What, like what Agent Pierce was after? In Montgomery and Las Vegas?"

"Yes."

Again, he chuckled; but it was more a sense of losing focus. "I don't know, Romilia. San Francisco, all of it . . . well, it's just very, very liberal, you know? If you're looking for a target for some domestic right-wing terrorist group, you can take your pick of places."

This thought, though swirling in my head, was not going any-where. "Okay, thanks, sir."

"You planning on going anywhere?"

"What? No, just check out some places here in the city."

"You know, you're not on your turf."

"I realize that, sir. I just would like to follow up on some things that Chip had been looking into."

"I see. Which was why you were in Tijuana. By the way, Special Agent in Charge Fisher and I have been talking quite a bit this morning. Playing a little phone tag. Lettie tells me she never had you go to Tijuana on assignment."

They were friends. Colleagues, of course, as both of them were SACs. He called her Lettie. I bet she called him Brucey.

"Tekún took you there, didn't he?"

I didn't say anything.

He looked at the door, as if to make sure it was closed. "Why am I getting this sense that your vision's blurred about this guy?"

"He didn't kill Chip Pierce, sir."

"How can you be so sure?"

I told him about the missing accent on Chip's stomach.

"I see. And that's enough?"

"No. Tekún's been kidnapped, I'm sure by the man who killed Chip."

"You're sure. So sure that you haven't considered that this kid-napping of your mother and son, all for the swap-out of Tekún, isn't some other cartel that wants to take Tekún out of their competition?"

The more I argued for Tekún, the more it was looking like I was his subjective lover.

"Did Tekún abduct you? Take you to Tijuana? Or did you go looking for him?"

"No. He had me picked up. He had me kidnapped."

"By whom?"

A pause. Then: "His workers. His boys."

"Took you and Pearl both."

"Yeah."

MacGunther was a head taller than me. He sighed, looked over my head down the hallway. "All right," he said. "I think you need to get on home now." His vaguely Alabamian accent came forth. "Special Agent Fisher's really anxious to get together with you and Agent Pearl. We'll get you and your family home as soon as we can." He smiled, got up, and left the door open as he exited the room.

All of which was Bureau administrative-speak for: *You're wacko, girl. That Tekún Umán abducted you and did things to you to either brainwash you or scare you into believing his tale. You're enamored with him, sure enough.* Here, I had done it: I had told the truth, or part of the truth, as best I could, while also trying to save Pearl's position for as long as she wanted it saved. And for that, MacGunther thought I was the Patty Hearst of the drug world.

So I walked out that door. I held confidence in my Bureau: I knew they would take care of my mother and son. They would follow procedure: make sure Mamá and Sergio ate well, rested, then get them to the airport, where I said I would meet them. I would meet them there, but I'd say good-bye to them and turn around. It all made sense to me: While my mother and child flew home, I, with all the skills of rationalizing that I could muster, would start looking for the man who had handed himself over to save my family.

At the airport, Mamá looked straight at me. "What do you mean you're not going?"

"You both need to go home," I said, and kissed Sergio on the forehead.

"What about you?"

"I'll be along soon. I just need to check some things out."

"You're going to look for him, aren't you?"

She said this with anger. She looked at me hard. I said nothing. So she kept going, "You know what I want, don't you?"

"Yes, Mamá. I know."

"So why don't you think about it?"

"Come on, *púchica,* we've been through this—"

"And your son's been through all *this.* Think about him."

She had pulled me away while saying this. Sergio stayed to one side, pretending to look at a *San Francisco Chronicle* headline, but really hearing every single thing we said.

"What, Mamá? I'm going to work for Chepe, then? Cook for the stars for the rest of my life?" I laughed, but nothing here was funny.

She stared at me. Longer than I was comfortable with. "Let me tell you something. I've lost one daughter. And I've been afraid of losing my other daughter. I haven't accepted that, but I've seen that it just might be inevitable. Almost lost you to that *pendejo* Minos—my God, he could have taken both my girls away." She got quiet, willing herself not to cry; she turned sadness into rage, like only a Salvadoran can. "But I'll tell you this right now, Romilia: If

I lose my grandson on account of your *jodido* desire to right the world, well, I'll never forgive you."

I heard all that. Then I put her on board, right in first class, in two of the three nice seats that MacGunther had bought for us. But I didn't just leave. No — I was responsible. "I'm Special Agent Romilia Chacón. I've put my mother and son on the plane, but the Field Office here has called me back, so I will not be boarding, if someone else would like to use this seat. I have no bags checked." I handed the attendant my ticket, after showing my badge and identification. They were pleased with that, in these days of higher security. After making sure I indeed had no bags checked, they let me leave. I walked out of the airport, rented a car, and drove back into San Francisco. Not back to the FBI Field Office, but to a small evangelical church downtown.

Tekún remembers the day he graduated from the Kaibiles, the Special Forces of the Guatemalan Army. It was a simple ceremony. The senior class all jumped into the river that ran through the camp. The officers started shooting as the cadets swam upstream. Those who made it to the finish line without getting shot, graduated. Those who did not, floated away.

It had been a hot day in September. He dove deep the first time, and touched the bottom of the river, from where he could make a quick reconnaissance: watch his mates, watch the bullets that pierced the water and slowed, three, four feet down. He had to think of two fundamental things: his lungs and the bullets. He formed a strategy—Stay away from the soldiers who panicked and bunched together too much, as they were easy targets. Those were the ones the officers wished to weed out: Those who would panic. The others, like Tekún, strategized quickly. Watch the bullets, watch the movement of the entire class. Plan accordingly. Tekún saw the trajectory he had to make: seven feet under the water, and swim like mad until he reached the finish line.

Which was a hundred yards upstream. Too far for one breath. Here, strategy had to succumb to chance. He pushed from the bottom, broke the water with his head, gasped, sucked in air, and went down again, just as an officer put a bead on him and shot. The bullet cut the water a foot from his face.

It worked well. Three times up, he could make it to the finish line. The strategy kept his mind busy, for years on end: Just reach that line, you'll graduate.

He remembers that, in the depth of the water, he escaped the heat of the Guatemalan jungle above him. In the swift, cold blast of current that ran along the bottom of the riverbed, he had never felt more awake, more alive.

He wonders if age has allowed him to see under that water once more. To feel, once again, how long he could withstand holding his breath, ready at one instant to blow it out, just blow it all out and suck in water and be done with it. Better than getting shot in the flank and left to float downriver, where his blood would be picked up by a wide assortment of predators, none of them human. He saw a fellow student, a guy named Enrique, who had done well throughout the weeks of training but who had acted a bit erratic as of late. Enrique had dived, but had gone up for air one too many times and there he was: two feet down, and the shots cut the water and pierced him. Enrique thrashed a few seconds longer, until his windmill arm movements slowed, and his heart, thumping with the energy only a good swim and a good panic can rouse up in a man, pumped blood from his back and into the current.

Tekún can remember men like Enrique now. This is a regret. The training, while leaving certain teachings permanent in him — the control of another person's fear; where to hit a man to kill him instantly, or not so instantly — cannot leave him completely inhuman. Mothers die. Godfathers get killed. A man like Tekún gets older, and tires of old ways. Sometimes there is temptation to run from all this, change his ways. A desire to be broken? A wish to break away from certain choices.

It's not the pain that makes him remember all this. The plastic handcuffs hold his arms wide apart and up, like Jesus blessing a crowd, his wrists cut with the splinters of the rafters. He is stripped to nothing, his clothes in a pile on a table. And not the abandonment; that, in some ways, leaves him almost tranquil. When the man's not in the room, it's better.

Perhaps it's the man who makes for the regret. Not fear of the man, but who he is: a past acquaintance of Tekún Umán.

Carl Spooner holds Tekún's Sorcerer Apprentice, the ten-ounce stainless-steel knife, shaped like a Harpy with its tip curving into a clean, needlelike hook. Spooner holds the knife by its jade handle, as if to stab Tekún. But this is just a desire. He then palms the blade. "I won't do what you did to me," he says. "I won't." He bends over slightly, and barely pops the curved tip into the skin of Tekún's thigh. Tekún doesn't even kick, can't kick, not with his ankles tied with rope to a metal ring in the old wood floor.

They are superficial wounds, though Tekún jerks from each piercing. But it's just enough to open the skin in long, clean cuts. Carl Spooner cuts as if out of duty, finishing up some strange ritual that's in his head. He carefully moves the blade over the back of Tekún's thighs, puts a few lines up and down his calves. He puts a few on Tekún's shoulders as well. "The branches," he says. He almost laughs. At first the blade is too sharp to be felt; but then the skin opens, wind hits the nerves inside. Tekún does not scream, though a moan slips out of him.

There are phone calls: Carl speaking to someone about a go-ahead, soon, just keep your hotheads from doing anything yet, "Don't jump the gun like your asshole buddies in L.A. It should be set for sundown." He hangs up. Though there is a curtain over the lone window of the room, Tekún can tell that it is afternoon, from the white rays of light that sneak around back of the curtain.

"Do you know why I did this?" says Carl, gesturing with the knife to Tekún's cut legs, his shoulders and biceps. "Prove a point. That's all. To prove to you what you are."

Carl goes outside. A vehicle door opens, closes again. He comes back in with a large wooden shipping box and a second, smaller box atop it. He places the smaller box to one side and opens the larger one. "You know what this is, right?" he says. He pulls one of the frogs out. A deep red frog, with black speckles. He walks up to Tekún, puts the frog close to his face. "Recognize it? Come on, answer me."

Tekún says nothing.

"Similar to the poison that you used on me. Yours was just the extract. And I suppose the Guaranee have their own way of reducing its toxicity. They don't use it just for hunting, you know. Medicines. Pain blockers. Better than morphine. But this isn't an extract. It's pure Dentrobatidae."

Carl takes a small butter knife from his box. He scrapes it

across the back of the frog. The frog tries to escape, and turns more wet, lucid, releasing more of its own slick sweat; it reflects the light from the lone bulb. "There it is," he says. "You can eat it, it won't hurt you. In fact, it'll deaden some of the pain in those cuts. Here. Go ahead. Eat it."

Tekún turns his head. But Carl insists. He holds Tekún's jaw with one hand, pries his teeth open with the butter knife and insists.

"You won't die from this. You don't have ulcers, do you? No, not you."

The slits in Tekún's legs and arms stop pulsing so hard. Something numbs them, soothes them.

Carl turns away, then pushes himself to say more. "That's what you are, you know. Just like the frogs. That's what all your business partners are. Drug lords, cartels. You're poison. Poison for us all. Look what it does to us."

Carl walks to the window and opens the curtain wide. The sun is bright above the Golden Gate Bridge. The bridge is so huge, close, right in front of them, towering over this building like a Titan. Carl is tired of metaphors. "I just want you to see what your drug money does to our country. Poisons our kids, our young people. Kills whole families, shit!"

It is as if a sane man fights through the thick membrane of one who is lost. Carl turns to the table, tips the wooden box over. The frogs jump and roll over one another, falling to the floor, hopping across the wood table. Dozens of them, spilling out in red and blue and yellow.

"They're tree frogs. Know why they call them that? They hide in the trees, whenever they're hunted." From the second box, Carl reaches in and pulls out a small constrictor: nonpoisonous, just big enough to wrap around Carl's forearm. He walks to the door, opens it, then peels the snake away and flings it to the floor. The frogs react; they head to the only tree in the room, the man spread and hanging from the rafters. Carl slams the door. From the outside, he yells, "There. Let's see how long it takes poison to kill *you*, you son of a bitch." And that is the sane man's voice.

Carl leaves the room.

Tekún concentrates on two fundamental things: the frogs, glistening with fear as they leap away from the snake and toward him across the wooden floor; and the young man up on the Golden Gate Bridge, who crawls over the side and walks carefully along a thin catwalk, positions himself, then shakes a can of spray paint up and down.

I had never seen so many homeless in one place. Either it was because the city, all bunched in like it was, also bunched up the people without houses or apartments; or something attracted all these men and women to downtown San Francisco.

On the same block where tourists grabbed hold of the poles on the trolley cars, black and white men sat at a string of card tables and played chess. Small piles of bills stood to the sides of each set, no doubt the money put down for the bet, which would get them through a night of drink or food. Next to them, shopping carts loaded with tightly folded blankets and plastic tarps. Nearby, a woman, just a bit older than me, white, sat at the corner of Market and Fifth, embroidering a scarf, talking down to her chest, "Please be so kind, give a woman with three kids something to get her through the night, please be so kind, give a woman with three kids . . ." Four men approached me before I reached the evangelical church. The last one was the most belligerent: "Yeah, fine-lookin' bitch come walking down *my* street and won't even bother to look my *way* much less toss me a dollar she ain't even used to wipe her *ass* with."

That broke the victim-image of poverty. I turned and had my badge in his face before he could blink.

"Sorry, Officer. No offense."

"What's your name?"

"Claude, Officer."

"Claude. I'm looking for a church, Claude."

"What kind? Catholic? Presbyterian?"

"Fundamentalist."

"What, you got religion?"

"An evangelical church, around here somewhere."

"Must mean the Saintly Word Church. It's around the corner."

Claude and I walked around that corner. He took me down the street. Claude was nice, when he wasn't cursing the bystanders who passed him without paying his toll. He somewhat apologized for his tactic. "You know, sometimes a man's got to use what he got to get through the night. Me, that's my skin color. Whites scared to death of it in the first place. So's I got my rap, adds to the flavor, shakes a boy down some, he gives more."

"You ever try the nice approach?"

"On Tuesdays. Yeah."

He told me a bit about the church before we arrived. "Pastor Menster, he's good people. Takes care of a lot of folks here. Mostly dope heads. I don't do any of that. Little liquor now and then. Especially when it's cold like this," he said, and he shivered for me. He was good.

Inside, Claude introduced me to the young girl at the front desk. She looked like college, some kid from Berkeley who was interested in Social Work and got this job through an internship program. "Hi, Claude. How are you?" A chipper voice; she sounded newly ordained.

"Hey, Brittany, this lady's with the F-B-I," said Claude.

"Oh, wow. Something the matter?"

I showed my badge, asked for the pastor in charge; as an extra credential, I said, "I'm an acquaintance of Brother Javier down in Tijuana."

"Oh, he's wonderful, isn't he?" said Brittany. "He was up here last month, giving a talk about their work on the border at the *maquiladoras*. He's really inspiring."

"Yeah, he is. Listen, is your boss in?"

"Brother Menster won't be in until later on. He does the evening watch this week, helps people settle in for the night."

That was too late to wait. It was already three in the afternoon, and I had no idea what could be happening, right now, to Tekún.

I looked around, out the front window of the small church, which had once been a Walgreens. Claude had sat down at one of the chairs in the waiting area and had picked up an old *Time* magazine.

"How long you been here, Brittany?" I said.

"About three months."

"You ever heard about a church called Ojalá?"

"Ojalá . . . that sounds Arabic, wait, isn't that a Spanish word?"

"Yeah. It is." But the look on her face showed she had no clue. "Not a church, no. Haven't heard of it."

"What you looking for?" Claude spoke from the waiting chair.

"Hang on a second," I said to him, then turned back to Brittany. "When I was in Tijuana, I heard about a church called the Ojalá. It was setting up a place across the border. I heard they had a church up here as well." I was floundering; there was no proof of this group except for that bitch in Tijuana. Her blatancy showed that she had no fear of me; what would her companions here, in the States, show me right now? They seemed hidden, too hidden to even exist.

"Ojalá? You mean O-*ha*-la, don't you?"

That was Claude, behind me. *Time* magazine in hand.

Claude liked bourbon, and I told him I did, too. But for now, Starbucks, and one of what Claude called their "funky sandwiches."

"Ohala. They're pretty new," he said. "Been walking around us, oh, two-three months now. I'm permanent San Francisco homeless. I know my streets."

"What do they do?"

"What a lot of those evangelical churches do. Promise you a warm meal if you go in and listen to their bullshit. Well, Brother Menster ain't like that, over at Saintly Word. He treats you with respect. He's also on the advisory council of the Housing Committee. Real activist."

"But what about this Ohala group, are they fundamentalist Christian, or what? It sounds Hawaiian."

He laughed at that. "No. Not Hawaiian. It's white folks who talk about Allah." He looked at me as if that should have shocked me.

"Go on."

"You see, at first I was confused. I went to one of their prayer meetings. Shit, the guy on the street gave me twenty dollars, said I'd get another *fifty* if I went and listened to the preachings. Fifty! So I went. They held it in one of those rental halls, down off Market. They started going on about Allah. I thought they were a bunch of white boys trying to get in good with the Niggahs, know what I'm saying? Young white boys talking with black people, trying to get to them through some of the Nation of Islam preachings. Which seemed crazy to us all, because only maybe half of us was black. But they had shitloads of money, so we stayed. And it wasn't Nation of Islam stuff, no, that wasn't it. They were, I don't know, kinda wild."

"Define 'wild'."

"Well, they were talking about that jihad stuff. You know. Holy War. Taking the holy war to the streets, changing America, bringing it back to what it used to be, whatever the hell that was. How our fundamentalist brothers over in other countries had it right, that it was time to bring on a Crusade again, right here in America. Then they got started on the government, how it's abandoned us homeless folks. Well, I couldn't disagree with that."

"What else?"

"That was about it. They finished up, gave us each a fifty-dollar bill, and we left."

"How many people were there?"

"Hell, I don't know. Maybe seventy, eighty men. A few women too, yeah."

"That's a lot of money."

"I'm telling you. They're nicely loaded, as they say in the Lexus ads."

"So they just hand out money, you listen. Then you leave. Seems to me they've lost out."

"They always get a few."

"A few what?"

"You know. Some don't leave. Some stay."

I leaned across the table. "Go on."

"Hell, Detective, you get a bunch of men together, all of them hungry, thirsty, needing a shot of something. You give them money, that's like instant hope. Know what I'm saying?"

"I think I do. But explain it to me."

"Groups like that, they don't worry about persuading everyone. All's they're looking for is a few boys who are willing to go whole hog for them. And believe you me, you'll find it out here. Lot of lost people. Desperate. And pissed off. Yeah. How you think the Moonies, or any other wacko group like that, get people to join?"

"Homeless people."

"Homeless. Drug addicts. Anybody who's lost. And college students. That's who was running the meeting, by the way. College boys. Just by how they talked, you could see that. They'd swallowed all that jihad shit hook, line, and sinker."

Claude was more than I had given him credit for just an hour ago, when all I saw in him was the homeless. "Ohala got an address?"

"You might want to check that hall, down off Market." He gave me the address.

I slid a twenty-dollar bill across the Starbucks green, round table. "Wild Turkey's my favorite label. Just a suggestion."

He took the bill, looked at me. "Should I wait up for you?" He smiled.

The hall that Claude pointed me toward stood between a Thai restaurant and a small bookstore. Both were open. The hall was closed. Through the large storefront window I could see that there was nothing inside, just some shelves, a waiting room, a kitchenette. The larger room, where Claude and the seventy other homeless men had gathered, must have been in the back somewhere. But there was no way back there. The building had no alleyway between it and the restaurant or the bookstore.

The more I lingered in front of the store, the more I knew I stood out, to anyone watching the place. I ducked into the Thai restaurant and ordered a small pot of black tea.

There I sat, trying to make decisions.

My mother and son were home now. Safe. Hanging out with my uncle Chepe. All of them cursing me for my chosen line of work.

My cell phone rang; the display showed Agent Fisher's number. I made to answer it and, whoops, hit the Silence button.

Soon another call, from a 415 area code number. I was willing to bet the field office not far from here.

"Shit," I said. They were all looking for me now, having figured out I had not flown back to Los Angeles. So I answered the 415 call. "Chacón."

"You're still in my city, aren't you, Agent Chacón?"

"Yes sir," I said to MacGunther. "I didn't quite make my flight."

"Where are you?"

I gave him the address.

"Why?"

"Because I think that group, Ojalá, they might have a dumping hole here, a meeting place. I think they're—"

"No. Why are you trying to save him?"

"I'm not just trying to save Tekún Umán, sir. I think this group is up to something. A terrorist hit on San Francisco. If Chip was right about this Ojalá Church—"

"This is your hunch. Not necessarily Agent Pierce's. And whatever you know, you should just hand it over to our Counter-terrorism Squad. Come on in, Romilia."

I was about to fall into that "You're breaking up" routine with the cell phone; but something told me not to. Something, I don't know . . . mature. Maybe his CT Squad could do something with this place, with the Ojalá leads. "Yes sir," I said.

"I'll have someone pick you up."

"All right."

He hung up. I sat and finished the tea.

Which made me ask for the bathroom. It was a small restaurant, a very clean hole-in-the-wall kind of place. I asked the proprietress, a young Thai woman who not only was the cook but who had also served my tea, if I could use their toilet. She led the way to the back of the building and pointed to the unisex bathroom.

It was clean, so I didn't bother putting paper on the seat. I washed my hands and dried them and saw, once more, Tekún, shattered with electricity, on the sidewalk in the Mission. Men running around, grabbing him. A white guy, a black man, and another who might have been Asian. The guy who had shot him with the electric water gun, he was white.

Three men coming out of the crowd. Ready for when Tekún got hit with the current. Ready to whisk him away.

Well planned. Organized. Different ethnic groups . . .

Racial superiority. Racial purity. That's what the Ojalá group in Montgomery wanted. That's why they had targeted the Southern Poverty Law Center. Maybe a neo-Nazi party. All white, no doubt.

Las Vegas. Planned Parenthood. Nothing said about race. All about abortion. Kill the doctors who kill the fetuses.

San Francisco. Men of different colors, kidnapping Tekún. In San Francisco. Where men kiss on the street. Where that is ordinary.

Ojalá. Fundamentalist Muslim. Fundamentalist Christian. Jihad. Crusade. Holy War.

Funded by drug money. Collected by the Crack Killer. Someone who hated drug runners. Who hated Tekún Umán.

Who hated Tekún Umán? Maybe better to ask, how many hated him?

I remembered a day three years ago, during the hunt for Minos, when a group of DEA agents stormed Tekún Umán's hideout in New Orleans. They hated him, and wanted to kill him, because he had hurt one of their own: Carl Spooner.

A renegade DEA official, maybe?

"This is really fucked up," I said to the sink.

Which perhaps was why I turned right out of the bathroom, instead of left, which would have taken me to the front of the restaurant. Right took me to the nice restaurant lady's back door, which would take me to her back lot, which I hoped would . . . yes.

A back lot shared with the back lots of the bookstore and the empty storefront house.

MacGunther's man, sent to pick me up and drive me to the airport, would be here soon. I could wait for him. We'd go in together.

I tried the door. It was locked. As if I could have expected anything else.

From the restaurant I heard the proprietress's voice, "Hello, Juan, good to see you, you want your tea?"

"Oh no, thanks, Miss Kim," said Juan. Latin name, California accent. Both were still in the kitchen. "I'm in a little bit of a hurry."

"You boys always in hurry, getting ready to see girlfiends, I am sure." And they both chuckled.

"That's right, yes ma'am," said Juan. He stepped through the back door and into the lot and saw me. I knew Juan, from the corner of Mission and Twentieth Street.

I knocked down three of Miss Kim's pots (one of them filled

with rice) while chasing him through her kitchen. She yelped in Thai. She may have been following us both, until I shucked my gun out of its holster and yelled for him to stop. She screeched, and stayed back.

But Juan ran. Through the front door, turned left, and sprinted down Market Street.

"Ay *hijo de la gran* . . ." I bolted down the street as well. And though he was younger than I, and thin, I was faster, so I didn't have to aim my gun at him and risk taking out one of the people we passed. I grabbed him by the nape of his neck and used his own velocity against him: He rammed through two garbage cans on his way down.

Now I had a fine aim, standing over him. "Where is the bomb?" I said between gasps.

"What? What bomb? Lady, you got the wrong guy." He shielded his face with his forearms, a fine way to stop a bullet.

"Your boss. Where is he?"

He didn't say anything.

"Juan! Answer the question."

"He's a faggot!"

I was confused. "Okay. So you boss is . . . gay?"

"No! Not the man! That guy. He's a fucking queer. He fucks men, he fucks boys."

This made me lean over to him, close to his pretty Latin face, his moussed hair, leather jacket, and a redolent cologne. "What guy?"

Juan said nothing.

"Latin guy?" I said.

Juan looked at me.

"Tall? Well dressed? The guy you kidnapped in the Mission?"

"He's a faggot. You can tell."

"That what your boss tell you?"

Juan kept quiet. There was a rage in his eye, a righteous one. Which scared me.

"Who's your boss?"

"Just some guy."

"What's he look like?"

"Tall, kind of, and blond. He's got all the money."

"Okay, and what did he tell you to do?"

"I just delivered a box. That's all."

"Of what? Explosives? Don't tell me you don't know what Ojalá's doing, Juan. Come on, you been painting little tags somewhere I should know about?"

"They were frogs."

I pulled back. "Frogs."

"Yeah. A box of frogs."

"What kind of frogs?"

"I don't know, he just told me they were frogs, and to bring them to him."

"Where were the frogs before you delivered them?"

"Down at the docks, below the Wharf."

"Any drugs with the frogs, Juan? Or explosives?"

"What? No, man. Carl doesn't mess with drugs."

"What? Carl?"

"Yeah, that's his name, that's all I know."

"Carl—Carl Spooner? Juan?"

"I said I don't know his last name!"

I was breathing shallowly, and remembering facts, phone calls with a DEA agent in D.C., about Carl Spooner being dead. But now, his death would be the only inconsistency in this entire picture.

But Juan seemed to know nothing about that. I said, "So, you didn't find that strange, delivering a box of frogs to your boss?"

"Listen lady, okay, okay . . . I've heard some things, all right? One off the other guys said Carl was all pissed off because he lost some frogs before. That he had them in a holding tank in that building down in Los Angeles, that got blown up. Some guy named Cowboy used to use the building for storage."

"You've heard a lot, Juan." I held him by the back of his throat. I tightened my grip a bit, lowered my gun so he could see the barrel.

"You got to believe me! Carl lost his frogs, so he had to order some new ones from Bolivia or Colombia or somewhere. And Jesus, they're just frogs, man!"

"Listen. Juan. Your boss is planning to murder Tekún Umán, if he hasn't already." And with that, I swallowed a bit. "That makes you an accessory. Those frogs you delivered? They're the Black Widow of the Amazon."

This woke him up a bit. Which told me that Juan here was not as plugged in to the whole Ojalá movement as I had thought. He helped the pro-hetero movement in his own little way. Juan was a lackey. A gopher. He delivered materials. Maybe went out and got the bosses, like Virginia Roberts, their cappuccinos. Got the frogs to the right place. But he didn't set bombs. Which meant, though he hated gays, and no doubt hated himself just a wee bit, he had yet to become a killer.

"You need to take me there," I said. "If Tekún's not dead, you'll be a lot better off. Why, I bet you could even finish off your college degree at Berkeley by next spring."

He looked at me, startled, in awe, as if I were the Salvadoran Sherlock Holmes of the West Coast. "Yeah . . . yeah . . . okay." So I reached out my hand and took his to help him up; you know—the hand with the U of Berkeley ring on it, and next year's graduating class.

We drove away, in Juan's nice Lexus. Before my FBI pickup arrived.

The sun had not set yet, but it felt colder. Young Juan drove obe-diently through the city, taking streets that I knew nothing about, though I had heard of them before. Lafayette Park. Union Street. I couldn't enjoy them very much now, not with the thought *It's already too late* running through my head, along with Juan's self-reassuring voice saying over and again, "So, Detective, you're sure I won't get in trouble for this. . . . I mean, my parents, they don't know nothing about me being in this group, and I thought it was just a Christian group, you know, like that other one, Real Men for Christ, which helps men who are gay turn straight? Not that I'd need that, that's why I didn't join that one . . . I learned about Ojalá in a place outside of the college, really cool group, and they're *doing* something about all the faggot-rights stuff . . ."

"Anything."

"What?"

"'I don't know anything'."

"Oh. Yeah. Right."

"You're in college. You should speak better than that."

Why I said that, I wasn't sure, except that it shut him up a second. "Where is he?" I said.

"It's across the Bay. My boss was waiting for me at the parking lot on the other side. That's all I usually do, deliver packages."

"Where across the Bay?"

"Just below where people walk across the bridge."

"Which bridge, you mean the Golden Gate?"

"Yeah."

"I've never seen it before."

"Yeah well, you're about to see it now," he said, and he took the 101 to Doyle Drive, where the arch of the bridge took up the windshield. For just a moment, I could almost forget the issues at hand, my friend in trouble, a terrorist group, and see the magnificence of a structure that I had only seen before in pictures.

But then I thought *terrorist*. I asked my new buddy, "Juan, wasn't there a terrorist threat on the bridge a while back?"

"Yeah, sometime last year. The governor said that someone was planning to fly a plane into it."

"Just like New York, and Washington?"

"I guess so."

"What happened?"

Juan seemed to enjoy the change in conversation topics, from gays to al Qa'ida. "The army came out. Or I guess the National Guard. I'm not sure. But they checked the entire bridge. They were on alert for a while. It's calmer now."

"It's beautiful," I said.

"Yeah, it is," he said. "I've walked it a lot."

"You can walk it?"

"Oh, yeah. Sidewalk on the east edge. Lot of people there all the time. Lot of suicide jumpers, too."

"It's a hot spot for suicide?"

"Yeah. Yeah, it is. They've counted thousands of people jumping off it. Something about the bridge attracts depressed people to it. Maybe it's the fog, you know, when it rolls in? It's like you're jumping into the clouds, or into heaven."

He was into this more than I cared for.

"And no one lives. Well, maybe one in a thousand. It's a sure thing. You either freeze to death in the water. Or the impact breaks your legs. Or your head snaps back so hard, it locks your jaw open and the water rushes into you." He lifted his hand to the back of his head, slapped it, simulating the water slamming there on impact. "You drown, with your jaw locked open. That's a horrible image, isn't it? The city's wanted to build a suicide-prevention net, or something, to keep people from jumping. Nobody wants it. It'd take away from the bridge's beauty."

"You seem to know a lot about this."

"It's San Francisco folklore. People jump. For a while the papers were keeping a tally of how many individuals had committed suicide off it. Then, when it got close to two thousand, they say some folks jumped just to be the two-thousandth person."

"Really." But I was losing interest. Or wanted to lose interest.

"Yeah. I've thought about doing it."

I was not surprised. But I didn't want to be the one to fill in the blanks for him: He wanted to die, to get away from his own homosexuality. Strange, in this city, and this guy could be so scared.

Juan got quiet, probably thinking about his walks across the bridge and his many chances to have jumped, while I stared from one end of the bridge to the other, the smooth arch of the red cables, the towers that held those cables suspended in the air. We turned a corner and went through some woods, right as I saw, in all that almost blood-orange, a tiny interruption, a white stain of sorts, on the far end.

On the other side of the bridge, in Marin County, we parked in a tourist lot. People were getting out of their cars, snapping pictures, standing next to a tall statue of a navy man, maybe a captain, who looked out to the bay. There was a gift shop behind us, round, one of those early-twentieth-century endeavors to look futuristic. "You met him here?" I said.

"Yeah. Well, down below."

"Show me."

I followed Juan. "Over here," he said, and pointed down the hill.

Below us, there was another parking lot, but I couldn't tell if we had access to it or not. "Was he parked there?"

"I don't know. I met him, right about here." He stepped a good twenty feet away from the edge of our parking lot. Some people who were heading to the bridge looked at us, but then turned away, perhaps thinking we worked for the national park, or the county. Or maybe they just didn't want to get involved.

"Where did he go, after you gave him the box?"

"He just stood here. He watched me go away. I remember, I

turned around before I got in my car. He was still watching me. I thought that was kind of weird."

"Yeah."

Or it meant he didn't go far. He waited for Juan to leave, so Juan couldn't see where he went. This was not just a pickup place; he was here, somewhere nearby.

I stared everywhere around me: at the bridge, as it was the most enticing thing to look at, with all those hundreds of cars, trucks, vans driving across it, hundreds in a minute. Maybe a thousand. The entire bridge stood in my sight, with no cloud in the area, and no fog for miles. I had heard that sometimes during a day, the bridge disappears. Not today.

It was still daylight. But the sun was going down. Which would make all this much more difficult.

There, in the Bay, small sailing ships. Privately owned. A few cars in that lower area, but they must have belonged to workers, people who took care of the park. Nothing much here except that small peninsula that jutted out from the embankment, which had a wire fence cutting it off, and beyond that fence, a small, old building. It looked like an old, tiny fort. And it appeared abandoned. Which made my imagination run a bit, especially when I saw above it, on the bridge, that one white stain that was no stain, but words.

"Juan. Let me see your driver's license."

"What for?" But he obeyed. He took it out of his wallet and gave it to me.

"Thanks," I said, and pocketed it. "If I were you, I wouldn't leave town."

"I've got a test tonight."

"You may have to ask for extra credit. You stay near, okay?"

"What do I do?"

"Sit in your car. Wait for me."

I walked down the hill and dialed back MacGunther's number, the one I had ignored for much of the afternoon.

"Where are you?" He was angry.

"Sorry sir, but I had to follow up on something. Sir, I think the bridge is under attack."

"Which one, the Golden Gate or Bay Bridge?"

"Yeah . . . yes sir. Golden Gate."

"Why so?"

"Because it's been tagged, sir." I said this while still walking down the hill and getting closer to the little building and the bridge.

"Tagged? What the hell are you . . ."

"It says, 'Ojalá: death to the faggots'."

He didn't say anything to that.

"Sir?"

"Hold your position, Chacón. I'm sending the Squad."

I thought about Chip, and his theory, written in his notes: *Tags sprayed near all attempted bombings*.

"I'd hurry, sir. I don't think it will be long."

"Just stay where you are."

"Yes, sir." And then I didn't. I jogged down the hill, all the way to the fence. It was closed, but the padlock was undone. Which was a bad sign.

He was already dead.

Something I didn't want to believe. Even as I ran through the gate and to the window. I said his name aloud, calling to him, almost barking it: Tekún. Tekún Umán.

There was a lock on the old door, a new one, just bought. Inside, the sound of nothing.

I hid as best I could to one side of the door, shot the padlock twice before it sprung open. Broke through the door to see him in a way I had never imagined or ever wished to see again.

Tekún, tied to the rafters, lifting himself as if doing a pull-up. But he didn't hold the rafter; plastic cuffs held him there. His legs, bloody, thrashed in the air, then swung around. One rammed down and his foot smashed against the floor. A small pile of rope before him, a metal ring, with old wood around it: he had been tied to it, and somehow, with strength or panic, had ripped the ring out of the wood. And then the stench, something I had never smelt before. Acidic, reptilian. And then his voice — yes thank god there was his voice — saying something strange: *he didn't cut my soul*.

I couldn't tell who he was talking to. And I was thrown, by the stink of something newly dead: all those tiny carcasses, blue and green and yellow, piles of them, squashed, most of them under and around Tekún's naked feet. Naked, except for the goo of crushed frog.

Then I could understand his broken voice: "He didn't cut my soles."

I wanted to cover him, right there, take my coat and throw it over him. But I had to get him down first. Step over this mess of dead reptiles, cut him down, somehow, find a knife. "It's okay," I was saying, "I'll get you down, it's all right, Jesus, oh Christ . . ." And for that moment, I got lost, which meant that I cared, too much.

"My knife," he said, "in the box."

I found it: his infamous Harpy Knife, tossed into a corner of the box. I slit the thick, hard plastic and peeled the cuffs out of the bloody wedges in his wrists.

"I have to wash it off my feet," he said.

He walked over to a sink, sat on its edge, and put his feet in it. I turned on the water. Pure cold and rust at first. Then it cleared.

He had no cuts on the tops of his feet, though the rope had burned him when he tore the metal ring from the floor. But he showed me his hands, bloodied from the cuts in his wrists from the cuffs. "I can't, can't touch it," he said. "Give me my shirt."

I took his shirt from the table, but did not give it to him. Soon, hot water came through. I soaked the shirt and started wiping the tops of his feet, then the bottoms. The shirt was wadded up enough to keep the blood and skin and ooze from me.

He laughed.

"What?" I said.

"I've waited for this day for a long time. Me naked, and you washing my feet."

I scrubbed. "Funny, that particular fantasy never crossed my mind."

I gave him his pants. He tried to put them on over his legs, but couldn't; the pain and the blood were too much. "My, *ropa interi-*

or," he said, as if embarrassed to say "underwear." He pointed to the black Jockey on the chair. His leather jacket was gone.

I screamed. Really loud.

"What?" he said.

"There's a fucking snake in here!"

"Oh, yeah." His voice was pure exhaustion.

"Why didn't you kill it, for chrissake?"

"It's a constrictor, *mi vida.* It's not poisonous."

The snake moved across the floor and over the remnants of frogs. It was moving toward a red one, still alive.

"Get that," said Tekún. "The frog, get it."

"What, why?"

"It'll take the pain away . . ."

"What, you want me to pick up a fucking poisonous frog with a snake on its ass?"

"Neither will hurt you, I promise. Do you have any cuts on your hands?"

"No."

"Then you're safe. Please."

That was a plea. I hopped around the little carcasses, cursing and saying things to him that I'm sure he wouldn't ever forget: basically, about all the fucked-up situations he had a way of putting me in.

"Go ahead," he said, "pick it up."

I did. It slipped out from my hands. I tried again. The snake was confused. It backed off, but still wanted its dinner. I cursed it, then stepped back and brought the frog to Tekún.

"Just hold it," he said. He took his knife and placed the blade delicately upon the frog's back, then scraped the glisten off its skin. Then he placed the blade to his mouth.

I turned away.

A minute passed. "Yes," he said, "yes, that's much better." He scooted off the table.

"The bridge," I said.

"I know."

"I've called the CT Unit at the Bureau."

"They won't make it. Carl wanted me to see the explosion, before I died. I'm surprised it's not gone off already."

"Carl Spooner, right?"

Tekún looked at me with weary eyes. "Yes."

"He's supposedly dead."

"Apparently not."

"So, he faked his death? He became the Crack Killer?"

"Tekún nodded.

"From DEA agent to serial killer . . ."

"No," said Tekún. "He's a vigilante. I'm not surprised, really. When with the DEA, he wanted to be the next drug czar. Now he's the business's Night Stalker."

I looked through the window, at the Golden Gate. "The bomb on Olive Street was plastique, with a simple timer on it, and a metal rod shoved into the dough."

"Unplug the rod, it won't go off?"

"That's my hope. But where the hell on the bridge . . .?"

"I'd say right there," he said, pointing to the new graffiti.

"What, right where the tag is?"

"No. To the left of it. There was a construction crew there for the past two hours. But they left, quite abruptly, about thirty minutes ago."

We ran. Up the hill, where Juan still stood — good, scared boy that he was, not moving at all, just like I told him. And then I noticed something about Juan: That leather jacket of his looked awfully familiar.

"That's mine," said Tekún. He jerked it off the boy, like pulling clothes off a wispy mannequin, with Juan whining something about his boss giving it to him that afternoon.

Tekún put on the jacket. He still had no shoes, no socks or shirt. But he ran ahead of me, fast. I had never seen a man run like that. A man with cut legs, wearing leather, no shoes, black Jockey, running to the bridge.

I followed, then I was beside him. We ran onto the bridge, with tourists from Japan and Kansas City gawking at us, a strange couple surely for them, but hey, they could say, this was San Francisco. That's how it went for the first few seconds, running down the bridge's sidewalk, just past the first art deco tower. "Where were they?" I said.

Tekún looked over the edge of the bridge, toward the little house that had acted as his torture center. He gauged, and said, "That's Lime Point, where he had me." He looked around. "Right about here," he said.

All I saw were a row of trapdoors, measured out a good fifty feet between each; but when I reached down to open the one nearest me, I couldn't, for it was welded down, its handle held fast with gray solder. Every door was like that, both up and down the sidewalk. We ran toward the tower. There, orange construction paint surrounded a trapdoor whose soldering had been snapped. "That one," I said.

Tekún reached down, pulled the metal ring out of its pocket in the door, and wrenched it open. Right when somebody yelled, "Stop right there."

A cop, I thought. But no: He had on a uniform, but it was brown, the color of a park uniform. "Back away from the manhole, please."

But he had no gun. He had only the façade of authority. Which, for Tekún, meant little.

I heard another yell, saw a second man running toward us. Wearing jeans, looking somewhat pained for the sudden sprint. Then his voice, yelling, "Stop. FBI!" And he, holding up a badge, which I knew wasn't an FBI shield, but a DEA one. The tourists scattered and ran, too frightened to take time to study badges.

Tekún moved, trying to ignore the cuts over his legs; still, he grimaced, as if the cold wind bit into his skin. He wrenched the door open wide and jumped through the opening. I followed, though I used the ladder.

Carl Spooner dropped his old DEA badge and opened fire. The park ranger fell. Half his body dangled through the opening.

"Jesus Christ," I said, but I kept going, turning, going up and down, looking. This was a world I had never seen before, never should have seen: the underside of the Golden Gate Bridge. And damned if everything under here wasn't painted the same international red as the rest of the bridge. It was a labyrinth of tin sidewalks, a giant Erector set of steel rafters, bolt heads the size of baseballs, cables as thick as my arm. Everywhere I ran, balancing on this catwalk, trying not to look through the slits between the metal at the ocean water far below. Everything was red, except for that poor ranger's body behind me, his head barely swinging. That, and the duct tape, strapped over a wad of gray substance that had been carefully molded in a metal corner, tucked under what looked like the midline of the tower above us.

"Over here," I said.

Tekún got to me, though he looked back, negotiating Carl's movements. Carl working hard to move the dead ranger's large body from the hole.

Tekún stared at the wad of plastique. "That's . . . very little."

"It might be a high-glycerin compound," I said. "No, wait. It's a detonator. The digital watch is the battery."

"Yes. But still, it's not enough to take down this tower."

I tried to get closer without disturbing it. The square battery was wrapped in duct tape, with wires running from it. A cheap black digital watch head was strapped by its edges under the tape. It showed thirty minutes. No. Three.

"That little wad can't do much," he repeated himself.

He followed the two wires around the corner, to the north side of the tower.

"Oh. But this is enough. Yes, definitely."

I ducked over there and saw it: an entire thick line of plastique explosives, one after another, over a dozen. They lined the corner where the tower and the bridge's support beams met. Names came back to me from bomb training: Semtex. RDX. C4 plastique. Not homemade. All bought on the black market. And enough here to snap the tower in two.

But if it were C4, it would be very stable. I could have shot into a wad of the plastique, it wouldn't have gone off. It needed a detonator. "The first one," I said. "It's the fuse."

The ranger's body slipped through the hole back behind us and slapped hard against the catwalk. "You know how to undo it?" he asked.

"Yeah. I think."

"Do it," he said. I turned, and Tekún was gone, disappearing into the red, steel forest of the under-bridge.

I studied the detonator. It was as our Counterterrorist Unit had figured from Olive Street: a simple wiring, a metal rod plugged into the plastique. Two wires, running to the other side of the tower. The small watch, used as the trigger, counting down two minutes from now. "Okay," I said, to no one.

Spooner behind me. I could hear him, could hear the metallic

cocking of a gun. But I worked, first on the two wires, discon-
necting them from the battery, then against the duct tape, pulling
it slowly, slowly, just as they had taught us at Quantico, so damned
slowly while I sweat in the cold of this city's wind. The wad behind
the battery didn't look like C4, which meant it was less stable.
Why had they put explosives onto the detonator? Unless they
wanted to stop someone from defusing it. I kept working. I was
hidden, partially, behind this corner of the tower. There, I kept
peeling the bandage of tape away from the metal skin of the bridge.

The duct tape gave way. The mass of clay bent forward. I
palmed it, like a baby.

"Put it back," Carl said.

I held it there, in my hands, the digital still running backward,
the metal fuse still punched into the gray dough.

"Put it back."

"Carl, we need to get rid of this."

A helicopter approached us, followed by another. They hovered near the bridge, at our height. I could see them, could see the
pilot who was staring through the spaces below the sidewalk and
trying to point me out to the agent sitting next to him.
MacGunther.

Then came the sirens. Behind them, SWAT would run their
black trucks around traffic. People were leaving the bridge above
us. Running. Obeying orders from the police. Obeying their own
fear of dying.

And though I did not believe it, I held on to that slab of explosive before me and said, "It's over, Carl."

"He did all this."

"I know. I know he hurt you. Badly."

"No. He did all *this*." And Carl shot at the tower, close to the
line of explosives. The bullet ricocheted into the water.

"Come on, Carl. Let's get out of here, okay?"

"No. I won't."

He was weeping. But his face, it looked as if rage meant to tear
it from his skull.

"Where is he?" he said.

"I don't know."

"Come on. You're his bitch." He flung the insult out there, but it had no sting, not coming from him.

"Carl, you need to stop."

"I'm almost done. Then I can drop Ojalá."

"You want them to blow up the Golden Gate, for God's sake?"

"I want him to see where his actions have taken us."

"Yeah, then what are you going to do after you stop funding Ojalá?" I glanced at the digital watch. Shit. "How are you going to turn them off?"

"They won't have money, they'll shut down. Now call for him."

"What?"

"Call! Yell for him." Carl was talking to me, but he turned his face away to yell through the helicopters and the sirens and at the entire subsection of the bridge. "Tell him if he doesn't come out now, I'll kill you right here." Then Carl walked up to me, fast, too fast for me to move, and pushed the barrel of his gun right into my forehead.

Just like he had done to Sergio.

The son of a bitch.

Right then, a *clank*. Metal on metal. Over to the right. An obvious sound, enough for Carl Spooner to turn. And for me to kick him.

He shot again, but it was hard for him to aim, doubled over like that, holding his crotch, the crotch that Tekún had cut into three years ago. I ran. Even as he fired again and again. I ran to the edge, then fell, for something had bit into my leg; but I threw that wad of gray clay over the edge of the bridge.

It fell into the water, in a tiny, silent splash. I could see it, through the grating of the catwalk. Just a splash, nothing more.

Then the water, how it rolled. It bubbled, as if it were boiling.

"I'm sorry, Agent Chacón."

I turned to find Carl standing over me, his gun aimed at my face and, indeed, a strange look of regret in his eyes.

And then I saw Tekún, taller, his face looming just behind Carl's left shoulder.

What he did to Carl Spooner, using just his hands, proved to me that Tekún Umán had been trained, thoroughly, in arts darker than war.

It was over. But it was not over.

Only a minute had passed since Carl collapsed before me. It should have been the moment in which Tekún and I reached to each other, and held on tight. But it couldn't happen. Not with Tekún's entire hand coated, as if he had dipped half his arm into a bucket of Carl's blood.

He stood. He watched the helicopters as they swarmed on both sides of the bridge's highway. From the one helicopter, MacGunther belted demands through an electric blowhorn, threatening, demanding Rafael Murillo to give himself up.

He looked at his hand, at his fist clutched around a small wad of Carl, as if he had not done that. Then he looked at me.

He said, "Carl was right. All I seem to do is destroy lives." He looked at me; that was the first time I had ever seen regret on his face. That, and pain: The toxin from the frog was wearing off. The leather jacket no doubt pressed sharp against the cuts in his shoulders.

We stared at each other. Though I said nothing, I was pleading, and he knew it; for he answered my plea.

"You know, Romilia, I just don't think it's going to work out.

"And not only that. But I am really very tired."

He looked down at the bullet wound in my leg and saw that I would live, just fine.

"Oh, Romilia. *Tanto que te quiero, que quiero quererte otro tanto.*"

He did a strange thing, then: He opened his fist and wiped the back of his neck. As if working a cramped muscle out. He worked it a good half-minute, completely staining the nape of his neck, turning his thick black hair red. And then he jumped.

I wonder if all those agents and police and SWAT teams up there on the sidewalk and out in the choppers heard me scream.

They verified Carl Spooner's body from his fingerprints. They called DEA in D.C., who then went through the files regarding Carl's death in the plane flight to the island off Florida. The plane had broken apart on impact with the water. They had found two bodies, Carl's wife and one daughter. They presumed the other daughter, and Carl, were dead.

A questioning of the flight attendants who worked the day of the plane crash put new light on Carl's death: Carl and his wife had had an argument in the airport terminal. Something about not being able to perform, and why waste money going to an island where lovers go? Carl had yelled at his wife, had screamed at her; she had turned away, but then tried to follow him. According to one flight attendant, she came back alone. "I thought he had already returned and boarded," said the attendant.

Thus we had one theory: Carl's family died in the crash. He had survived. A good reason for a father, a husband, to go nuts. He disappeared; and a year later, the Crack Killer murders began. One drug dealer after another, dead, and their cash-on-hand gone. Carl collected the money, used it to travel, to find more drug dealers, to kill them and collect their monies, in a path that took him to Tekún Umán.

The San Francisco Bomb Squad successfully unstrapped the belt of explosives from around the tower. I was right: C4 explosives, manufactured by the U.S. military. Wrapped with Semtex, the same explosive used in the downing of the plane over Lockerbey. Both plastiques, especially C4, are hard to purchase.

Black-market prices, affordable only by those with a large cash flow. Something Carl had, from all those dead drug cartel leaders. Money he handed over to Ojalá, in exchange for loyalty, for henchmen who helped him hunt Tekún.

The following day, traffic resumed on the bridge. Though it was leaner for a while. People took the Bay Bridge, and drove the long way home to Marin County. Then, soon enough, the need for convenience won over the fear of death. The Golden Gate once more choked with late afternoon traffic.

We never found Tekún's body. "Out of all the suicides on the bridge, one in a thousand make it," said MacGunther, repeating little Juan's statistics. "No doubt that guy's fish bait now." And then he said what many agents, in one form or another, with similar clichés, would say for the next few weeks: "Good riddance to bad, bad rubbish."

Bad rubbish. The man who helped me save the Golden Gate Bridge.

I went home.

Fisher had words for me.

"The new mayor of San Francisco would like to meet with you," she said. "He's very excited about recognizing your valor in the line of duty, and your saving the lives of many a taxpayer, while also saving one of our country's great monuments. So I told him you would. After your suspension."

"Yes, Special Agent Fisher."

"Have you heard from Pearl?" she said.

"What? No."

"I think she's going to hand me her badge."

"Is she okay? I mean, was she okay?"

"I think the abduction really messed with her. I told her to take some time off. But she was really torn up. And she said something about having to take care of family. So I've sent her to Quantico, to do some desk work for a while, and make a decision if she wants to stay in the Bureau. She'll be doing what she does best: hacking into computer hackers' computers. And seeing a shrink. Sorry I stuck you with her."

"What? Oh, that's fine. Live and learn, right?"

Fisher filled me in on as much as she could about the group Ojalá. "That boy you picked up, Juan Dominique Martínez, he's in jail. He was low in the chain. A lackey. He said others were higher up, and they did Spooner's dirty work, like finding your son, trailing him from school to home, when your mother dropped him off."

Something I would not tell my mother, that members of a fundamentalist zealot group followed her to and from Sergio's school. Images I'd rather not have Mamá thinking about.

"But that name he gave you," said Fisher, "'Cowboy.' We went back to the Van Nuys jail, talked with Bradley Pack. Seems Pack and Cowboy had their own little cartel going. Cowboy was into exotic animals. Maccaws from Guatemala. And tree frogs from Brazil. Poison frogs. Cowboy ran coke, and used Pack's building as a storage facility."

"Olive Street," I said. "The Hang."

"Right. So when Carl killed Cowboy, and took Cowboy's frogs, he kept up with Cowboy's connections. Pack said he got a call from some guy who claimed to work for Cowboy. Carl, sure enough. He stored the frogs here in Los Angeles. He may have been planning to kill Tekún here. But then Ojalá got overzealous on him. They blew up the building before he had a chance to get his frogs out."

Which was why they found both coke and frog toxin in the rubble: Cowboy still had kilos of produce in Pack's building. "What about that woman in Tijuana, Virginia Roberts?"

"They found her. Dead. In that nice little church you met her in. The church that housed her own private Jacuzzi and apartment suite, where she kept lots and lots of cash. They suspect someone from her own group. I don't doubt Carl ordered it done."

Fisher wanted to know more about that little conversation I had had with Virginia Roberts. I knew that, come soon, she'd be grilling me on that, and how it dovetailed — or didn't — with the rest of my week. Or maybe, just maybe, she'd leave it alone.

"They're a ruthless bunch," I said. "And Machiavellian. Chip was onto Ojalá. But looks like they knew it, and had him killed. A little tit-for-tat with Spooner, I suppose. And a perfect setup for getting to Tekún. Killing Chip was meant to bring Tekún out of the woods, and make him easier to hunt down."

After saying that, I got quiet for a minute; I was thinking about Chip, and about what it meant now, Ojalá. A radical extremist group that was both homegrown and imported. A mix of the worst in religious beliefs, all rolled into one live piece of hot rage. Maybe they'd burn one another out. But along the way, I suspected, and worried, that they'd take a lot of us with them. Now, however, without Carl Spooner's money, they'd probably revert to making fertilizer bombs or crystals from heated bleach. Or, for an infinite supply of cash, they'd make more drug connections.

"Hello?" said Fisher.

"What? Sorry. Just spacing."

She could have read it many ways: me thinking of Chip, or terrorism; or perhaps thinking of Tekún. She would have been right whichever one she chose.

She turned another way. "Your suspension, for disobeying a direct order from a Special Agent in Command of another region, is for three weeks. Paid. Get some rest."

I took the advice. There was a lot to do in my home. My mother was angry, very angry. So angry, she could hardly speak. And my son, he was not sure what to do with me. Here I was again, wounded. Not a cut in the neck, but a bullet wound, small, in my calf. His mother, limping around the house.

Perhaps Mamá was right. It wasn't good for a kid to see his mother hurt on the job. And yet, years had gone by since the cut to my neck. Back then, Sergio had said, "You got the bad guy. But the bad guy got you," and he pointed to my neck. Nowadays, he doesn't say things like that. He didn't say anything about the bullet wound. Even when one of his friends, a kid named Ben, a cute guy with glasses and hair like Harry Potter's, came over from school to play one day, and said, "Wow! So it's true, your mamma got *shot!*" it didn't cheer him up. Not that it should have. But one kid's fascination and curiosity, and even pride, was my boy's nightmare.

We had never talked with him about Minos, or any of the other cases I had been on. But he knew. He could feel it, in the house, in my mother's fearful, angry eyes.

I would go back to work. It was hard to define my life any other way. But for now, I did stay home. Didn't call the office, and Fisher left me alone. Three full weeks. I taught Sergio how to play the card game Demon. He's already beat me twice.

At night, I have thought about Tekún, what he said in the end, and how right he was. It would never have worked out. And yes, I have cried myself to sleep.

Sometimes Sergio hears me. He comes and crawls in bed with me, holds me tight, like no other man can. He knows what it is: My leg must be hurting. "It'll all get better soon," he says to me.

I've learned to believe him.

Once, while working on a few lines of his own poetry in his journal, he wrote this:

> *There is a venom beneath the skin*
> *That cries at night.*

He wrote that the day after finding Beads. He did not know why he wrote those words. Only that he was weeping when he did, and those words came out.

Then there was Carl Spooner in the little homemade torture center below the bridge on Lime Point. Telling him, *You're just like the frogs. You're poison.*

It was the closest he had ever felt to being cursed. While crushing all those frogs under his feet in an act of trained survival, he had almost stopped. He had, in one moment, meant to take one of those frogs in the clutch of his toes and slap it up against the other leg. One slap. The venom seeping into the cut in his thigh. And he would have been gone.

He hadn't. He had crushed them all, but is still not sure why he chose to keep killing them, one by one. It smacked of hope.

Something he doesn't believe in. Especially now, with Carl Spooner's words ringing through his head. That's why he looks at her there, holding her wounded leg, SWAT and police and FBI all around them, assuring him a permanent separation from her.

They would have killed him. He knew that. Before dragging

him up to the bridge's highway, one shot from a fed-up sniper. He would not have blamed them.

So he chose. At least he got to say the line that he had written and rewritten in his journal, all for her, Oh Romilia: *Tanto que te quiero, que quiero quererte otro tanto.*

Even in such acquiescence, his body braces with old trainings. Some habits, a soldier just can't break:

He remembers the cold current of water, in the depths of a Guatemalan river.

He remembers teachings. He has always remembered teachings. One cause rouses an effect; a man with a gun makes him move left, or right, only after a flash of thought that has informed him which is better.

The training shunted emotion and heightened awareness.

Yet there has been emotion. He has known love, and loss. He has mourned Beads, his mother. Since the first day he saw her in a bookstore in Nashville, he has longed for Romilia.

So when he jumps, he knows things: the velocity of a body falling straight, feet first. The estimated distance: a good two hundred feet. The possibilities on impact: broken legs. Exploded testicles. Even worse, a snapped neck, due to the skull popping against the table of water. Paralysis of the open jaw, an easy rush of ocean, a quick drowning. Or, simply, hypothermia. The chances: slim. Which is fine.

Still, blood and viscera are like oil. Rub them in, over the neck, so the skull has a better chance, not of avoiding impact, but of slipping into the waves. Cut the losses. Thicken the chances.

There are no promises. As he falls, he knows there is nothing guaranteed. Her scream, its echo, follows him all the way down, like a ghostly tether.

There is the cold blast, another current — yes. How it reminds him of other rivers, and the safety of their depths, and how he, while burying himself in the deepest, coldest current, felt most awake.